HEAT NOT A FURNACE

Jerome Kiely

Printed in Victoria, Canada

Note for Librarians: a cataloguing record for this book that includes Dewey Classification and US Library of Congress numbers is available from the National Library of Canada. The complete cataloguing record can be obtained from the National Library's online database at:
www.nlc-bnc.ca/amicus/index-e.html
ISBN 1-4120-1720-3

TRAFFORD

This book was published on-demand in cooperation with Trafford Publishing.
On-demand publishing is a unique process and service of making a book available for retail sale to the public taking advantage of on-demand manufacturing and Internet marketing. On-demand publishing includes promotions, retail sales, manufacturing, order fulfilment, accounting and collecting royalties on behalf of the author.

Suite 6E, 2333 Government St., Victoria, B.C. V8T 4P4, CANADA
Phone   250-383-6864   Toll-free 1-888-232-4444 (Canada & US)
Fax 250-383-6804   E-mail sales@trafford.com   Web site www.trafford.com
TRAFFORD PUBLISHING IS A DIVISION OF TRAFFORD HOLDINGS LTD.
Trafford Catalogue #03-2097   www.trafford.com/robots/03-2097.html

10   9   8   7   6   5   4   3

For my sister,

Mary.

Be advised:
Heat not a furnace for your foes so hot
that it do singe yourself.

KING HENRY THE EIGHTH.

William Shakespeare.

Contents

Chapter 1

THE FIRST NAIL

The first nail in my own coffin was driven into it at the funeral of Stephen Burke.

Stephen and his wife Catherine were Yanks as we disparagingly called them. Of course, they were nothing of the sort: Catherine was born within bell toll of the parish church of Kilbroney, and Stephen no further away from it to the west than a thirsty walk on a fair day. I think we called them Yanks not because they had lived in Chicago for thirty years but because of what they wore when they returned to Kilbroney for their annual vacation. Stephen wore a hat almost as large as a small umbrella and God knows that a small umbrella would have been more practical in the summers we had waiting for him, and Catherine wore flowery dresses where the flowers were so clashing and undisciplined that they used to remind us of a grave after a big funeral in the churchyard.

Strangely, we always said "The Yanks are back" never "The Yanks are home" when they settled into their customary flat in Gobnait O'Brien's papershop cum guesthouse in the village every July, but it was their fixed intention to change our word 'back' to their own word 'home' in a year or two; and to show that that wasn't just Yankee talk but native fact they had bought a plot of ground near the village with a fine view of the church, the mountains and the sea.

However, as bad luck and a severe Chicago winter would have it, the better half of their plan was wrecked: Stephen got pneumonia and died, so instead of coming home to a new bungalow he was coming home to a new grave.

Although I didn't know it at the time my reputation was lying inside in Stephen's coffin with his remains as it rode unsteadily in Donal Clancy's hearse from Shannon Airport to

Kilbroney on the day of the removal. I remember the date very well, February 26th, because I had a double, not just a single debacle on that day.

It was the custom of the parish that when a parishioner died in the County Regional Hospital forty miles away the priest drove to the mortuary and recited the prayers there before taking his protocolled place in front of the hearse and leading the cortege homewards at roughly half the speed of his outward journey. However, when a funeral was coming from Shannon which was considerably more than a hundred miles away what used to happen was that the priest would drive to the parish bounds and wait for it there until it rounded Cotter's corner and then he would angle his car sharply out in front of the hearse, take up his pride-of-priestly place and lead the procession at a sanctified pace the rest of the way to Kilbroney.

So it was that on that afternoon of February 26th I burrowed my Toyota into the fuchsias on the side of the narrow road just west of Cotters, switched off the engine and waited. How long the wait would be would depend on whether the engine of Donal Casey's hearse was in the humour for going or not; all other considerations were secondary to the old Ford's temperament on the day. My rear mirror would be my ignition key.

As always on these occasions I brought my breviary along with me to kill the time and at the same time as I was killing it to fulfil the obligation of reading the Divine Office. It was a habit I had in common with many priests of plugging any old gap in the day with a bung of Scripture. It certainly did not measure up to the triple standards of digne, attente ac devote which the Latin rubrics set for us, more particularly as regards the demand that the reading should be attentive: how could it be attentive when I would be lifting my eyes from the sacred text to the rear mirror about as often as a robin would be lifting his head from the cake crumbs on the bird table to the crows in the trees above him?

The scripture reading for the day was the account of the fight between David and Goliath but there were so many gaps in the narrative that it was like being in a cinema in the Thirties with the projector breaking down every other minute. However David eventually killed the giant and I went on to the psalms.

"Watch and pray" the Lord said to the apostles in the garden of Gethsemane but I fancy that what he meant was "stay awake and pray", whereas what I was trying to do was literally to watch and pray at one and the same time: to watch the road and to pray the psalms. The monks of Solesmes with their dignified robes, their attentive eyes and their devout bearing would certainly not have been impressed at my performance in the car with an anorak around my shoulders, my eyes lifting and lowering like a child learning the piano and my right foot poised over the throttle for a quick getaway. Sooner or later I would be punished for the lackadaisical liturgy and as things turned out the punishment was fast approaching Cotter's corner.

My timing let me down. My eyes were scanning the page when they should have been scanning the mirror; I was racing through psalm 50 when Donal came racing around the corner at 50 miles an hour. Only in the last hundredths of a second did I catch a glimpse of the bluff bonnet of the hearse coming up the middle of the road almost astride of me. There was a real danger that I would find myself wriggling in the lower intestines of the cortege instead of at its head. I chucked the breviary onto the floor as if it was a parcel bomb and I launched my Toyota out in front of the Ford. It was the nearest I ever came to simulating the action on a grand prix circuit, when a Ferrari dashes out of the pit lane a mere wiggle of a tail in front of a procession of cars clattering down the straight.

Donal, somehow realising at the last split second that he was driving for the same team as myself, applied his brakes and let me through to take the lead. But the brake lights at the rear of his hearse set off a chain reaction which had cars and people screeching for three hundred yards down the road. The car containing Stephen's widow, Catherine, and the following car containing other close relatives braked without trouble or twisted metal because they were keeping a safe distance behind the hearse out of respect for the dead, but behind those two cars the rest of the drivers were mindful neither of the dead nor of the rules of the road and there were jarring consequences for five of them. The funeral procession did something it never does in Ireland: it came to an unscheduled stop.

I had careered the best part of a hundred yards before I realised anything was amiss. Then looking up at my mischievous rear mirror to see how the retinue was shaping up behind me I discovered that the mobile part of the funeral consisted of only four vehicles: my own, the hearse, and the two cars with the relatives. I wound down the window, gave Donal a distress signal and brought the head of the funeral procession to a halt in sympathy with its detached tail.

I got out of the car and walked to the hearse. Donal was one of those people who had been brought up on versified Victorian counsels to the effect that one should always strain forward for what lay ahead and never look backward to damage and dread. He had a puzzled look on his face: clearly he had no idea what lay behind my mysterious hand signal.

"What's up, Father?" he asked.

"Tisn't so much what's up as what's down", I answered, "back down there I mean" and I pointed to the mechanical mayhem down the road. It was only then that Donal who obviously wasn't on better terms with his rear mirror than I was with mine, swivelled his head and shoulders about and looking through the large window behind the coffin took in the plain fact that the snake he had brought in one healthy piece from Shannon through three counties had met with a cleaver at Cotter's corner.

I left Donal to his sulky snorts and moved along to Catherine's car. I hadn't seen her since the previous July so I almost expected to view a floral landscape in the passenger's seat, but if she was decked out in the latest prints of magnolias and petunias from Chicago they were covered up under a winter wrap of black leather. What she was wearing as usual was her sharp, peaky expression: she always reminded me of a school marm who sets her face in the mirror at five minutes to nine every morning and says to her image "You must not smile in school today". I am not suggesting that in the stalled funeral procession of her husband she would be greeting me like a mother-of-the-bride but I was hoping to meet something more mollient than a mask. Her set expression stultified my vocabulary and all I could think of to say was the million-mouthed "I'm sorry for your trouble, Catherine."

She said a limp "Thanks".

I gave her the hand and the pressure of my fingers on hers must somehow have set off a minor explosion in my mouth because I heard myself saying what any sympathetic priest would have said in the circumstances. "It's a shame he didn't live to see the bungalow" I began, and I continued "he deserved a few restful years before the eternal rest. He was a good man, was Stephen. Very friendly. Never missed Mass, and he had the homing instinct. You did the right thing, Catherine, to bring him home and not leave him like a block of ice over there among the skyscrapers. I'm sure he is thankful to you"

She said "Thanks" again and this time she added "Father" as a sort of mark of approval for my sentiments.

I left her saying that there was a bit of a collision back the road, but nothing much, and walked up to the stalled cars and the stalking drivers to see how accurate or otherwise were my words.

A pileup would be much too strong an expression for what had happened, but there was no doubt that a fair bit of nudging, bumping, sandwiching and fender climbing had taken place. There were fragments of red lamps and yellow lamps scattered around the road like the coloured tableware in a children's game of chanies. In one case there was a perfectly straight, deeply scored black line right through the middle of a registration plate as if some local government official had dramatically cancelled the number. In another case a curvaceous white car had a red weal across its rear end as if someone had mistaken it for an impudent child's bottom and had applied a birch.

The worst damage was to Jim Lacy's car: the front bumper had done its job so enthusiastically that it was now lying prostrate on the road, but no one was surprised at that because it had been attached to the brackets by some makeshift engineering in Jim's own shed after an earlier bumping competition with a stone wall. Jim was a true philosopher: Qoheleth of the book of Ecclesiastes, the most famous of all the proponents of the transitoriness of created things, would have admired him for his reaction: Jim's car was full of passengers so he merely picked up the bumper, chucked it in the ditch and said "I'll be back for it some other day".

There were, of course, odd dents and scratches here and there but nothing drastic: there was no sign of any steam rising as a result of friction between hot water and a cold road, nor as much of an oil leak as would stain a leaf of a mountain ash. Summing up the evidence as they saw it collectively the injured parties decided that there was nothing that would warrant the weariness of filling out claim forms for their insurance companies.

In any event whom could they blame? Not the priest, for sure! If they combined to instance his spectacular manoeuvre to challenge the hearse for first place in the procession, wouldn't it sound like a plot, a conspiracy, a religious rebellion, the start of another western schism?

I moved around from one afflicted driver to another, from Dave Murphy to Eddie Collins, from Eddie Collins to Stan Hyde, from Stan Hyde to Peter O'Rourke, from Peter O'Rourke to Damien O'Grady and from Damien O'Grady to Jim Lacy, and in each case I used the bereavement phrase I had already used when I greeted Catherine Burke on the perceived ground that it was their funeral too: "I am sorry for your trouble" I said. But the blush on my guilty cheeks made me add "'Twas my fault. I am to blame".

They wouldn't hear of it. One and all of them pointed the fingers, thumbs and entire fists of blame down the road at Donal Clancy.

"The fool should have known you are always in that nook", Eddie said to me, loud enough for the words to be carried in the wind to the fool he was alluding to.

"Certainly" said Paul, taking up Eddie's point; and then addressing the assembly as if it was evidence he was giving in a court of law he said "Father Laide has not parked his car anywhere except under those fuchsias for a funeral from Shannon since he came to the parish".

"He was going far too fast" Jim said and the heads that nodded agreement were considering a broad smile because they felt that Jim was referring not so much to the unseemly haste of a Christian funeral as to the demands that had been made on his own senile engine.

First one and then another backed up Jim with more than nods.

"What rush was he in when he was half an hour ahead of the time in this morning's paper?" was Damien's argument.

But the most colourful statement of all came from Peter. "You would think it was a feather he had in the coffin instead of a heavyweight of a man like Stephen", said Peter and we all laughed.

They had virtually arrived at a consensus when the laughter ebbed, and their consensus gave way to unanimity when Jim whose experiences in life had been mostly blunt ones, said bluntly, "Only that he's guilty he'd be back up here with us".

"You're right", "You're damn well right", "What else?" were the phrases that came across the roofs of every car except one.

That one belonged to Peter, the acknowledged wag. "Ah now, be fair," he said, "sure he had to mind the corpse!"

That was the cue for all of them to return to their cars, and when I left them to walk back across the gap between the many and the few they were reversing a little here, edging forward a little there and generally sorting out the tangle everywhere.

The jury had brought in a verdict of 'not guilty' in my favour, but I knew in my heart as I sidled past Donal in his Ford and slid into my Toyota that the angel who operates the traffic camera in heaven would have handed in a very different expert opinion to the Judge of all.

* * *

Even including the forced stop for the scrimmage and even allowing for how approximate the word 'approximately' on a death announcement can be, Donal Clancy was still an astonishing quarter of an hour ahead of the paper time when he pulled into the sandstone bay at the gate of Saint Brona's church. Why he had made such good time from Shannon to Kilbroney only Donal himself could say, but when we all got out of our cars and encircled the hearse it gradually became clear that there was more to the speed of the journey than the heaviness of his foot on the throttle.

In fact from the moment that Donal threw up the hatchback door of the hearse in that squeaky arc which was the signal for the four picked men to come forward and shoulder the coffin into the church, the key word was lightness not heaviness.

To begin with, the coffin seemed to shoot off the rollers of its own momentum like a train out of a tunnel instead of being pulled, as it always was, like a hesitant calf out of a trailer. Then when the four men, facing each other, two and two at the tail of the hearse took it onto the palms of their educated hands before hoisting it on their shoulders they looked across at each other with a look of bewilderment as if to say "What's this coffin made of? Plywood?"

Not everybody in the circle was watching the four men, of course — many eyes were fixed on the unusual sight of Catherine in her leather coat and zipped boots — but to those who were following the movements of the men it became obvious in the next twenty seconds that there was something very mysterious about that coffin. Normally when men hoist a coffin what happens is that, after a nervous shuffle or two, the inside edge settles firmly into a sort of traditional groove in their clavicles, and their outer shoulders lift as their inner shoulders buckle. But what happened at the church gate on that surprising February evening was that the four men all together, as if they had rehearsed it beforehand, gave a sort of a heave of their inside shoulders, as soon as the coffin rested on them and the coffin bounced up in the astonished air three, four or five inches before it settled back again. Then, without the customary pawing of the ground to get the feel of it under their burdened feet, they moved off as smartly as bank clerks in the direction of the church door. I almost had to reproduce my Cotter's corner manoeuvre on foot to get ahead of them for the prescribed solemn march up the church.

Solemn it wasn't. It was the nearest thing you would ever get in a church to four strong men carrying a light canoe with a brisk air as if to say "This is real child's play". Always up to that evening I sensed that the pallbearers were following me; on that evening I felt they were pursuing me. It was a bit like what used to happen during the solemn procession of the Cross from the door to the sanctuary on a Good Friday when I would be placing my feet fastidiously in every diamond of the tiled floor in order to maintain a reverent pace but the altarboys behind me would be nudging me with their candle sticks and stampeding me with their impatient shoes.

When we arrived at the top of the church the four men placed the coffin on the trellises with a nonchalant, almost a dismissive flourish, and I shall always remember the pitying look that one of them, Ned Burke, Stephen's first cousin, threw at me as he genuflected in front of the altar: it said "I hope you know what you're at, Father!" To be honest I wasn't sure whether I was involved in chapter one of a strange novel or chapter two of the book I had in my hands: "Christian Burial — Reception of the remains".

What I was absolutely sure of was that I never had to wait so long with that melancholy book in my hands for the congre-

gation to settle down quietly and peaceably so that I could recite the opening words of the service: "My brothers and sisters,
we believe that Jesus died and rose again and that it will be the
same for those who have died in Jesus". The reason was that
people in one pew had their heads slung around to people in
the pew behind them, and some faces had entirely disappeared
into the coat lapels of their neighbours. I never thought I would
be recalling, however inaccurately, the words of a Puritan poet
in a Catholic church, but what I was looking at was a couplet
from John Milton:

"Quips and cracks and wanton wiles
Nods and becks and wreathed smiles".

Nods and becks and wreathed smiles there were by the
score.

I have to admit I was never so unfocussed at a funeral rite
as I was that evening. No; 'unfocussed' is the wrong word: I
was very focussed on the coffin but very distracted in the read-
ings, and it was the words of Horatio rather than the words of
Hebrews that came echoing back off the walls of the church at
me: "O day and night but this is wondrous strange!"

When, one way or another I got to the end of the prayers
the buzz that had preceded them started up again. Of course
it is a common occurrence, funerals being social occasions, for
a social rumpus to follow the religious calm. Knots of people
twine together, and chatter takes over from chant, but I never
experienced anything to equal the intricate knots at the bottom of the church that evening or the animated volume of the
chatter.

I walked down through the church to waylay a few mothers
for neat altar boys for the funeral Mass on the following day
and as I did so my eyes locked with the eyes of a man to whom I
had been speaking at Cotter's corner only three quarters of an
hour earlier. It was Peter O'Rourke. He gave an amused glance
which being interpreted meant: "Many's the word spoken in
jest -----. Do you remember what I said about a feather? "

* * *

The Christian Burial book made provision for a vigil but I never turned those pages. We all of us figured that a cup of tea at home or a few pints at Florrie's were more of a consolation to the bereaved than passages from Matthew or Mark. But we did have a vigil of sorts that evening and as with a lot of things in Kilbroney the first notes were intoned in Bill Driscoll's shop.

The best way I can describe Bill is to say he was the spitting image of Dylan Thomas in that famous photograph of the Welsh poet which shows him with a cigarette dangling from his lips at so steep an angle that the half inch of ash at the end of it is touching his chin. Like Dylan, Bill loved a companionable cigarette and although he didn't indulge in wine or wenching he too like the Dylan of the photograph was puffy, pleasant, perceptive and above all personable.

Bill was a formidable man in an argument. Shopkeeping is a great whetstone to sharpen the mind, and Bill's was so sharp that he was credited with trumping even the Master's verbal aces. As well as that he was the parish's most exuberant curser. The Welsh bards who preceded Dylan as the eloquent soul of their country were always noted for their powers of cursing but Bill could knock a gaggle of those geese into one of their mother's conical hats when it came to malevolent mouthings. He was usually as calm as a lake behind a dam but if some missile hit that dam the man or woman who launched it was likely to be submerged in a spluttering cascade of abuse. To use two local expressions, he was 'touchy' and 'hard to time'. Too big a crowd in the shop on a Sunday or nobody at all between one Angelus bell and another on a weekday could equally detonate him and you had to be careful where you placed your elbow lest you touch off a trigger button.

A request for something he hadn't got such as Algerian dates — he had the Tunisian variety but they weren't shiny enough according to the impudent shopper; a challenge to the cost of his corned beef; a farmer leaning across the counter staring into the nothingness behind the pearl barley; or the bitches in his kitchen on a Sunday toasting their hammer toes at his fire, reading his paper and stirring pots of his tea for themselves, all of these could put the curses swirling like froth on a mountain stream. But that is all it was really: froth. Everyone knew that under the passionate froth there was happy water.

The shop was the very essence of an auctioneer's sales talk — it was small in size but big in character; and the name on the facia described it to perfection: Driscoll's Emporium. It was said that Bill got the word from a learned parish priest twenty years before. Fr. Quinlivan went into the shop one day shortly after his arrival in Kilbroney and "Do you know what?" he remarked to Bill, looking around at the miscellaneous merchandise, "What you have here isn't a shop but an emporium. Down in the village they have a meat shop and a paper shop and a sweet shop and a clothes shop but you have everything in the one shop. An emporium that's what it truly is.

"A what?" Bill asked, his Latin not being on a par with his cursing.

"An emporium", the parish priest repeated "you know, a shop that sells a huge variety of things".

"And how would you spell that?" Bill asked.

"E-m-p-o-r-i-u-m" Fr. Quinlivan answered and as he spelled out the letters slowly Bill wrote them down in his pass book, and the next time he got the shop painted DRISCOLL'S EMPORIUM was emblazoned in big red letters on the white facia.

As the parish priest remarked and as the facia proclaimed that is what it truly was. Bill sold bullseyes for big mouths, liniment for strained backs, exercise books for children, pink bloomers for traditional women, bacon and cabbage for the Sunday dinner and battleboard for the fast days. You could buy yourself six inch nails, oil for an outboard engine or five cigarettes if you hadn't the price of ten. And there was something charmingly timely about items that came and went with the seasons: Christmas cards — he had such a stack of Hands-across-the-sea that if they were all joined edge to edge they would have stretched from Rosslare to Fishguard; sprigs of shamrock for Patrick's Day which the children picked for him on their way home from school in exchange for some of the aforementioned bullseyes; flower seeds in their exotic packets as soon as the midday sun had awakened them from their winter sleep under the counter; swimming rings and smiling rubber ducks for the summer; yard brushes for the autumn leaves, and a good supply of habits for the winter in anticipation of a big mortality rate among the elderly.

Bill's best day was Sunday because his shop was strategically situated opposite the church gate to command the immediate attention of the Mass leavers, and also because his kitchen had become a sort of unofficial waiting room. Before Mass it provided heat for the women who had come in from home too early and had no notion of being frozen to stone in the draughty quarry of the church; and after Mass it provided amnesia for the women whose husbands were slowly sucking their pints down at Florrie's. He also picked up a big share of the casual trade: during the week women who weren't dressed up enough to submit to the eyes of the scrutineers in the village would do all their shopping in Bill's; people who were going home with their Saturday parcels would shop there when they suddenly remembered they should have got a bar of Lifebuoy soap to scrub the children and would then buy unneeded tea and jam as well to cover up the fact that they had passed him by on the way in; and because, like the Broadway babies, when Bill said goodnight 'twas early in the morning, the queer characters who came out only at night, like the owls and the bats, and every closing time transgressor on his way home on a wobbly bike called into Bill's for their bottle of milk and their pound of sausages.

I can't remember if it was for milk and sausages that I went into Bill's that evening but I do remember with the sharpness of an etching that I was there about an hour after the church had emptied of gossipers. May Connell the chapelwoman — a term that covered everything from ringing the bell and washing the albs to snipping the altarboys' hair when she thought it was liturgically too long, and throwing stones at my bedroom window when I overslept on a winter's morning — was resting her elbows on the counter. It was clear that she wasn't ruminating at what she needed for the supper but that as the custodian of the coffin she was delivering her cargo of guesses to Bill's entrepot of gossip. I was immediately drawn into the line of commerce.

"What do you think, Father?" Bill asked me with the directness of a horse's rear leg. "About what?" I answered Kerry-like with another question trying , vainly I knew, to protect my groin.

Bill was never one to go beating about a topical bush; he always butted his way head first into the trunk of the matter. "About what Catherine did with Stephen" he came back bluntly.

I laughed defensively but my tactics were no match for Bill's. "The coffin is empty" he said with the certitude of Simon Peter reporting on the tomb. And as there was a woman to back up Simon Peter on the morning of the resurrection there was a woman to back up Bill on this occasion. May said "I went to straighten up the coffin because they left it a bit sideways, and when I moved it, it put up no resistance. I could do what I liked with it".

There is an unwritten rule in every parish that no matter whom you quarrel with you never contradict the chapel woman; otherwise you might as well write to the bishop requesting a transfer. So I had to agree with May that the coffin was light.

"Empty, you mean, Father" said Bill, dismissing my vagueness. "So, if it's empty, where is Stephen?"

"Maybe she dumped him in the Atlantic," May said. At least that is what I think she said, because her words were being buried in heaped waves of laughter.

Bill called her to order; there was a serious matter being discussed here. Had Catherine buried him cheaply in Chicago, he wanted to know, and was the coffin only a blind to fool the yobs in Kilbroney into thinking that she loved him so much that she had gone to the expense of hauling him across half a continent and a whole ocean. "It has to be so," he argued. "That's not an American casket; that's one of Donal Clancy's specials, so he must have brought it with him to Shannon, driven around to the mortuary and nipped in and out with it with the help of some coffin traffic controller when nobody was looking".

It was my turn to laugh. "Impossible, Bill" I said "That's more ridiculous than May's idea of opening up a hatch in the plane and dropping him into the Atlantic".

"Well then" said Bill, throwing the sprat that he was sure the salmon of a priest would rise to, "you're an educated man, Father, you tell us what's behind it".

"I think it may be a cremation job" I answered quietly.

The two of them looked at each other and then back at me with more shock on their faces than if they had actually seen Stephen Burke being fired from the jet like an aerial torpedo into the ocean. Cremation was something practised in India or by people who didn't believe in the resurrection of the body, and there were neither Hindus nor heretics in Kilbroney, praises be to God.

I felt I had to massage that look of shock off their faces so I said, "Ah now, a good many Catholics are doing it in America these times and some few in Dublin too, I heard. The Church allows it so long as it isn't done in defiance of the doctrine of the resurrection of the body".

I wasn't at all sure that my catechesis had relieved their sense of shock, so I brought them back to more practical matters. "The thing that is bothering me about this cremation, if cremation it is , is what about the urn?"

"The urn?" both of them asked together.

"A sort of a container", I explained, "something like a jam jar that the ashes are put into after the body is burned. And

I would have thought that Catherine would have brought the urn with her on to the plane and then put it into the coffin at Shannon".

"Do you mean to fool the yobs in Kilbroney" — it was the second time in five minutes that Bill had used that phrase — "into thinking that there was a regular corpse in the coffin?" he asked.

I didn't have to voice an opinion on that suggestion because May broke in. "I can tell you this much". she said, and she paused like an orator, "there is no jam jar in that coffin, because I lifted it fore and aft and nothing rolled up or down inside in it".

"Well, in that case, I just don't know", I said weakly.

Bill pounced. "But would you like to know? he asked.

"Not as much as ye would" I answered smilingly, "but yes, to be honest, I would like to know." I had opened a gate and Bill shot through it.

"You can open a coffin, can't you, Father?" It was more of a statement than a question and more of a wheedle than a statement.

"Well, yes, but only in limited circumstances", I answered like a law book.

"Such as", Bill prompted. He was like a cheetah's teeth around a gazelle's windpipe: he wouldn't let go.

"Well, the usual case is when a relative turns up late because he has been delayed by a traffic jam or fog or business or something like that, and he requests it".

"I'm a relative, you know". I didn't and if I had been in the parish for fifty years I wouldn't have been able to get out of their maze of relationships. "What am I to Stephen, May?" he asked the resident guide. "You're a third cousin, once removed through your mother's people", May answered as promptly as if she had been asked "two and two?"

"There you are, and I was delayed by business: the shop was crowded when the funeral arrived," Bill announced triumphantly "and of course I request it," he added, latching on to the second condition.

"Come on, Father. No one will ever know except us," May urged me.

"Alright so," I said, as the gazelle was garroted.

I get these mad moments from time to time and that was one of the maddest.

* * *

Curser-in-chief and arguer almighty Bill Driscoll may have been but he was no nerveless warrior. That's for sure. He dearly wished to take the lid off the mystery of the corpseless coffin but he funked to take the lid off the coffin itself. He suffered from nightmares, he said, and he had no wish to add the lid of a coffin hanging over his bed at night to his other customary horrors.

Therefore, as he wouldn't take an active role in the unveiling of the secret, the plan we devised was that I, as the official binder-and-looser in the church, would remove the six screws which secured the lid to the box; May, as the custodian of the church movables would lift the lid off; and Bill who knew more about the church door than anybody else, having lived opposite it all his life, would stand guard there until the operation was completed when he would join us to have his desired peek at whatever, if anything, lay inside.

Unlikely as it was, there was still a chance in a million that one parishioner out of our thousand might decide "to look in on the Lord" which was why Bill's job was to stand at the door, keep a steady eye on the gate, and give us nix if necessary.

I can explain why I didn't call it a day and shut the church for the night: it was a Friday in Lent and we had Stations of the Cross scheduled for 7 o'clock. But I can't explain why the three of us set off from Bill's shop with chuckles and chatter like some grotesquely overgrown school children in an Enid Blyton adventure unless the explanation is that the devil of the unthinking mind had taken possession of us.

May and I left Bill at his post and walked up the aisle to where the coffin was resting on the trellises in front of the altar. Immediately there was a snag. I couldn't get a stir out of the screws. "Your hands are too soft", May said with a splutter of laughter. I chafed them against each other and tried again: no good. The screws were as secure as wheel nuts on a car after a power brace has tightened them. Donal Clancy must have used a vice grips to squeeze them into such a locked position, and for all we knew of the workings of his secretive mind maybe he did it to prevent the nosey parkers of Kilbroney — Us! — from doing what we were attempting to do now.

We took Donal for some class of a fool but the unbreached coffin proved that he wasn't and if he was clever we would have to imitate his cleverness. If a vice grips was used to tighten the screws a vice grips could be used to loosen them. Out with me to the boiler house to fetch the tool box.

With six jerks of the vice grips and six gentle twists of my right fist the six screws were soon nestling in my left hand. "Now, May," I signalled. She raised the lid with just a faint whimper of silk on silk as it came off. I stepped back and she walked off with it as if it were a small swing bridge and rested it on the front bench. Then the two of us looked over the brim of the coffin with a grip in our stomachs like Carter and Carnarvon in the Valley of the Kings. And what we saw was as astonishing to us as the gleam of gold was to them.

Lying between what I would call the hips of the coffin and attached to the silk padding of the base by a strip of cheap office adhesive tape was a bag. It was just like a freezer bag, transparent, small size, 24 by 17 centimetres I reckon, with a write-on label on it and twist-tied at the top with a white ribbon. The name on the label read "Stephen Burke". Inside was a grey-black powder.

"What is it?" May asked with the child-like wonder of a first experience.

"Ashes, May, the ashes," I said, "Don't you see the label? Stephen Burke".

"My God, is that all that's left of him?" she said, shaken. "We'd have four times as much for Ash Wednesday".

It was not the time for the imagination to trace the noble dust of Alexander until it stopped a bung hole as Hamlet did in the churchyard of Elsinore, so I simply agreed and said "We would".

Then for one instant some movement at the back of the Church caught the corner of my eye, a mere speck of undefined movement which had disappeared before I could blink and at the same instant I thought I heard a faint click as if someone had gone into the confessional.

"Bill, come up," I called, but no Bill came. Instead, a woman, who of all the women in the parish was the last one I wanted to see, came in the door.

"Gobnait!" I yelped between my teeth,

"Jesus!" May exclaimed.

Jesus didn't come to help us, but after a momentary glance at the confessional Gobnait strode up the aisle towards us. She was wearing her winter anorak with the hood up and she looked like one of those menacing figures in the Holy Week procession in Seville. To give May her honest due she reacted to the situation much more quickly than I did: she hurtled herself at the front bench and she swung her small swing bridge back into position faster than you could put a lid on a saucepan, but alas, the quickness of her hands couldn't find any time for finesse and the lid fell onto the coffin with such a bang that not only ourselves but the four walls of the church recoiled. I hadn't a chance to do anything: the screws remained in my hand but they were no longer screws: they were shafts of guilt.

I got the awful feeling that May and myself were two small timber boats in an alien ocean and that a gunboat was bearing down on us. And I was right. Gobnait blew May out of the water with one salvo. "I wouldn't expect anything better from you, May Connell," she spat, "and ye living like limpets on the rocks beyond in Cuasdhú without book or breakfast".

Then she opened up on me with such a protracted shelling that not only did she sink the boat but she blew holes in the sea as well. "A nice priest you are," she sneered, "invading the privacy of the dead. There were people hanged for robbing graves, but what you have done is even worse: you have robbed Stephen's coffin of its secret. What a hypocrite you are! I heard you giving out a few weeks ago because people were talking during the prayers in the churchyard. Every word they spoke, you said, was a stone thrown at the coffin. So what have you done to this coffin? Emptied it of its contents, that's what. Tipped it up like a cart of manure. Another time you said we wouldn't go to any funeral if there wasn't a swig of free whiskey at the gate on the way out: mocking the dead, you said it was. Taking the cork off a bottle or the lid off a coffin, which is the worst? Who is doing the mocking now? Curiosity killed the cat, they tell us. Well let me tell you, Father Laide, that when people hear about this curiosity it will kill you off as a priest in this parish".

She ended the bombardment. I was floating in the water like slivers of bait. I couldn't say a word. She had shot the tongue out of my head. Then as May and I slumped onto the bench, shaking from the violence of her attack, Gobnait knelt at the coffin to pray for the happy repose of the dead. She blessed herself with the slow and exaggerated features of a windmill on a day of light winds and lowered her head in rapt reverence. If anything, it was a more galling performance than the tirade itself.

"You can replace the screws now," she said as she rose from her knees: that one missed nothing. Then she floated down the church with the smug visage of an avenging angel, gave a sidelong glance at the confessional, and went out the gasping door.

I did indeed replace the screws in the coffin. What's more, I used the vicegrips on them in the desperate hope that Gobnait might not inform Catherine and Donal against us that night.

When that was done May and I walked down the church with curses in our hearts for the curser. Where had he scuttled to, the rabbit, in our time of need?

We hadn't long to wait for the answer because as we approached the confessional a bare arm protruded through the violet veil screening the door and Bill followed into our view.

All I could say was "So that's where you were" because I was still more or less shell-shocked after the pounding I took, but May laid into him. "You are some friend, I must say," she stormed — and there was a ton weight of sarcasm in the way she leaned on the word "some". "You ran off to save your own skin while we were being torn to bits by that wildcat. I don't mind for myself: another scratch on my old pelt isn't going to shorten my life, but the tearing she gave poor Father Laide was beyond the beyonds. I don't know how he had patience with her. If I had a priest's power I'd have clung her to the ground, so I would, and left her there like a statue. But that's not the point. The point is that none of this would have happened if you had done what you were supposed to do. And 'twasn't we stood you at the door: that's the job you asked for yourself, so why the blazes didn't you do it?

Bill's defence wasn't very convincing but such as it was I record it here. He said "I had my face towards the gate, but she didn't come in the gate. That's the way any ordinary human being would come, but she's not an ordinary human being. She isn't foxy for nothing and the fox doesn't walk up the main road when he is raiding the henhouse. She came around on my blind side, by the south corner, and I didn't see her till the last minute. There was no time to shout a warning: she would have heard it before ye did. There was no shift but to make for the confession box in a hurry. I'm not a bit sure even that she didn't see my face at the door or my heels at the box".

May picked on the weak point in his argument straight away: "If you were so clever as to know that a fox wouldn't come up the main road why didn't you watch the boreen?" she asked angrily.

"How was I to know a fox was on the prowl?" he responded reasonably enough, but we weren't assuaged. We turned our backs on him and walked out the door. He followed pleading "Ah, Father. Ah, May" and as he stepped outside, the sharpness of the February evening must have stropped his cursing razor because he began to slash the air in the direction of Gobnait's papershop cum guesthouse with swipes of ferocious curses.

"That your papers may catch fire," he cried "and that you may be cremated in the blaze!"

"That the devil may shove his fivepronged fork up your arse," he screamed, "and not be able to pull it down again!"

"That you may get uglier even than you are already" he positively bellowed "and die a yellow spinster!"

I haven't yet figured out what is so specially loathsome about being a yellow spinster rather than any other colour of spinster, but I do know that, as I walked up home past Bill's shop, it wasn't his curses that were ringing in my ears so much as the hammer blows that Gobnait struck when she was driving the first nail into my coffin.

Chapter 2

THE YELLOW SPINSTER

She didn't tell Catherine that night. She had every chance to do so because Catherine stayed in her guesthouse, but she left the lid resting on the coffin. That became clear to me three times on the following day. First of all, when Catherine arrived in the church for the funeral Mass I gave her the hand of welcome and she took it without any tingle of revulsion. My pulse went back to normal.

At the end of Mass when I came down from the altar to stand at the coffin I diplomatically opened page 56 not page 158 of my book and I read "With faith in Jesus Christ we reverently bring the body of our brother, Stephen, to be buried in its human imperfection" rather than "As we prepare to bury the ashes of our brother, Stephen, we are reminded of the words of scripture which tell us that our bodies are but dust and ashes". Then I gave the coffin a fine generous April-showered spatter of holy water — was I attempting to wash my own sins not Stephen's away? And I enveloped it totally in a soft pall of incense smoke — it seemed to me that May had put more and sizzlier pieces of charcoal into the thurible than ever before: as her peace offering to Stephen's spirit, perhaps?

Then the four men came up the church to take the coffin to the graveside, but before they lifted it on their shoulders Catherine stepped out of the seat, walked up to the coffin and kissed it on the lid. I watched her very closely as she did so and I knew for certain by her composed face — something I had never seen before: the sharpness had softened, the peakiness had pinked — that she knew nothing of the violation of the evening before. I drew a deep breath of relief.

But the most dramatic moment of the funeral for me came just before the coffin was lowered into the grave. Donal Clancy produced a vice grips from his jacket and made a circuit of the coffin loosening the six screws as he went.

The loosening of the screws came as no surprise to anybody. It was a custom in many parishes. Some oldtimers said it was to ease the emergence of the faithful from their coffins on the last day, before the trumpet would stop sounding, but the cynical, the scientific and the pessimistic said it had to do with the fact that many people are buried alive and so it was designed to give them the chance, when they woke up in the coffin, to push up the lid and burrow their way out: no one wanted to be another Thomas á Kempis who was put into his coffin facing up but was found with his face down when the body was exhumed years later.

One way or another the loosening of the screws was nothing new but the sight of a vice grips was very new indeed; it was the first time ever that a shovel and a vice grips were workmates at a burial. All eyes were on Donal as he moved from one screw to another, all except one pair of eyes: they were the eyes of Gobnait O'Brien and I could feel them boring into me from where she stood directly opposite me at the graveside.

When all was finished, when the grave was filled in and the earth was greened with a sod from Stephen's place and the two shovels were placed on the sod in the shape of a cross and the decade of the rosary was mumbled I stepped over to Catherine and I wished her a safe flight back to Chicago and a happier journey eastwards the next time she would be coming to Kilbroney, and she thanked me "for all your kindness", as she put it. It was with a much lighter step that I passed Bill Driscoll's shop on the way up home.

The crisis was over but I was left with a problem and it followed me around the house all evening. The problem was: why hadn't Gobnait carried out her threat?

The first thought that occurred to me was a spinoff from Bill's name calling: yellow spinster. Yellow suggested Chinese and Chinese suggested slow torture. No doubt about it, there would have been a lot of satisfaction for her if she could have seen Catherine push away my proferred hand, if she could have heard her say "Hypocrite" out loud when I got to the words about reverently bringing the body of our brother Stephen to be buried, and especially in the climactic moments as Donal was circling the coffin, vice grips in hand, if she could have witnessed Catherine turn to me and say, with a bitterness that would yellow the green sod, "Fr Laide, would you like to have another look inside? Now is your chance".

She had waived the satisfaction of all that, so she must have had a keener pleasure in mind. Chinese torture, that's what, I reckoned: the kind of thing where a victim is stripped naked, shackled to clamps, and spreadeagled on the floor under a faucet, and he doesn't know, hour after manic hour, when the single drop of water will fall on his tense body. If she had told Catherine and the funeral had become an exercise in fury, the drop of water would have fallen straight away and there would have been nothing further to fear from the faucet, but as things stood now she could keep me spreadeagled for months in dread of the day when the word "lid" would fall from her lips.

In other words, Greek rather than Chinese, the sword of Damocles was hanging over my head. Instinctively I looked up at the ceiling of my living room to see if it was dangling from the plaster by a single hair. It was a long time since I had first heard of it in Fr. Roche's Greek class and I went over to my bookshelves to find a book that would refresh my memory on the menace. The Oxford Companion informed me that Damocles was a flatterer who pronounced Dionysius, the ruler of Syracuse, the happiest of men. Dionysius was indeed the most successful of men: he had conquered half of Sicily, he had put a Syracusan boot on the toe and heel of Italy and he had even won an award for an original play at a major drama festival. It isn't often that you find a man with a conquering sword in one hand and a conquering pen in the other, but success wasn't the same thing as happiness, Dionysius stated.

"Come with me, flatterer", he said, "take my seat at the banquet tonight and experience the happiness of a ruler. When you are nicely ensconced among the viands and the wines, look up and see what you will see". Damocles looked up and saw a naked sword directly above his head hanging by a single hair.

I certainly wouldn't account myself a flatterer and even if my tongue produced the sweetest of honey I wouldn't put any of it in a pot for Gobnait, but I got the point of the story: one couldn't be happy with a sword hanging over one's head, especially a sword hanging by a hair. That hair was the whim of Gobnait O'Brien.

And as for being a "ruler", I was one only by default. The parish priest, Father Mac, as everybody called him, was away in hospital for months being treated for cancer. His chances of recovery looked as pale as his face but the bishop had shown him the courtesy of not asking him to resign, so I found myself promoted by circumstances from curate to acting parish priest. However, with Gobnait's threat to kill me off it didn't look as if my reign would be a long one.

So, with that sword constantly above my head, whether I sat in the house, walked through the village, attended a meeting or preached about right and wrong, I was an unmissable target, as unmissable in my own way as that pathetic Goliath whom I had been reading about while waiting for the funeral at Cotter's corner the day before. There he was, silhouetted against the morning sky on the hilltop of Socoh as big as a brown bear, only weighted down by a museum of armour: he didn't have a chance against the nimble skill of David. Several details stood out sharply in the account in the first book of Samuel: David picked up five stones, not just one, from the bed of the stream; he put them into his pouch one by one; he bided his time until Goliath was off his guard; and when eventually he did let fly it was because Goliath insulted him personally. So, equally, couldn't it happen that Gobnait would collect more than one stone to fling at me, stow them away in a bitter pouch, bide her time, and eventually bring the sling of her tongue into action because of an insult to herself rather than an injury to Catherine Burke?

What they all added up to — the Chinese torture theory, the sword of Damocles and the stones in David's pouch — was that Gobnait had no notion of throwing away the hammer with which she had driven the first nail in my coffin.

* * *

Gobnait is an uncommon but a jarring name for a girl to have and in my experience Gobnait O'Brien was the only one I ever met whose parents saddled her with such a strange life-long burden.

As a matter of fact, not being a Corkman myself I never even knew the name existed in the calendar of Irish saints until one day I was in Cork city and I went to the Honan Chapel to see the Harry Clarke windows. It was the first time I made the acquaintance of any Gobnait, sainted or otherwise, and Clarke's Gobnait was indisputably a saint with her nimbus, her crozier and a toy church instead of a worldly handbag in her left hand. However the more I looked up at the figure the more she came across to me — I won't say 'down' to me; I doubt if she would defer to anybody — as an imperious woman who would quickly convert that crozier of hers into a javelin if you crossed her. She had what I would call a prying nose and a tumble of fiery red hair. Our Gobnait took after her in her bossiness, her interrogative nose and her hair, more tinkerish red than regal red, I will admit, but still fiery from being neighbour to a hot tempered cranium.

What interested me mostly about Harry Clarke's Gobnait, however, wasn't so much what she looked like as what she was doing, and what she was doing in her mistressy fashion was avenging the intrusion into her monastery at Ballyvourney of a band of would-be robbers. They didn't get farther than the cloisters, poor misguided fellows, because she unleashed a swarm of bees at them, and there are marvellous vignettes in the window of those diminutive robbers racing in terror from bees which are as big as hawks; I don't blame them for being gripped by terror, having been chased by hornets once myself, and they were fearsome enough, goodness knows, although they lacked the preternatural power of Gobnait to fuel their fury. What I learned from all of this was that Gobnait of Ballyvourney was the patroness of beekeepers; she was not a woman to be trifled with; and she put men in their place, and that place was paltry and penitential.

That was many years before I made the acquaintance of Gobnait of Kilbroney but very soon I was struck by the fact that her parents who apparently had no interest in beekeeping had shown extraordinary prescience in giving her a name that, however unmusical, was remarkably apt. I was only in the parish a few weeks when she came into the sacristy to have a Mass said, and she attached so many conditions to it that it was like signing for travel insurance. When she left, May who had overheard the whine of her instructions said to me "That one is like the bee". What struck me at the time was that May didn't say "That one is like a bee" but "That one is like the bee" as if there was only one bee. Later on I came to see this as a brilliant piece of phrasing because the definite article removed her from the ordinary working class category of bees, conferred regal status on her, made her the bee of bees, as big in fact in the world of bees as Gobnait of Ballyvourney's robber-chasing species.

To most people the word bee signifies two things: honey and sting. To most people in Kilbroney the lady who was like the bee signified one thing only: sting. She didn't have any honey sac in her gullet; she secreted only venom, what Saint James called the deadly poison of the tongue.

When it came to James's turn every three years to speak at Mass I hoped she was listening. Other epistles have become dull and dated but not James. The only thing that was dated in his epistle as far as I could see was when he said that salt water cannot yield fresh but he could hardly have been expected to know about desalinisation in the first century. For the rest he was as contemporary as a current affairs presenter and when he spoke about the tongue there was no need to follow it up and preach a homily on the topic: James said it all with vigour and striking imagery:– "If you put a bit into a horse's mouth he obeys you. There are mighty ships sailing the seas but they are steered by a small rudder. The tongue is our human bit. The tongue is our human rudder. A forest fire can be started by a match; the tongue is that match. Elephants and lions can be tamed by human beings, so why can't human beings tame their tongues? A spring doesn't pour forth clear water and brackish water from the same source but the tongue does. It is a capricious organ, full of deadly poison."

Whatever about the other horses, ships, forest fires and springs that I could have named in the parish setting on the Sunday of Saint James, I have to admit that Gobnait was the first who moved down the page, line by line, as I read it. I could think of a huge fire that she started in a family with a little match of a false suggestion. I could think of a pregnant teenager that she drove on the rocks because of the way she steered local opinion. I could think of a case where she used a whip and not a bit and a young man emigrated. And I could certainly think of the kitchen behind her paper shop where she held court and the tap ran a lot more brackish water than clear water.

She had a mouth as big as a letter box, the only difference being that letters went in through one and gossip came out through the other, and the livelihood that she had was the perfect setting for her expertise as a gossip monger: she ran the paper shop and she kept guests.

The paper shop was much more than a means of making money; it was the inspiration of her life. Reports, speculation, dispatches, rumours and scandals were all around her on the counter, on the shelves, in the magazine rack and on the display table: they were the organs of news and she was the heart that was pumping blood into them all. The butcher didn't turn into beef, and the publican no matter how hard he tried didn't liquefy into beer, but somehow she saw herself as an impersonation of news. This was particularly true of the local scene: to sell the "News of the World" in defiance of the priest was exciting but to be the centre of the news of the world that mattered, the secret and sometimes sinful world of Kilbroney, was much more exciting.

She was a news agent (two words) as well as a newsagent (one word). The news she sold was a magnet for the news she sought. When a farmer called in for his "Journal" on his way home from the creamery she skimmed him of all the creamery gossip he had accumulated while he had been waiting in the queue there. When a schoolboy called for a comic it was she who had the smile on her face as he left because she relieved him not only of his dull pennies but of the bright coinage of the day's happenings in the school as well.

She never laundered news; on the contrary she fouled it up some more. What she was really good at was tailoring it according to the pattern and the shape that she liked herself.

A classic example of her method was what happened when young Brian Mescall, aged six, called in for his "Beano" on his way home from school.

"You are early to-day, Brian", she began.

"I am because the lady doctor was in school",

"I see". She said it tamely; it was stale news.

"But I won't be so early tomorrow", he added with the honesty of childhood and the effusive nature of the Mescalls.

"Why is that?" she asked, feeling a nibble on the line.

"Because I'm going to be kept in".

The pace quickened. "And why would you be kept in?"

"Because I'm in trouble with Miss Feehan, that's why".

"What kind of trouble, Brian?"

"O, the same kind of trouble" he said with a sad shake of the head.

"You mean you hit Kevin Coughlan again?"

"I did".

"How?"

"With a bottle".

"With a bottle, Brian!"

"Yeh, but sure that's how I did it before too".

"And was he hurt?"

"Naw".

"And did he tell the teacher?"

"Naw".

"So who told her?"

"That old Josie Long."

"And what did Miss Feehan say?"

"She said to tell my mother I'd be kept in tomorrow".

"And did she say anything else?"

"She said I was one right little bastard".

Frank O'Connor couldn't have done much better if he had made it up; it was a piece of dialogue to be savoured for its own delectable sake, bottle or no bottle. But by the time Gobnait had finished twisting and turning it inside her convoluted mind, Brian had really become one right little bastard, Josie Long was a sly telltale, the doctor had been called to the school to examine Kevin Coughlan, and Brian's mother and father had no control over their children.

The original conversation sparkled like a clear stream with chuckle after chuckle as it leapt the boulders of question after question, but what she did then was to pour slurry into it and kill off its humour, its freshness and its innocence.

Her other occupation was running the guesthouse and again news was the chief profit motive. The guests were more important to her than the house and their importance was measured much more by how they filled her ears than by how they filled her purse.

She had two year-round guests, Jim Lacy the bus driver and Rose Feehan the schoolteacher. Jim was a particularly generous contributor to her bank of knowledge because bus drivers not only move buses and passengers from place to place but they pick up the most varied and interesting parcels of information along the route. A woman who scorns a handy place next to Brigid Finn in the front of the bus and instead risks a broken hip lurching to a seat at the back tells a lot about herself, about Brigid Finn and about the relationship between them. Three people get off at the doctor's cross: two of them look as healthy as mountain sheep, so they are suffering only from imaginitis but the third has trouble lowering herself down the steps so either she has very bad phlebitis or her womb is fallen. The woman who comes back from town hugging so many parcels that she looks like a donkey with panniers has surely got dollars from her daughter, a nurse in Boston, and the man who comes back with nothing but a sour look on his face has discovered that the price of a pint in town is no cheaper than it is in Florrie's.

What is more, when Jim got into Kilbroney at night with the late bus he was always so hungry for the supper which Gobnait had ready for him that if he were a superintendent in the Gardai he would have waived the Official Secrets Act in order to get his mouth around her lambchops. Gobnait invariably sat opposite him while he was having his meal and for every forkload of gravied potatoes that he shoved back his throat she picked up with delicate nicety the dainties of his day behind the wheel.

With Rose Feehan it was different. She had a self-contained flat and prepared her own meals so she wasn't exposed to a daily frontal assault. Besides, she hadn't become a teacher without first learning about the stratagems of nosey women. But from time to time the abuse of irate parents got her down and when Gobnait saw the grey mood settled on her face she outflanked her defences by dint of womanly support and a pot of freshly wetted tea and the doors of the school flew open.

Summers brought a run of haddock to the fishermen and a netful of visitors to Gobnait but the French mullet and the Spanish tuna were no use to her apart from their crisp banknotes because she could read all they could tell her in the Foreign News pages of the "Irish Independent". The fish that Gobnait had her long nets spread for were the salmon, the men and women of the parish who had crossed the Atlantic and later on returned for a visit to their native streams in Kilbroney. Some of them such as the Burkes arrived annually although she realised that with the new bungalow planned to be ready for the following year she would be losing the grist that Catherine had always brought to her mill. Others arrived only once in a while when they had the dollars to match the nostalgia or for a wedding of a sister's child: when that happened and the relatives considered that their houses "weren't swanky enough for the Yanks" they used to ask Gobnait to put them up and Gobnait not only put them up but she beat them up like an egg in a tumbler and swallowed them, leaving only the shell.

I don't know if she had a favourite poem but if she did the chances are that it was Robert Browning's "Home Thoughts from Abroad" because when she was quizzing these people from abroad the thoughts she had in her mind were home thoughts: her aim was to get information about the young people who had left Kilbroney and had settled in New Bedford, Mass. or Norfolk, Virginia. A drop of punch which she gave the visitors in the kitchen before they went to bed was a great loosener of tongues and although she didn't always get all the pieces of the jigsaw that she was looking for she had no trouble completing the picture because her bad mind could shape the missing pieces and her imagination could colour them. In that way by doing a verbal tour of the churches, Irish centres, feiseanna and factories of New Bedford and Norfolk she was able to compile a list of the people who were drinking heavily or had given up going to Mass or were on State Assistance, in jail or shacked up with a Puerto Rican.

When the summer work was over and her guests from far and near had gone off with the swallows and the fieldfares, the kitchen settled down to being the winter quarters of her regular cronies. The cronies were her condiments and the kitchen was where she cooked up her own successful recipes of news to be carried by these special agents of hers to the four quarters of the parish.

It is no wonder that when Brian Mescall, swathed in scarfs, called into the shop for his "Beano" another day and she asked him why he wasn't at school, the unfortunate child, trying to be respectful to her and not realising how disrespectful his parents had been about her, answered "I have swollen tonsils, Miss Newsy".

* * *

From time to time Gobnait not only marketed news but she made news. Those were the periods when she was pursuing a man rather than Mercury, when she broke out in a sort of emotional rash, the underlying reason for which was some youngish fellow she took a fancy to. She was, as the saying goes, mad for a man but at 38 years of age the digits were rising and her hopes were falling. When this madness possessed her, the cronies had their visas cancelled and the kitchen space for a week or two was reserved for the male target of the moment. All of her fancies had three things in common: they all had good farms, they all lived on their own without fathers to direct them or mothers to distract them and none of them ever got a mark of more than three out of ten in school. She inveigled them with her threestorey house, her dazzling knowledge and her curranty cake, but none of the affairs lasted very long because stupid and all as they were, when the men got a close up view of her maw they used their legs to get away fast before the shark took one of their legs off.

One evening late in the spring, when kings go forth on their conquests according to the scriptures, there was a knock at my front door. I opened it, and standing in so close to it that I thought he was going to rub noses with me was a man of about 35 with a freshly washed appearance and cheeks so puffy that they seemed to be the foundation on which his eyes and forehead rested. I moved back to create a space between us but he moved forward and occupied it. "Come in" I said but he hadn't waited for the invitation. I had no option but to step to one side and give him the right of way.

He went down along the hall without saying a word and turned unerringly into my living room. It was as though he was a regular visitor of mine but in fact I had never set eyes on him before. I closed the front door slowly to give my mind a chance to get into gear and then I followed the mystery man into the living room.

He had settled himself in my red leather easy chair and his hands were patting its arms as if they were two red setters one on either side of him. I had been trained in the necessity of putting callers at their ease but there was no need in this case: he was as much at home as my cat.

Funnily, the fact that he had chosen the best chair gave me an advantage because I then pulled around the high stool I had for keeping myself awake when reading the Office and I sat on that and so I was able to look at him closely from a bit of a height without giving the impression that I was staring at him, which I was. What my stare focussed on was his smile: it appeared to be painted solid on his face and only if the pigments cracked, it seemed to me, could his expression change.

Not surprisingly he took the lead in the conversation, but very surprising was his first sentence. "I am Derry Russell of Moulabranna" he said, and added, "You haven't seen me before, Father".

"No, indeed", I said nearly falling off the chair with the shock, and when I recovered my balance I said, all manners, "I am glad to meet you, Derry" but if my mouth had followed the prompting of my mind it would have said, all interest, not all manners, "I am fascinated to meet you, Derry".

No wonder: it had taken five and a half years for this to happen. That was the length of time I had been in the parish and apart from some bedridden Church of Ireland people, I had made the acquaintance of everyone else from east at Cotter's corner to west at the heaving Atlantic, young and old, Protestant and Catholic, native and alien, everyone except Derry Russell.

The best chance I had was when I first got settled in the parish. Fr Mac put me through the care-of-souls book, as he called the register and explained where the various bodies were that housed the souls. When we came to the page headed Moulabranna his index finger hovered over the name Derry

Russell and he said "Poor fellow. He's not so well in the head. He has some fine grazing over there but after his father died he sold all the stock and the only things moving over the land there now are the brambles and the nettles". Then curling the finger to draw me closer to him and cocking an ear to make sure that Nellie his housekeeper wasn't dusting outside the door he said, in a low voice, "He is away at present in the Mental".

As things turned out that was my best chance to see him. My plain duty demanded that I should visit him in the asylum but I excused myself on the poor grounds that I didn't know him and he didn't know me and that my visit would be more of an intrusion than an act of Christian charity. The fact of the matter is that I didn't and when he was discharged after two years he secluded himself more stringently in Moulabranna than all the double-lock systems, male nurses and security heavies had been able to do in the Mental.

I can testify to that. I called to see his mother many a time but the only sign of him I ever saw was his shirt airing in front of the oven. Whenever I asked her how he was she invariably answered "Better than yourself, Father". She was a bit of a wag and I could never be sure whether it was his physical health or his mental health that she was comparing with mine. It was well known from my finicky picking and choosing at Station breakfasts that I had a stomach ulcer, but equally she might have been referring to the juvenile capers I indulged in from time to time when the Roman collar was close to choking all the creativity out of me. Indeed on balance I think she was probably referring to the pranks because on the first occasion when I visited the house after his discharge and I asked her if he had received a clean bill of health she rivetted me to the kitchen floor with a remark that was a quarter humour and three quarters judgment on myself. "He was told", she said, "that he was as normal as three quarters of the people who think they are normal!"

With a mother as staunch as that, he wanted for nothing. She fetched his Guinness from Florrie's, his tablets from the dispensary and his comics, yes comics, from Gobnait's. She cooked for him, washed for him and especially mounted guard for him. What system she employed to alert him I do not know — it was more successful than Bill Driscoll's obviously — but nobody, postman, mobile shop driver, ticket seller, electioneering canvasser or myself ever caught a glimpse of him. I asked her one time if he ever went outside the door at all and she answered "Of course he does. A body can't live without sunshine" but no one searching for a breachy animal or the makings of a pot of blackberry jam on a sunny day ever discovered the warm nook in which he stretched himself.

I mentioned Stations. The best job that Ciss Russell ever did of shielding Derry from the public eye, that is from several dozen private eyes, was when it was her turn to house the Station Mass and act as hostess to the neighbourhood of Moulabranna. No purdah in a Muslim palace was ever so strict and certainly was never so successful in shielding a beautiful princess from the gaze of outsiders as was the security system she put into effect at the time of the Station to protect Derry's psychological virginity. With workmen coming and going for a fortnight beforehand the measure of vigilance required was enormous. He couldn't be in the kitchen when they were painting the walls; he couldn't be in the room when they were laying the new roll of linoleum; he couldn't be anywhere inside when the electrician was putting in new wiring; he couldn't be anywhere outside when the Cantys were spreading shingle from Tránagloch over the path from the gate to the front door; and he couldn't be in his upstairs refuge when Pete-at-the-Cross who had a very sharp eye from playing whist every Sunday night was whitewashing the outside walls.

If the planning period presented difficulties to her defensive system that was nothing compared to D Day itself: assault followed upon assault from neighbours, returned Yanks, suppliers of apple tarts, altarboys, free beerers and the merely curious. I wasn't any great trouble to her except when in a sudden flash of piety I suggested to her that it would be a splendid opportunity for Derry to go to confession and communion "in his own room, of course" I quickly added "not down here with everybody gawking". But not even that sort of Holy War assault could breach the walls of Derry's citadel. "I thank you for the kind thought", she said in reply, "but no: sure he has no chance of committing sin, poor fellow, and he would get a seizure if you walked in on him".

Not being a Godfrey de Bouillon I abandoned my scaling ladder and let the Lord attend personally to the sacramental business in His own good time. Everything else went according to plan — Ciss's plan. Nobody got to go upstairs except Ciss herself. Unfortunately as the toilet was upstairs this proved to be a great inconvenience for the women who were present and it was noticed that a number of them left early saying that they would be back later when they got some chores done at home. It made no difference to the men who came to terms with the profusion of porter in the haggart.

That Derry was upstairs nobody had any doubt but not a geek or a meek was heard from him all day, not even during the quietest parts of the Mass. Some people figured he was creeping around the bedroom in his socks to muffle the sound; others that he was lying in one position in the bed like a patient after an operation. One way or another, there would have been more noise from up there if a butterfly had floated in through the bedroom window and landed on the quilt. The day ended as it began with the veil of the purdah unruffled, the walls of Jerusalem intact and the Omaha Beach still in the hands of the defenders.

But life plays the cruellest of tricks on the kindest of people. In February around about the time when Stephen Burke's coffin was heading for legendary status, Ciss Russell suffered a crippling stroke. She had to be moved first to hospital in Hilltown and then to a longterm nursing home and in a real sense the vehicle that carried her away for ever from Moulabranna was more like a removals van than an ambulance: it shifted out of sight every stick of furniture of their former lives and it left

Derry with virtually a new house which he would have to furnish for himself.

The first result was that the "siege" ended. I have to enclose the word in inverted commas because in actual fact no one ever put him under siege. He shut the gates on himself, hung out a banner on the battlements saying "Siege on here" and invited a little army of curious people outside to take up their tactical positions. When, three days after his mother was moved, the hunger got to him he surrendered to his situation, he took in the banner, opened the gates and walked out to find that there wasn't even a platoon waiting outside to ambush him.

That first day, when he went on the morning bus to Hilltown to visit his mother and came home on the late bus with an awkward weight of parcels was something of a sensation, but it was a frustrating trip for the other passengers because he pushed every other topic except himself out of their minds and by his presence he kept that pressing topic behind their teeth. It was a tense silent journey both ways; it was like having a time bomb on the bus.

But Jim Lacy the bus driver didn't see it that way at all. When he arrived in Gobnait's that night he didn't need her Irish stew to lubricate his speech organs: the wheels were already spinning on the sensationally new brand of oil that Derry brought on to the bus with him. He was impressed. He told Gobnait "I had the wrong notion of him altogether. I thought he would be like the sweep at the end of a sooty day but he wasn't. He had a very nice jacket on him, a mack over his arm, and a crease in the trousers that you wouldn't find in a clothes shop. And he looked like a man who came straight out of a bath before he got dressed: there was a shine on him, I tell you, like the shine on your plates. But what I noticed most of all was his smile: he smiled at me when he got on the bus — very few do that — he smiled at me when he was getting off — even fewer do that — and a few times when I looked back at the passengers on my inside mirror he was still smiling like a child on his first bus ride". And he concluded, not realising that he was splashing some of Gobnait's own stew-gravy over her face "You can never believe what people tell you about other people".

As time went on and Ciss got no better Derry got better and better in himself. He went on the bus to Hilltown every Tuesday to look in on his mother and as that was Martday he sat on the auction benches leaning forward with everyone else but unlike everyone else with a smile on his face for the proceedings in the ring. From time to time he walked to the village and spent a leisurely hour or two getting his tablets at the dispensary, his six pack of Guinness at Florrie's and his comic at Gobnait's. He liked to leave the comic till last because then Gobnait crowned the day for him with a cup of tea and a slice of currany cake in the kitchen.

How I failed to meet him in the nursing home when he was visiting his mother or on the road to Kilbroney when he was coming in for his triad of essentials I do not know; I can only speculate that Providence had something more dramatic in mind for me than a casual encounter. And so it was that on a May evening I was looking down from a high stool at a man with a neat suit, a scrubbed appearance and a permanent smile who was lounging in my red leather armchair and I was wondering to myself what I would say next after saying "I am glad to meet you, Derry".

In common with every other priest I had three fillers for gaps in conversation at weddings and Stations and they jumped to my mind now in order of yeoman's service: the weather, football and the price of bullocks.

"Good weather we are having, Derry", I said confidently, leading with a king of trumps.

"Not for apple trees", he responded, slamming me with a knave.

"Well, it's good for footballers anyway", I came back tentatively. "Firm sod underfoot. Makes for an open game". And then warming to my subject and calling on all the sports journalese I could think of, I said "I saw the Owen Roes in action on Sunday. They had a resounding win over the Brian Borus. I fancy them this year to go all the way and get their hands on the cup. They have a nice blend of youth and experience".

"Blend of cuckoos and terriers if you ask me", he said, "and fellows as old as myself running around in short pants chasing a bag of air".

He was a strange bird, surely, stranger than the cuckoo he mentioned, and as for the terrier I couldn't be sure whether he was biting my leg or pulling it. I simply couldn't determine the man's mood: his tone of voice was sharp but his smile was gentle. For the first time in my life 'ambivalent' wasn't a word in the dictionary; the experience was like being drenched under a sunshower.

I didn't trot out the bullocks, that's for sure; they would probably have been slaughtered right away. But I didn't need to. He led the next card. And it was a surprising one. "I want to talk about myself", he said.

"Go ahead, Derry".

"There are two things I want to do," he told me, "but I don't know which of the two I want to do the most".

"And they are?"

"The first is I want to be a monk, but I'm not sure if it would suit me or not".

"What sort of monk have you in mind, Derry? There are all sorts of different breeds of them: Carthusians, Cistercians, Benedictines . . ." I hesitated at this point, not knowing for sure if the others I was going to add to the list, the Dominicans, Franciscans. Carmelites and Augustinians were monks or not.

"The Melleray monks are the ones I am thinking of. I was there once and I liked the look of them and the way they were dressed".

"How long did you stay, Derry?"

"Oh, just an hour. I was on a bus tour".

"Spending an hour there and spending your life there are two different things", I reminded him, finding myself immediately drawn for everyone's good into the business of dissuasion.

"I know that, but do you think they would suit me?"

I didn't want to act as the master of novices and point out severely that it wasn't so much a question of whether they would suit him as a question of whether he would suit them so I contented myself with saying "It depends on whether you would like to do what they do", which drew the further question from him "And what do they do?"

"Well, the main thing they do is to chant the Divine Office seven times a day". And I went on to explain that what I could say by myself in three quarters of an hour would take them several hours all together in the abbey church sending the words across at one another from side to side, like table tennis, over and back, over and back.

It wasn't a very accurate account or a very elegant simile so it was no wonder that he asked me "Why would they do the like of that?"

"To give glory to God", I answered.

"I don't see much glory in that", he remarked, "lobbing words across at one another like table tennis balls".

"It's in the singing that the glory is", I said, trying to extract myself from the bog I had walked into. "The singing lifts up the words to God".

"You mean the balls hop so high they rise to heaven?"

"Something like that", I said resignedly, knowing I would have to get away from the ping pong table.

"Seven times a day", I repeated, "and the first time is three o'clock in the morning".

"Three o'clock in the morning" he roared, his eyes full of exclamation marks.

"Or maybe four," I said "I can't remember exactly".

"Three or four, what's the difference? Sure that would be right in the middle of my sleep."

"Well, Derry, that's what makes the monks what they are. They turn the day on its head".

"More likely they would turn me on my head", he said sadly. I felt I was winning, in a perverse sort of pastoral way.

"What else?" he asked.

"Well, they eat only bread and vegetables"

"Bread and vegetables!"

"No meat".

"No meat!"

"Sometimes they have fish".

"I hate fish".

"They never talk".

"Never?"

"Except for Christmas dinner".

"Christmas dinner! What good is Christmas dinner without turkey?"

"Well, the talk makes up for the turkey, I suppose".

"What else?"

"Well, the priests study all day in their cells but as you have no Latin you would be out on the mountain a lot".

"Doing what?"

"Looking after the sheep. They have more sheep than there are people in Galway".

"My God!" I could see his eyes running up and down the mountain like a pair of frantic sheepdogs.

"Of course you could be on the farm too".

"On the farm?"

"Yes. Setting parsnips. Thinning turnips. Digging potatoes. You remember I told you about all the vegetables they eat."

"Couldn't they buy the vegetables with the money they get from the sheep?"

"Oh, no, they buy nothing. Everything they eat they grow themselves. Wheat. Fruit. Vegetables. Their farm is the most intensive, the most productive and the busiest in the whole of the county of Waterford."

"Busiest" was a whack on the point of the chin to him. I could see his dizzy mind wandering among what the poet called "the unlaboured fields" of Moulabranna where the ferns held sway and the furze bushes smelled like the spice groves of Araby.

Punch drunk, he could only say a hesitant "yes".

Seeing my mission as the mutual welfare of Derry and Melleray I went for the knock-out.

"And every day," I said, summoning to my aid the popular and, in the popular mind, incontrovertible belief, "they look at their graves".

"Their own graves, you mean?"

"Yes."

"Before they are dead, you mean?"

"Yes. They dig their own graves, bit by bit, day by day".

"By God, do you know what? They are more mental than the fellows in the Mental".

It might not have been the conclusion that would be reached by a writer on the contemplative life, but it was a punch line worthy of a literary pub. And it was also the end of his vocation to the Cistercians.

But if it solved a problem for the abbot of Mount Melleray it produced a problem for myself. There was the second preference. "What other plan had you in mind, Derry?" It was a question that expected no more than a flick in the ear for an answer but it was my turn to get a punch straight on the chin.

"I was thinking of getting married," he said.

"I see," said I but I could see nothing except spots in front of my eyes. When I recovered my balance a little I retreated to my priestly corner to get my head cleared and I sneaked out the conventional first sentence of the instruction that I gave to intending couples when they called. "Marriage." said I, "is a big step and requires a lot of thought beforehand". He agreed with a cursory nod of his head.

"How long have you been thinking about it?" I asked.

"Oh, two or three weeks", he answered.

"Two or three weeks!" I repeated, the exclamation mark rocketing my voice. It was my equivalent of his "Three o' clock in the morning" shout. Then I said lowering the volume to a civilised level, "All the experts recommend a period of two or three years."

"Two or three years!" The volume went up again. "I could change my mind in that length of time"

I could think only of a cliché in response to his adventurous honesty. "Better change your mind before rather than after". He had me on the run.

I tried again hoping to stem the retreat. "Are you just thinking of marriage in general?" In Cricket that would be called a dolly shot and he dispatched it for six. "Good God, no," he said, "I'm not talking about marriage in a book, I'm talking about marriage in a bed".

Not for the first time that evening I was taken off my feet by a flash of lightning from his lips. There was the crack about the ancient footballers in short pants chasing a bag of air; there was the snigger about the monks being more mental than the fellows in the Mental; and now this balanced Joycean beauty about marriage in a book and marriage in a bed. He was mad in the general direction of Hamlets's north north east and you couldn't help thinking about the turbulence in the clouds that caused the lightning, but there was no denying the brilliance of the flash.

"Oh, fine," I said, "fine." Although there was nothing fine about being pummelled in my corner; and finally getting to the only question that mattered I asked "And who is the lucky woman?"

"Gobnait O' Brien," he answered.

As I used to say when a child, before I got to making my own metaphors, you could knock me down with a feather.

"But does she know?"

"Of course she knows. Isn't that why I'm here?"

"You mean she sent you?" I was out in the middle of the ring again.

"She said to come up and sound you out". He didn't have the peasant cunning to match his patches of brilliance. In the last analysis he was, poor fellow, an innocent.

"Has she been talking to you about marriage?"

"Oh, yes with the tea and the curranty cake these nights."

"I see" and this time I really did see as clearly as a spy satellite.

"Usually the two people come together", I pointed out to him. "Why didn't she come up with you?"

"I suppose she has to mind the shop."

"Well, I'll tell you what I'll do. Someday that she is minding the shop I'll call in to her and I'll discuss it with her."

I think he could sense the closure of the interview and he rose up out of the armchair. "You can tell her to expect me" I said, as he preceded me to the door.

And then at the very door itself I remembered that I was supposed to be a pastor more than a proctor. I asked him how his mother was and I said how really nice it was to have made his acquaintance.

* * *

I delayed my visit to Gobnait for three or four days. This was a calculated gambit to keep her on the edge of her seat and give her a tense backside before we got seated opposite each other in the kitchen. Also I needed to go over the ground of the likely encounter very carefully so that I would be the one setting the ambuscade not the one being ambushed. So I was wearing my proctor's wig rather more than my pastor's biretta during those days.

My first consideration was a humane one: to protect Derry from what I could only call child abuse. He was an adult in years but a child in outlook, and the control she was trying to exercise over him was nothing short of an abuse of power. I had no doubt in my own mind that her greed for land was one bird and her need for a man was another and that she aimed to kill the two birds with one stone — the well flighted weapon of a wedding.

Moulabranna was a fine holding even if the rabbits were the present tenants and if she got Derry up her own twisty staircase she could make it produce revenue not ragwort. The house would be ideal for an English couple in retreat from the onslaught of noise, muggings and grandchildren in Britain; it had a view of the sea to the south, it was sheltered from the north and east, and it was about as far 'away from it all' as a clay road is from a motorway. Alas, because of Derry's foolishness the land had no milk quota going with it but she could easily lease it to fellows who were into barley or beef or even into the vanity of having more acres to their name.

Everyone knew she was mad for a man and even if the man were a little mad she didn't seem to mind so long as she could move over in the church from the single women's side to the married women's side. But it mattered to me because I could see that the marriage bed would become a procrustean bed in a very short time. Procrustes of old expected his visitors to fit his guest bed exactly, and if they didn't he either stretched their limbs if they were too short or he chopped them off if they were too long and I could see Gobnait doing something similar to Derry: either she would stretch him to utter insanity or she would reduce him to an utter nonentity. As a defender of the weak I was determined to foil Gobnait's scheme.

Better still, as a priest I had the means to do so. The first thing I had ever learned about marriage in canon law was that it is a contract and if there wasn't free and full consent the contract was invalid. If consent was absent, the only thing that was present was a sham; if consent was forced the injured party was entitled to have the marriage annulled. The core of the marriage ceremony was the exchange of consent, just the few seconds that it took the bride and groom to say "I do"; the whole apple took maybe an hour to eat but without that core it was a hollow apple. And the lead-up to that exchange of consent was the vital question they were asked: "Have you come here of your own freewill and choice and without any compulsion to marry each other?"

It was clear to me that Derry didn't have the necessary freedom of choice; on the contrary, he was being conditioned by attention and currant cake, he was being fitted into a wedding suit the way a toddler is fitted into a rompers, and he was being steered to the church door. There are more subtle ways of urging a man to the altar than a shotgun. I knew all about Gobnait's subtlety and I knew the bludgeon that could blunt her rapier — canon law.

But I also knew that there was a big risk involved for myself, personally. If Gobnait lost her man I could lose my reputation. There was a very good chance that she wouldn't want it to be generally known that she was leading this three quarter wit by the nose up the aisle, but in the event of her having to let go of Derry's hand, it would give her another stone for her pouch, and it might even provoke her into revealing the secret of the ashen coffin. I would have to walk the narrow line between self preservation and the sanctity of marriage very carefully.

Another consideration was nettling my mind as well. Was it all a façade? Was it a plan to fool me into thinking that she was serious when in fact she wasn't? Did she figure that I would approve of the marriage in order to get into her good books and to wheedle her into forgetting that she ever saw those coffin screws in my hand? Would she then delate me to the bishop for using the sacrament as a bribe? Was she simply using Derry as a pawn to draw out my rook into a position where she could assail it? She was clever enough and unscrupulous enough to plan all of that, which was why I spent several days planning my own strategy.

The first thing I decided on was not to trundle up the heavy artillery of the canon law but to keep it in reserve. Instead I would try a few spatters of rifle fire over her head and see if she would duck. So on the day when I went into the papershop I went in wearing my commercial face — the one I wore when going in to pay the monthly account for the papers — and not my judicial face.

Gobnait was standing there right in front of me when I entered, shuffling the magazines. "Come in to the kitchen, Father Laide," she said "I have been expecting you". She walked before me into the gossip chamber and shut the two doors linking it with the shop. Then she pointed to a chair at the far end of the kitchen table and she sat at the near end herself. Good: the distance between meant that she was on the defensive.

"You know why I'm here" I began, with a 'Let us get down to business' tone of voice. I had no intention of woolying the situation with the preliminaries of weather, football and bullocks; in any case with the grazing of Moulabranna at the back of my mind, bullocks wouldn't have been a cosy topic.

"O, yes, Derry Russell told me you had a matter to discuss with me," she said, lifting her chin.

Better and better. The fact that she mentioned his surname meant that she was uncomfortable; it was as if she was putting him at the other end of the table too.

"I must compliment you on your interest in him," I said "and on your kindness to him. It is very good of you, in view of his history, but in my opinion you shouldn't humour him into thinking there is anything more to it than that".

"How do you mean?"

"I mean: don't give him any notions". I silently thanked God that one could say so much in the vaguest of English. Gobnait was silent, astonishingly silent. Could it be that she had been expecting a kicking match in hobnailed boots and that the pirouetting in soft shoes was wrongfooting her entirely?

I continued "As you know he was in the Mental for some years. What that means is that there is a fault in his brain like a fissure in the earth's crust. It can stabilise for a while like at present but it is never fully healed. It can open again just like the fault in California. A whole new way of life to him would bring on crushing, unbearable pressure. He would crack up like an earthquake. You could find yourself visiting the Mental every week for twenty years."

"You must take me for a fool" she said.

"O, no," I replied, "that isn't why I am here. I am here precisely because I do not take you for a fool, Gobnait". It was the first time since I entered that I used her Christian name; my confidence was growing. "You are a highly intelligent woman, Gobnait" — I used the name again — "and it astonishes me that a person with a brain like yours could think for even one instant of having an alliance with a man of very inferior intellectual capacity. He is a very nice man, but well . . . he is still reading comics at the age of 35. Can you see yourself in one chair" — I gave a quick glance and saw "Guests of the Nation" on a chair under the window — "reading Frank O'Connor and Derry in another reading Beano?"

The vanity argument was good; she smiled.

"Well, can you?" I repeated.

"No, not really," she answered. It was as good as saying to me "Continue with the soliloquy". I did.

"If a child came along, you can surely guess how it would be with him as regards his brains and you would hardly want a child of yours being kept back in 2nd class and 3rd class and every class and not being confirmed till he was 15, would you? That might be alright for a Russell but not for an O'Brien, with teachers in your family".

Every moment I was expecting her to say "Now look here, Father" and make a stand and begin a counter attack but the shameless arguments that I was using based on doubtful genetics and outright snobbery gave her no chance to look anywhere except at the doom I was prophesying for her. Also it could be that as I was speechless when she found me with the coffin screws in my hand so she was speechless when I found her, as it were, with an imbecile in her lap, and for the same reason: shamefaced embarrassment.

Whatever the reason might have been, there was no fight in her and my final argument was the feminine equivalent of kicking a man when he is down. What a gossip dreads more than anything is the knowledge that she is the object of gossip herself and I used that dread as my coup de grace.

"I think you should also consider, Gobnait," said I, "that if you were to pursue the idea of a marriage such as this, seriously, Doctor Morgan would have to be consulted". It was the first time that I bluntly mentioned marriage; I had spoken of it in vague terms such as notions, alliance, a child coming along but I hadn't actually used the term marriage. Now the very word was an extra weapon because it had acquired at this stage of the discussion a pejorative meaning. And I continued "The doctor would have to be asked for a certificate of mental fitness. It is very very doubtful that he would give it, but what isn't doubtful at all is that Alice would hear about it. Pillow talk and all that, you understand. What a husband knows his wife knows. And what she knows tonight the parish will know tomorrow". I paused, "Am I right, Gobnait?"

"Yes, you're right, Father".

It was checkmate. The townland of Moulabranna was wiped off Gobnait's map forever. I outmanoeuvred her on the day. I won the battle conclusively. But what I forgot was that Kilbroney wasn't one battle field. Kilbroney was a theatre of war.

Chapter 3

THE DAY OF THE ARAB

Four weeks later a day arrived out of a June sky that came to be known as the Day of the Arab. But really it began not with a crazy idea in the priest's house on the hill above Kilbroney church but at a much higher elevation in the Wadi Musa in the Jordan Desert.

Years before I became curate in Kilbroney I went on a fifteen hour trip by car from Amman to the Wadi Musa. For most of the way the road was a mere consensus of tyre tracks. I had three companions, two Englishmen and an American, and we were driven by an Arab who was not the most skillful pothole skimmer I have ever known.

From the time we passed through Dhiban about noon the road never again got a mouthful of tar. We angled up the sides of the hills, we bucked along the plateaus and we minced our way down into the next canyon as if we were on horses rather than on wheels. The heat was sickening; I got to know why a dog sticks his head out of a car window. But you didn't stick it out when a truck was approaching because if you did you got shawled in thick dust. The tyres left marks in it as exaggeratedly deep as those in advertisements.

South of Karak the road did the impossible: it got worse. Joseph abandoned the course he was following parallel to a dried up river and he drove the car right into the riverbed itself. He shouldn't have: something snapped and the car sagged at the rear. He blasphemed in Arabic gutturals, tore the doors open and shouted at us to get out. A broken spring, that's what it was. In my elementary knowledge of car mishaps a broken spring meant a breakdown lorry, but where would you find a breakdown lorry in a wilderness? Joseph found an alternative in the boot of the car — a piece of strong rope. He jacked up the Opel, got under her and after half an hour of grunting the repair was completed. We were ordered two into the front and two into a perspiring corner in the back, and off with us again.

In the late evening the eastern sky was like a strip of wall on which you try out colours. Then the sun set, the moon came out in muslin and cream flowed on the top of the mountains.

At last we got to the Wadi Musa and arrived at Elji the nearest inhabited place to Petra which was what we wanted to see. Elji consisted of a scatter of mudhouses and a police station straight out of a Foreign Legion novel. It doubled up as an unofficial inn. We got a room in the watch tower and we climbed to it by an outside ladder. We each got three blankets, one for under, one for over and one for bundling up as a pillow. There was a manhole in the ceiling which was open and the stars were looking inquisitively in. But I for one didn't look at them for long.

At sunup we were up too: up through the manhole on to the flat roof of the watch tower. We looked out on five eucalyptus trees, a dust heap of countryside, a village that had been planned by a child with a sand bucket and off in the distance a lower jaw of sharp mountain teeth. Behind those teeth there was a small tongue of level ground and that is where Petra was. There was only one way in: through a gap between the teeth, a gap that the Arabs called El Siq — the Pass. We slid down the ladder to where four of those Arabs were waiting with horses for us to ride through the Siq into Petra.

A legionnaire from King Hussein's Arab Legion rode with us as an escort, booted, brassbuttoned and bravadoing down the trail but I was much more interested in the man who walked alongside the horse that I was riding. His name was Abu Ali. He was about fifty. He had cavernous eyes and a thistly beard and he was dressed in a black smock and white pantaloons. A goathair cord about his middle held himself, his clothes and his dagger together. That dagger was almost the death of me twice: my eyes were magneted to it when they should have been watching the flinty trail. It was about 12 inches long; the sheath and the handle were of silver and it was studded with five ruby stones and four emeralds. It was shaped like a sword-fish all thrust and dazzle. In the safer parts Abu Ali handed me a succession of Roman coins that he was trying to sell me but even if he had as many on offer as would pay a Roman Legion I wasn't interested. The dagger was what I wanted. I didn't see it as a weapon of death, only as a thing of beauty. It wasn't Abu Ali's reins I wanted to hold but Abu Ali's dagger.

When we got through the Siq and out into the theatrical clearing, I marvelled, of course, at the building carved out of red sandstone and glowing in the sun which gave English po-etry one of its greatest lines: "rose red city half as old as time". It was called Pharaoh's Treasury and it was said that at one time the Bedouin riflemen used to snipe at the great stone urn on top of the building in the hope that they could riddle it and bring down upon their heads a shower of the Pharaoh's gold. But the only treasure that I coveted was the treasure hanging from Abu Ali's girdle.

I got lucky. The other tourist fare on offer was a climb to the Great High Place, but the others decided they had eaten enough for one day and so the only ones who set foot on the goat track leading to the mountain top and the altar of sacrifice were Abu Ali and myself. I wanted to see it because for years I had been reading the thunderous words of the prophets blast-ing the life, present and to come, out of any Israelite — and there were many — who dared to worship on the High Places. I had always had the feeling that the Israelites took part in the local pagan rites to save themselves the bother of traipsing hundreds of miles to Jerusalem but when I got to the summit, after much tearing of the heart and shoe leather, I realised that there was a great deal more to it than that. There was the altar, very much like the altars I said Mass at myself with steps, a platform and a table hacked from the solid rock at the very tip top of the mountain. There was no higher you could go to offer anything to God, and if you stretched your hand upwards in the air there was a real chance that He would stretch His hand down to clasp it. Thousands of feet below a bush moved; no, it was a man; no, he was an ant on the path of history.

Abu Ali and I sat down in the hewn out court of the priests and it could be because we were in a place of sacrifice that I focussed my attention once again on the dagger dangling from his girdle. If it was withdrawn from its silver sheath one slash of its blade would rip open a sheep's throat. I recalled the sardonic principle that if you need something badly enough it is for sale.

"I would like to buy your dagger, Abu Ali" I said looking into the twin caves of his eyes, and knowing that the Arabs, like the Irish, love poetic exaggeration I added "It outshines the sun for splendour".

"Ah, my dagger" he said with a smile, the first of the day, that brought the brown eyes to the mouth of their caves and with one hand on the silver sheath and the other on the silver handle he pulled them apart and held up the dagger to the pierced sky. The blade was of grey steel and the point of it was so sharp it would make three sticks of a match stick.

"It is an inheritance" he said — I knew he meant an heirloom — "I got it from my elder brother when he died and he got it from our father."

He hadn't marvellously said an outright "no" so I cut in with "You have other inheritances, other daggers".

"Oh yes" he said. "Many. Our daggers are your women". I knew what he meant, even if the compressed syntax gave it a Joycean flavor alien to the desert. He explained it, anyhow. "One comes, another goes. One is lost, another is found." I began the next sentence of the series in my own mind "One is sold, another is — " but I didn't finish it because he said "This one has much value".

I knew that, but obviously I wasn't tamely going to confirm his opinion. The important thing was that we were in a bargaining situation.

"I can get as fine a dagger in the bazaar in Damascus," I said, trying to lay him a false scent.

He was too clever for me. "No, you can't," he replied. "You can get maybe a boy dagger or a cripple dagger but not a young man dagger the like of this." The change of sex in dagger talk from female to male was confusing but again I thought I knew what he meant and I didn't like the sound of it: this dagger, he was implying, was intended to be used. I proceeded on that understanding; if he thought I intended to pin it to a wall along with a brace of pistols he would have threaded it back on to his girdle.

"Yes, the young man is vigorous" I said. "He is strong. He fights well" and then I asked the question "How much value is much value?"

"Fifty English pounds", he replied without hesitation. "I won't take a pound less".

I pitched my bid to where splitting the difference would still be very big money for him and not outrageously big for me. "Thirty English pounds," I said. "I won't give you a pound more". We looked at each other with the alert glance of men who know a good thing when they are assessing it, be it a woman, a horse or a dagger. "Forty English pounds," we said simultaneously. The dagger was mine!

From deep inside my clothes I pulled out the pouch that was my travelling bank. I counted out forty pounds sterling into his snug hands — he would walk a good many miles with his horse in and out of the Siq to earn money like that — and he lowered the dagger, handle first, into my tingling right hand.

I remember thinking what a pity it was that the ancient cistern for ritual baths hadn't any water in it; otherwise I had no regrets leaving the Great High Place. I almost glided down the shaly slope and it wasn't because it was downhill going but because every now and then I would halt, pull the dagger out of its sheath, look at the Arabic squiggles on the blade that named the name of the smith who shaped and tempered it, and then, holding the sheath in one hand and the dagger in the other in front of me I would see them as two stretched wings that carried me to happiness.

A fortnight later I was indeed in the bazaar in Damascus and there I bought two further pieces of Arabic embellishment, a headcloth and a headband.

As regards the headcloth, a small tablecloth that I could have bought in Hilltown would have been every square inch as functional, although it would have lacked the sinuous embroidery but the headband I couldn't have bought anywhere except in Arab lands. I went for a green one because it was a balm for the mind in the oven heat of the Syrian day, within that circle of brown hills in which the city was sitting as in a great baked pot. Extreme heat does that to me: I go colour blind to every other colour except green. "Green, green, I want you green," Lorca wrote in one of his poems and that is what I said too when I saw the headbands stacked up like coronets in the bazaar. Later on I was really pleased with my choice when I read that green was the adopted colour of the descendents of Mohammed's daughter, Fatima.

So now with the dagger, the headcloth and the headband all I lacked to fancydress myself as an Arab, if I ever took the notion, was a long offwhite shirt stretching to the shins. I didn't ever get around to buying one; and a grubby alb which would have doubled convincingly for it would have identified me too readily, but when indeed that mad notion seized me I had at hand a robe which would elevate me from a poor Bedu to a Sheikh.

It was a dressing gown, to be honest about it, but the only thing it had in common with the dull, the loud, the crumpled and the cheap wraparounds in which you see men walking up and down hospital corridors was the name. Where Fr. Bergin, a former parish priest of mine, got it, I have no idea: maybe as a present from a cousin of his who was on the Chinese mission. The material was shot silk; it would have pleased Polonius: it was "rich not gaudy". The only way I can describe its colour is to say that it would remind you of the final phases of a cloud-bossed sunset, still glowing but artistically subdued. It was trimmed with a nervous black band and if it had been turned inside out the lining itself would have done a cardinal proud on the day of his investiture.

Fr. Bergin's sister told me that he never wore it; he put it away for the emergency that would land him in hospital, but when the emergency came he was dead before the ambulance arrived. His sister reckoned that I had been nice to him as his curate and asked me if I would like to have it as a keepsake. I said yes, of course, and then I did with it what Fr. Bergin had done: I put it on a hanger in the wardrobe and waited for the occasion to wear it. That occasion came on the Friday in June which went down in the annals of Kilbroney as the Day of the Arab.

* * *

I can remember every detail of the day except one thing: what precisely it was in the first instance that prompted me to dress up as an Arab and stalk through the village. In Saint Luke's gospel it says that Satan entered into Judas; the question is: what got into me? A poltergeist out for a bit of fun? There I was like a sedately parked car: what was it that turned the ignition key in me and got me to move down the road in a totally erratic manner? Something picked me up like a clockwork toy and wound me up; but what?

I can't remember if I had been to see the film "Lawrence of Arabia" shortly before my own change of dress, or if that was the year when a book club edition of Wilfred Thesiger's brilliant "Arabian Sands" came out, or if somebody simply had come from the city and brought me a present of a box of dates with palm trees romanticising the lid.

I have often read of a crime without a motive. What I did was certainly not a crime, unless it was a crime of indecency in the old sense of the word, meaning something unbecoming, in my case something not becoming a humdrum man of the cloth, but if so I had no motive I can think of . . .

Unless it was that I suddenly tired of being a spancelled horse and kicked at the traces . . . Unless it was that all the world except Kilbroney was a stage and I desperately needed deep within myself a bit of drama . . . Unless it was that the boredom of routine as a priest had blocked the arteries of my personality and the only way to get the blood flowing again was to do something daft . . . Unless it was that I wanted to see a dead village come alive and the indifferent villagers to actually look at me for once, instead of merely noticing my presence.

On the other hand I could just have been out for a bit of crack like a boy who throws a stick in the stream to see how far it will get.

At all events, whatever the reason or the lack of it , whatever the forces that were at work in me or outside of me, at 3 o'clock in the afternoon of that Friday in June I went upstairs to doff the priest and to don the Arab. I took off the Roman collar and all my black gear — trousers, jacket and stock — and I put on a grey trousers that I had for discarding my label in faraway places. Next I went to the wardrobe, took down Fr Bergin's dressing gown and put on the sheik's desert coat. And then I went the short cut to Damascus and took the headcloth and the headband out of the locker. I draped the cloth over my head remembering the heat of the Syrian sun as I did so and I pulled the splendid three-hooped band down over the cloth to keep it in position, recalling the evergreen memory of the daughter of the Prophet.

I looked at myself in the mirror and I asked myself the question: could I be recognised? In profile, certainly not, although the somewhat bulbous sunsmeared nose might very well indicate west of Ireland origin rather than Middle East. But when I looked at myself head on, even though I was cropped of my ears and my forehead the answer that came back from the mirror was: yes, the eyes give the game away. So down I went to the car to fetch my old-fashioned heavily opaque sunglasses and when I put them on for the benefit of the mirror even I myself had trouble recognising the curate of Kilbroney.

One thing now remained to be girded on to complete the outfit — the dagger. I went downstairs and opened the door into the dining room where I never dined, junk room rather, which was so cluttered with bric-a-brac from everywhere that I never brought a parishioner in there. The happy result was that no one had ever seen my "armoury". Clipped to the wall above a brace of pistols was Abu Ali's dagger. I unfastened it and hitched it to the belt of the robe, recalling the day when it shone like a meteor in the blackness of the Siq. And then giving myself a swirl of unreality I went out the door, and the robin who came six times a day to be fed, and waited for me on the pillar of the small gate took off in alarm when he saw me. It was the perfect start to the adventure that was to sweep me into legend — and trouble.

I headed first for Bill Driscoll's Emporium. Not that I had any intention of going into the shop or into anywhere else for that matter because my voice would give me away as sure as the magpie's. Luck was with me. A shopping bag was propped up against the outside wall of the small garden that fronted the shop. I recognised it straightaway as belonging to Maura Mescall.

Maura had this habit — well known to me, to several other amused locals and, in all probability, to Bill himself who never alluded to it presumably because he felt that it was better for him to get some few pence from her than no pence at all — of leaving her bag outside his shop when she entered to buy some few small items on her way home from the village where she had already done the bulk of her shopping. She did so because she was afraid that if he saw the well filled bag he would top it up with curses choicer than the groceries she had bought elsewhere.

I made a dog-line for the bag knowing that it would provoke a reaction from Maura, knowing for certain also that as my eyes were focussed on the bag, two pairs of eyes inside the shop would be focussed on the billowy figure floating down the hill towards them.

I guessed correctly. As soon as I reached the low wall and bent my swathed head to look into the bag, Maura came rushing out the door and through the gap in the wall shouting "Hi!

What are you doing?" For an answer I raised myself a little with a pound of sausages in my hand, not high enough for Bill to see them but high enough for me to see that they were the same variety that Bill stocked, only maybe a halfpenny cheaper. She gave a sort of a coyote howl out of her which made me drop the sausages back in the shopping bag but, more dramatically, brought Bill pounding out of the shop with red combat in his eyes, and cursing as he came. "The devil cripple you for a foraging foreigner," he roared.

I wasn't at all sure how an Arab would respond in the circumstances but as I was armed with a superior weapon I drew it. I pulled the dagger out of its sheath and pointed it in the general direction of his belly. "Holy Christ, save us", Bill gasped. It was probably the most fervent prayer he ever said. I took two steps forward, following the direction of the dagger, and they turned and fled, Bill showing a fleetness of foot even more remarkable than on the day when he ran from Gobnait into the confessional, and Maura following him squealing as she went as though I had stuck her with the point of the dagger.

Bill must have hit the stairs a wallop in order to pull up because I could hear a tumbling avalanche of apples and I knew it was on the stairs that he kept the boxes of Granny Smiths. Then the door was slammed shut and the bolts that he used only for a hurricane were driven home with a force that shook the whole ground floor of the house. I too turned on my heels not because there was no more I could do just then to bring further Billian curses down on my infidel head but because I couldn't keep the smile off my face any longer.

Bill wasn't the only coward, however. My intention was to carry my unrehearsed drama to the theatre of the village by way of the hill road but when I came level with the church gate, still not crippled by the devil, thanks be to God, I saw three children coming up the road in my direction. Children live so much in the authentic world of make-believe that they can detect a fake twenty yards away, let alone eager face to Arab face, so to avoid their expert scrutiny I shot through the cowardly gate and made for the roundabout foot path to the village. That was the way that Gobnait came up on the evening of the ashes when she surprised Bill, and that was the way that — surprise, surprise! — two priests were climbing up now as I started down.

Which of us got the bigger shock I can't say for sure but I rather fancy they did, to judge by the ferment on their faces. Somebody had told me there were "two strange priests", as they were called, staying with the Clearys in Ardbrack, and presumably these were the two, but once I realised that they didn't know me or I them they became actors fortuitously pushed on to my stage and I pulled back the curtain for the start of Act 2. They never took their eyes off me as we got closer; I felt like a visitant from another world.

"Salam alaikum", I said, in greeting, the words bubbling up out of my Jordan memory like a very small spring of knowledge in a very large desert of ignorance.

I wasn't the only one who was ignorant; the priests' faces looked vacant as plates on a wall.

"Peace be with you", I translated.

"And also with you" they replied together, parroting the response of their own Mass congregations wherever it was they came from.

I halted right in the middle of the pathway with a grassy bank on one side of us and a stony wall on the other, and they had no option but to do the same.

"In the name of God the Compassionate, the Merciful. Praise be to God, the Lord of the worlds," said I , quoting from the opening of the Koran, and I bowed profoundly to the south east, figuring that Mecca must be in that general direction.

The two priests looked like farmers in a racing yacht, utterly baffled by what was going on.

"You, are, imams, here?" I asked, inserting pauses like commas after each word in the hesitant way that I reckoned an Arab would be speaking English. And because the word 'imam' was a block to their minds as my dress was to their bodies I asked the question another way. "You lead the prayers here in this mosque?" and I gestured with my shot silk arm back over my shoulder at Saint Brona's.

"That's not a mosque , that's a church", one of the priests said, losing his rag a little.

"Yes, yes" I said with a conciliatory smile. "I forget. Yes. Not a mosque. A church. A Christian church. You lead the prayers in this Christian church?"

Appeased, the father with the short temper said "No. We are here on a visit."

"Allah be praised. You are on pilgrimage," I said, all the time carefully clipping the syllables so as to orientate my words and disorientate my hearers. "It is one of the five pillars. You do well."

"And yourself", the second priest asked, finding his voice, "are you too on pilgrimage?"

"Yes", I answered, "I am on pilgrimage to Ireland, the country of the most green in all the world. Green is the sacred colour of Islam. When I touch green" — and with that I leant across and pulled a fistful of grass and dock leaves out of the overgrown bank — "I touch all of our people back to Fatima, back to Mohammed himself. "La ilaha illa allah; Mohammed rasul Allah."

I had the two priests more or less stupefied at this stage, so I went for broke.

"Ireland is of the soul of Islam," I proclaimed. "Three times every day the bell calls you to prayer." I regretted that it was between 3 and 3-30 and not 6 o'clock or 12 o'clock when the Angelus bell would accentuate my argument. "Two more times and you would be like us."

This was altogether too much for the priest who had had the bad lunch. "Numbers have nothing to do with it," he snapped. "You are reducing religion to a matter of sums. Ridiculous. I could just as well say to you 'If you had two more persons in your God you would be like us'."

He was sharp, sharp in mind and sharp in tongue. I had no answer to his riposte so I withdrew from the numbers game and returned to the conciliatory tone I had used earlier. "We must not fight", I said, "on the path of peace. I am a man of peace."

But he hadn't finished with me yet, this acrimonious priest. "If you are a man of peace" he countered, "why are you carrying that knife?"

A good point indeed and one that I couldn't blunt so I fell back on pure invention. "Christian imam" I said "you are unfair to me. I do not carry this dagger as a weapon, but as a reminder of God's wisdom. It is written in the Koran and it is also written in your own sacred book" — thank God, he didn't ask me for chapter and verse in either — "that the wisdom of God penetrates the soul like a sharp knife," and for the second time in half an hour I pulled the dagger from its sheath.

The two of them stepped back from me somewhat alarmed but I reassured them. "Christian mullahs," I said, "do not be afraid. This dagger is not for action, like so" — and I pointed it directly at them — "but for contemplation like this" — and I cradled it quietly in the palm of my hand with the point towards myself.

"Yes, well, we must be going," the quiet one said, having had more than his share of contemplation for one day. I slipped the dagger back in its sheath and I stepped to one side to let them pass. As they did so, I raised my hands to the level of my head with the palms forward as I had seen the worshippers doing in Damascus and I used the only other bit of Arabic I had picked up. "Allahu Akbar!"

"Good luck", "All the best" they said and away they went with a story that would keep the Clearys of Ardbrack amused for the evening.

If an arbiter had been present I think he would have decided that the two priests had won the theological debate by a shade, but all that mattered to me was whether my disguise was convincing, not my arguments, and clearly it was. In fact, so far it was carrying all before it, like an engine in a shunting yard.

I continued down the pathway until it met the road into the village from the direction of Croghan, almost exactly opposite the site where Catherine Burke's bungalow was going up by leaps and bounds, except when Seán O'Donovan, the village's unofficial advisor on everything from bingo to bungalows was present, as he was now. He had his back to me as I emerged through a cutting of fuchsias onto the road.

Seán always reminded me of the passage in Paul's second letter to the Thessalonians where he lectured them about busybodies, people, he said, who do no work themselves and mind everybody's business but their own. He could be found wherever there was a bawling baby, a smoky chimney or a flat tyre with advice on how to soothe the baby, sweep the chimney and shift the stubborn bolts on the wheel, and his interfering nose was so big that it got in the way of the mother, the householder and the motorist. He was on a disability pension himself, but he had an outstanding ability to be everywhere he wasn't wanted.

So, as I crossed the road to the other side there he was lecturing the two Downey brothers who were up on the scaffolding on how they should proceed with the placing of the lintel over the front door. "What I would do if I were you" he was saying, but what they were actually doing was looking at me as I approached the low ditch. And one of them must have said to him, "What I would do if I were you, Seán, would be to turn around", because he pivoted quickly on his supposedly disabled feet and looked me straight in the sunglasses, hood and headband.

"A poor life this if full of care
We have no time to stand and stare" wrote W. H. Davies and that is what I did when I got to the ditch. I stood and I stared. I stared at the building. I stared at the crumpled concrete bags. I stared at the two Downey brothers and I stared at Seán.

But there is no fun or fluidity in that. I had my hands hanging from me by my side in what I took to be the approved W. H. Davies fashion, but then acting on some memory I had of the warlike Bedouin posing for their photograph I raised my hands to the level of the belt around my waist, one above the other with my left hand curled around the sheath and my right hand firmly gripping the handle of the dagger.

That was the prompt from the wings that Act 3 needed. "Christ, there's no one with my mother", Seán shouted, and he took off across the rubble, over the ditch and up the road towards the village at a rate that would disqualify him from his pension but qualify him for the steeplechase in the Olympics. It was the second best laugh of the day. The best was still to come.

I followed Seán at an uncompetitive distance up the Croghan road and the first house I reached was the village's one and only public house. Somebody claimed one time that we were unique in Ireland in that we had only one watering hole for the parched herdsmen; be that as it may, it was better situated than most, discreetly placed at the entrance to the village for those who had no wish to penetrate further and strategically located for the benefit of those who had to make a quick retreat in the event of a a raid. The name Keane was over the door but everybody knew it simply as Florrie's.

As soon as I came level with the door I knew one thing for certain: that Seán had shouted a warning to the clientele as he rushed by on his mission to protect his mother. Not a man jack of them was looking at his pint: they were all looking out the door in anticipation of the Islamic menace, and Florrie himself was outside the counter in the company of his customers to get an unimpeded view of the Arab.

I made it easy for them all: I halted on the pavement directly opposite the door and looked brazenly in. It was the first time in my five and a half years in Kilbroney that I had done that; protocol demanded that the priest should never stare in the door of the pub lest he discover who the aforesaid parched herdsmen were, as if he didn't know already by their eyes, noses, breath, staggers and upended machinery.

Florrie had the floor, not surprising when it was his floor, and his message needed no expert interpretation. "What next?"

he was saying. "We have Brits, although they are not the worst of them by any means" — in fact, they were his best customers which was the extenuating circumstance that lifted them from the bottom of most people's racist pit — "We have French. We have Germans. We have Dutch. We have Swedes, and now an Arab. Will ye look at him? What a get-up. Women in trousers, and this fellow in a dress. We won't know what country we are living in soon. It will be like London airport, without the planes."

I shifted a little from foot to foot and I looked over the house several times in a general survey from east to west and from bar to bedrooms wondering all the while how long it would be feasible for a deaf-and-dumb Arab to stand at the door of an Irish pub without either going in or going away. But the next voice made me prolong my stay, however ridiculous the stand off appeared. It belonged to Riobárd O Luasa, an Irish Irelander who came from the city on his holidays every summer and whose father was one of those eleventh hour Republicans who left the comfort and safety of their beds only when the British forces left the country in 1922, and whose actual service was confined to the burning down of military barracks when there were no military manning them. Riobárd was lamenting the futility of such heroism. "What fools they were to strike for liberty," he was saying, "when you now have I.R.A. men shut up in Portlaoise Prison and tykes like your man out there walking around in freedom."

"Shush," somebody said, "he'll hear you."

"Not at all." Florrie corrected him. "How could he know what we are saying with a face on him like a fish."

It was perhaps the best compliment yet to my disguise. But rather insulting to my physiognomy, so I left, carrying with me their present of a flagon full of racism and seedy nationalism. But if that was unexpected — and it was — what I saw when I rounded the corner and went into Main Street was more unexpected still.

The village was deserted except for Bill Peter's terrier: evidently Arabs didn't kill and eat dogs! It was going on for 4 o'clock in the day and the place was as empty as it would be at 7 o'clock in the morning. In fact it looked like the set of a Western film just before the bad guy comes into town to get the sheriff, with just one stray dog snapping at flies and all the citizens behind their curtained windows.

Sure, there were days when Kilbroney took a long nap but this wasn't meant to be one of them because on the following Sunday, just two days away, we would be having the Corpus Christi procession through the village from the church to the grassy mound behind Seán O'Donovan's. It was the occasion that brought out the paint brush, the windolene and the buckets of sudsy water. In fact, when I went down to post a letter before lunch there were more people outside the houses than inside, climbing ladders, standing on chairs and making the pavements gurgle with sudsy water.

The ladders were still there, three of them, angled against patches of unpainted walls, but there was nobody on them. Tins of paint stood near them and paint brushes stretched out on old newspapers but there wasn't an amateur splasher to be seen. Seán O' Donovan's white tailed signal had worked well and all the rabbits had bolted for their burrows. There was nothing I could do except stroll up along one side of the street and back along the other, halting for a moment or two outside the grocer's, the post office, the meatshop and the property office to note how the preparations were going for Sunday's procession and then I decided that as there was no welcome for the Arab at sea level the Arab would go back to his own high place. It seemed like a limp finale to my escapade but I was wrong.

I rounded the blind corner out of Main Street into the hill road and even if I was half blind itself the shock that I got would have restored my sight fully. There on a ladder was Gobnait leaning bodily against it to keep her balance, with a paint brush in one hand and a tin of paint, foolishly, in the other. Evidently she hadn't heard the tocsin or else she had been inside at the time for a surreptitious cigarette when the village ran for cover. Whatever the reason there she was on the ladder seven rungs off the ground touching up the red letters of NEWSAGENT on the facia.

Not for long! At the very moment that I looked up she looked down. I saw a woman in a precarious position; she saw a man in a menacing garb. My mischievous urge was to skirt the ladder as closely as a racing yacht rounds a mark. Luckily for me I didn't get nearly as close as that or I would have been the first Arab in history to get a lick of face paint. What I think she attempted to do was to drop the paint brush into the tin and then grab hold of the ladder with her right hand, but she was watching me, not the tin and the brush glanced off the top of it and fell. She made a lunge to catch it, failed, lost her footing, let go of the tin and slid down the ladder, rung by shrieking rung. They hit the ground together, the tin on its open mouth, and Gobnait on her heels and bottom.

I forgot that I was an Arab but she didn't. I quickened my pace to go to assist her but she saw that as a stratagem with intent and she shrieked again, picked herself up and scuttled into the shop with a slight hobble.

Self-preservation was the thought that hit me next. There was no way I could now simply stroll home with the leisurely lope of the timeless desert. Speed was of the essence. Phones could be ringing. A posse could be assembling. I put my head down and lengthened my stride. The head cloth streamed out behind me like a manta ray. I passed the church gate without thought of Yahweh or Allah. I gave only a sidelong glance at Bill's Emporium: the shopping bag was gone but the door was still shut. I reached my own door with as much relief as if it were the first palm tree in an oasis.

Upstairs with me in a clatter. I slid out of the robe, belt, dagger and all in one swerve of the body. I pulled the cloth and the band off my head as if bees had made a nest of them. I got out of one trousers and into the other with the speed of a schoolboy. Lucky for me I did. A car drew up with a squeal of brakes outside. I looked out: it was Florrie Keane's Ford. I thrust my arms through the bands of the stock and clamped velcro on velcro as I twisted the Roman collar around my neck. The doorbell rang. "Blast," I said. Actually 'twas worse than that! I grabbed my jacket, wriggled into it and made for the stairs.

The bell rang again. "Coming", I said with sham composure, as I opened the door.

Florrie was standing there, almost filling the doorspace with his six feet three and sixteen stone.

"Are you alright, Father?" he blurted.

"Of course, Florrie. Why? Come in".

"No, I can't. I'm on a manhunt."

"A manhunt?"

"Yes, there's some class of a foreign lunatic around. An Arab we think he is, by the way he is dressed. He is dangerous."

"Dangerous?"

"He has a knife on him that you could skin a seal with."

"God bless us."

"He threatened Bill Driscoll with it."

"Good Lord! Is he alright?"

"Yes, he is alright, but he is in a frightful state of nerves after it. He is up in the bedroom afraid to come down."

"Will I go down to him?"

"No, don't . Stay where you are. We rang the sergeant in Hilltown and that's what he said: everyone to stay in till the Arab is caught."

"Ah, it can't be that bad."

"It is, I'm telling you. He has no respect for man or woman. He tumbled Gobnait off her ladder."

"He did?! Is she hurt?"

"Not too bad, but her ankle is blowing up like a balloon!!"

"My God, where is he now?"

"That's what I'd like to know, but he came this way. Gobnait is sure of it. Up Hillroad, she said."

"Maybe he ducked into the church?"

"Church! Not that fellow. Hell, more likely. As soon as I saw him I knew 'twas trouble ahead".

"Saw him! You actually saw him?"

"Yes. A quarter of an hour ago. He stood at the door of the bar and he looked in as bold as brass".

"What did he look like?" I asked. I was hoping he would say "like a fish" again.

"He was like a fish you'd see head on in a tank. All mouth and nose. He had a sort of a scarf all around his head and you couldn't see his forehead or his eyes or his cheeks or his ears. He was an ugly yoke, and by the time I'm finished with him he'll be even worse looking."

"What do you mean, Florrie?"

"I have a bit of a crowbar in the car, and if I can get near him he'll have a very sore head, I'm telling you."

"Well, be careful, Florrie. You can never trust these foreigners. Any of them."

"Exactly what I say myself, Father. Well, I'd better be going. I'm glad you are alright, anyhow."

"Good hunting," I said "I hope you will track him down."

He got back in the car and rejoined the crowbar. Where the search would lead him I had no idea. The only thing I knew for certain was that the Arab would not have a cracked skull going to bed that night.

* * *

The two people I fixed my eyes on most intently during the eucharistic procession on Sunday were Sergeant Miller and Gobnait.

The sergeant was there by annual request to act as a sort of dam holding back the flow of the tourist traffic from the east while the procession was moving through the village to and from the mound of the Blessing. He never looked very devout — I don't blame him for that: our straggle lacked the discipline and the devotion necessary to raise anybody's thoughts to God let alone the thoughts of someone who was present for a purely vehicular reason — but on this occasion he was transparently vexed. He gave me a bad look.

He had spent all of Friday evening searching for the Arab, from the time he had received the s.o.s. until the last glimmer of light and hope went out of the midsummer sky. Every trail went cold. In fact there was no scent anywhere except the scent that livened the hill road and evaporated in the region of the curate's house.

He had returned on Saturday but the only vibrations he felt in his moustache were vibrations of the excitement the Arab had generated — the scene at the creamery resembled that of a morning after a general election — and the only leads he got were leads to sheltering hills, about fifty different hills, and leads to a fanciful ocean where the Arab was supposedly cruising in his yacht.

Both on the Friday and the Saturday Miller called to interview me. On the Friday he asked me if I had seen any sign of the Arab. On the Saturday he asked me if I was quite certain I had not seen any sign of the Arab. I answered "no" to the first question and "yes" to the second, and when on the Saturday he suggested how strange it was that the Arab had apparently disappeared into thin air in the vicinity of my house I counter suggested that it wasn't so strange at all, telling him that the big rock at the rear of my house was sacred in the minds of the old folk of the parish who claimed that Mass had been said on it during the Penal times. "Do you know, Sergeant" I asked, "that sacred rocks are a very significant feature of the Islamic faith, and that Mohammed himself ascended to heaven on his winged steed called Lightning from a black rock in the middle of Jerusalem?" He didn't, and when I further suggested that our Arab had perhaps done likewise from the sacred rock behind my house, he left in pain, hugging his offended intelligence.

Gobnait also was in pain when I saw her during the procession standing on the pavement outside her shop. Her right ankle was very heavily bandaged, she was wearing a cutaway slipper on that foot and she was flagrantly supporting herself on a crutch. In spite of the fact that I was carrying the monstrance and should have had eyes front at all times I shot her an inquisitive glance as I slowly approached her position. In return she gave me what novelists call a long knowing look. It had the effect of derailing me from the second glorious mystery of the Rosary, the Ascension of Our Lord, which we were rattling off as we walked down the hillroad. Claudius got the better of Gabriel the Archangel: "my words fly up, my thoughts remain below," and "below" was surely the appropriate word, because in spite of the monstrance obstructing my view to some extent I could see the red trade mark that the tin of paint had imprinted on the tarmac. Much scrubbing with paraffin had failed to eliminate it, and as I passed by abreast of her I could almost hear her saying with Lady Macbeth "Out, damned spot. Out, I say."

The touch up of the inscription on the facia had got no further than when the Arab rounded the corner with the result that the first four letters of "Newsagent" were highlighted thus, NEWS, and the other five were faded. The big news everywhere was the fall of the newsmonger. Even if she had been tumbled off the ladder, as the propaganda had it, very few had any sympathy for her having felt the lash of her tongue. In fact the great majority of the people believed she had fallen off herself and that she was a straight forward example of the words in the popular love ditty which went: "I didn't slip, I wasn't pushed, I fell."

Although I wasn't speaking to Pat O'Mahony, the local correspondent for the "Western Orb," that weekend, I saw him doing his research wherever heads were being put together between the church and the gate after the procession. His account of the incident appeared among the weekly "Clippings from Kilbroney' in the following Friday's issue of the "Orb". It was remarkably restrained, and presented the Arab more in the guise of victim than villain. I quote it here exactly as it was printed, poor punctuation and all: —

"Visitors.

Chapter 3 – The Day of the Arab

The week-end brought in a big influx of visitors locally to hotels, guest houses and private houses. A big number of caravans have also arrived. At Sandy Cove all the villas have been occupied. Two Capuchin priests from the priory in Kilkenny, Frs Romuald and Mel are spending a short holiday with John and Mrs Nora Cleary in Ardbrack. A visitor in Eastern costume made a brief appearance at Kilbroney on an evening last week. Many wondered what the purpose of his visit was, was he a passing tourist or maybe a judge of Tidy Towns? There is much support for the latter opinion because it was noted that he spent most of his time making a survey of the premises in the village. Some others felt he was a diplomat from the Middle East, if so the cool reception he was accorded won't help to improve East-West relations".

Pat O' wasn't given to saying things with his tongue in his cheek so he must have almost swallowed it in his attempt at humour, but he was much closer to the bullseye than he thought or imagined when he threw that dart about East-West relations at the skulking citizens of Kilbroney, not indeed the relations between the industrialised West and the oil producing countries of the Middle East which he had in mind but the relations between Gobnait and myself which he knew nothing about.

In point of fact my house was west of Gobnait's and her house was east of mine and that particular east-west relationship was deteriorating fast. I heard about it from one of the cronies who thought I looked gloomy one day and needed a laugh to cheer me up. While Gobnait was resting her ankle she was activating her brain and it occurred to her that the Arab walked just like Fr. Laide. The more she thought about it the more certain she became that the gait gave the game away. It fitted in perfectly with the disappearance of the Arab in the vicinity of the curate's house: the Arab and the curate were one and the same man!

"Do you know what I think?" she said to three of her entourage as they sat in a semicircle around the propped up ankle.

They straightened up because with her that rhetorical question was always the 54321 countdown to a rocket being launched.

"I think that the Arab was Fr. Laide or Fr. Laide was the Arab, whichever way you want to put it. Don't laugh. I'd know his walk anywhere."

"Ah, Gobnait, you can't be serious," one of them said.

"I'm dead serious," she replied. "I tell you if he was in a sack race and the sack was up over his head I would still know him by his walk. There's only one person walks the way he does and that is the way the Arab walked."

"Do you think so?" the second of the trio asked, handing her another pellet for her air rifle in the amusement arcade.

"I don't think so; I know so," she answered. "He could cover up his forehead. He could cover up his eyes. He could cover up his cheekbones. He could cover up his ears. He could cover up his vocation. But he couldn't cover up his walk. Below the robe I saw the shoes: they were enough for me."

"Ah, he wouldn't do the like of that", the third woman said, putting up an unmissable clay pigeon.

Gobnait shot it to smithereens.

"He would then," she said viciously. "And he did. A lot worse than that. In the month of February this year, if ye only knew."

Chapter 4

SERGEANT KILLER

The next occasion on which the sergeant and I met up close was the day when the whale was beached in Sandy Cove. By "up close" I mean we had a stand up fight, snarling at each other like enraged wolves. I suppose I was lucky that I walked off the beach alive and that he didn't turn his gun on me, because that would have been his way of dealing with wolves, enraged or otherwise: he would have shot them with only the one moment's hesitation that he would have needed to get them unmissably in the telephoto lens of his rifle. Whenever I had correspondence with him I addressed him by his correct surname, Sergeant Miller, but in the conversations I carried on with myself I always referred to him as Sergeant Killer.

That is what he was, a ruthless killer of wild life; and the confrontation that we had on the grey sands that day was not the first round of the contest between us involving God's creatures: it was nearer to the tenth. In that context it always got my rag out when I heard references to the Gardai as an unarmed force; as for myself I would have been much happier to see Sergeant Miller walking about at all times with a revolver in his belt knowing it to be for the defence of the community than to see him in the winter months skulking behind rushes at Heaskin Lake waiting to ruffle it with bloodied feathers.

To him the hills of three parishes were merely clinics where the foxes had to be taught a stern lesson in birth control, and the marshes were only outdoor laboratories to determine whether a straight bullet could outthink a zigzagging snipe.

Miller was the secretary of the Hilltown Gun Club and that is how the relationship between Church and State at our small local level first became strained. From time to time he used to send requests to have notices concerning the activities of the Gun Club called out at the Sunday Masses. I always ignored them.. When Father Mac was in his health he used to copy the sergeant's text into the notice book but I always skipped on to the next item, and when Father Mac had to go off to hospital and the notices came directly to me I used them to give the fire a bit of a boost.

I was happy to call out any notice that came my Sunday way from babyshows and G.A.A matches to judo classes and the theft of a red lady's bicycle — we had great fun about that one not being sure whether the bike in question was coloured red or whether the lady in question came from a reservation in North America — but I never read out anything that might swell the numbers or the coffers of the Gun Club, be it an annual general meeting, a special outing or a concert organised to raise funds on its behalf. The result was that his members in Kilbroney who didn't buy the "Western Orb" but depended on the church notices to double up as newspaper advertisements didn't get to the meeting, the outing or the concert.

Not surprisingly, Miller was irritated when he heard that none of his notices was hitting the target, and one day when I was in Hilltown on some business or other and we met on the street he asked if he could have a few words with me.

"Sure," I said, "what about?"

"I hear," he said, "that you never read out the notices from the Gun Club and I am interested to know why not."

"Because I do not agree with the activities of the Gun Club, that's why," I answered bluntly.

"But you are only one person," he argued. "There are many people out there in Kilbroney who do."

"That may very well be," I answered. "If so, I suggest that you contact them by post."

"Ah, now," he said "be reasonable, Father. With our limited resources that's not possible. The church notices are the ordinary way of informing people about what is going on".

"Yes, but not about everything that is going on," I countered. "If the Lesbians hand in a notice to say they are holding a jamboree at Sandy Cove do I call that out? What you have to remember is that the church notices are Church notices" — and I emphasised the word Church — "and the priest in charge is the person who decides what is called out in church and what is not."

"But that is a form of censorship."

"In a way, yes, but no different from the censorship you exercise yourself when you decide to display some notices on the window of the barracks but not others."

"You are comparing two completely different things, a barrack and a church. Why don't you compare church and church?"

"How do you mean?"

"I mean that Fr Lucey reads out our notices here in Hilltown, and you don't. Is something which is right in Hilltown wrong in Kilbroney?"

"It's wrong everywhere."

"So Fr. Lucey doesn't know the difference between right and wrong, is that it?"

"It's you people who don't know the difference between right and wrong."

"You didn't answer my question about Fr. Lucey."

"Fr. Lucey doesn't want to offend you. I suppose. But in this particular matter it doesn't worry me at all if I offend you, Sergeant. I would rather offend you than offend a foxcub. I think that is the best answer I can make to the question you asked me first. I'm on the side of the cub, not the Club. Simple as that. So far as I'm concerned, the fifth commandment includes foxcubs; and anything that imperils them, whether it is a gun in your hands or a church notice in mine, I repudiate utterly. And if you will excuse me now . . . " I said, knowing that my passion had reached its peroration, "I have a few things to do."

The first thing I had to do before going into any shop was to bring down my blood pressure. When I get into an argument about animals my engine overheats and I blow a gasket. It is not the way to make converts; rather, is it the way to make en-

emies. I had the distinct feeling as I moved away from him that
day that not only had I increased the firepower against the foxcubs but I had put myself on the sergeant's list of unprotected
species.

* * *

If I was asked at any stage of my life, from the Christmas
when I got a present of a child's book on animals to that day in
Hilltown when the passersby on the pavement passed by twice
as quickly as usual to avoid the stray bullets, what it was that
roused me to that sort of sacred fury that sent the Crusaders to
Jerusalem I would have said: cruelty to animals. The oldtimers
in Kilbroney used to speak about a former parish priest who
literally danced on the altar with temper about an unmarried
girl who got pregnant but I was never tempted to make that
dance a pas de deux. However, if I heard of a badger being
dug out of a sett to be mangled by a pack of dogs, that took the
leash off my tongue. The first I regarded as human weakness
to be met by understanding; the second I regarded as inhuman
viciousness to be met by rage.

I preached in public that the way to heaven was by the wide
road of prayer and the sacraments but privately I felt that I
had a better chance myself along the narrow path flattened out
by the webbed feet of the otter. I didn't agree at all, either in
private or in public, with the theologians' view that animals do
not possess souls. How did they know such a thing? Had they
been to heaven and come back with an insider's report on the
matter? After seven years in a seminary I knew no more about
God than I did at the beginning. I knew a lot about theology, of
course, but not about God: He refused to get in between their
bookends. What the theologians were trying to do was to tie the
hands of God, those hands that had created the speed of the
cheetah, the elegance of the swan, the grace of the dolphin and
the majesty of the eagle. Human clothing was a poor effort on
the part of men and women to emulate the astonishing spread
of colour to be found in the creatures of earth, air and sea and

the denial to them of souls was little better than a bit of crafty play to level up the score.

Of course I should never have allowed myself to bring my private views into the public pulpit in such a way that I was giving the impression that protecting the fox was a matter of faith and morals to be held by all the faithful. Contrariwise I was outraged whenever I heard of other priests extolling in church the manly virtues of the G.A.A. as if they were the cardinal virtues of temperance, prudence, justice and fortitude, or when I heard of them directing people to vote for a particular candidate in an election as though the finger of God was writing no.1 opposite that name in the ballot paper. I could see the speck in their eyes but I couldn't see the beam in my own. The result was that whenever I referred to the slaughter of foxes or the butchering of woodcock, I handed the Gun Club in general and Sergeant Killer in particular another nail for my coffin so that when the boards were finally to be fastened together they had a bag full of nails for the job.

The pogrom of the magpies, as I called it, became for me a four inch nail. It was planned by the County Committee of Agriculture and in our area the implementation of the plan was put into the trigger fingered hands of the Hilltown Gun Club. Two very large posters appeared on the windows of the post office and the creamery exhorting the farmers to wipe out the plague of the magpies, describing the birds as vermin and promising a bounty of a few shillings for every magpie killed. A letter arrived from the County Hall asking me (1) to bring the eradication scheme to the notice of my congregation and (2) to request them to cooperate with the Hilltown Gun Club who would be organising the shoot in various townlands on successive week-ends.

On that occasion instead of simply ignoring the letter I saw it as a major attack on my principles and I mounted a counterattack at Mass on the following Sunday. I concentrated my firepower on the word 'vermin.'

"I don't want to act the school master," I began, "and turn the Mass into an English lesson but perhaps it is as well for ye to grasp clearly the meaning of the word 'vermin'. It means something vile and contemptible. Now if ye have studied the posters at the post office and the creamery ye will have noticed that magpies are described there as vermin, and in a letter which I have here from the County Committee of Agriculture the same word is used to describe them — vermin.

"The first thing I want to say about the word is that it is an insult to God the Creator. It is bordering on the blasphemous to suggest that God could or would devise a form of life which is vile and contemptible. You all learned in your catechism the question "Can God do everything?" and the answer "Yes, God can do everything," but the answer didn't go far enough: God can do everything except to create something vile and contemptible. Even the devils, the orginators of evil, jumped out of God's hands as good. Unlike the devils the magpies are now as they were when they left God's hands, acting within their nature and out of their given intelligence. So that's the first thing: banish the word 'vermin' from your minds.

"The next point is: they are described as a plague. In other words, there are too many of them, according to the County Committee of Agriculture. And again that is offensive to God: it is telling Him that He has given His creatures wrong instructions. In the very first chapter of the very first book of the Bible, God said "Let birds fly above the earth" and He created every kind of winged creature, including magpies, and He saw that they were good and He blessed them and said "Be fruitful and multiply." "Be fruitful and multiply" is the direct opposite of the instructions from the County Committee of Agriculture: "Shoot and exterminate."

"The idea seems to be if there are too many of anything, especially too many of anything that doesn't bring you a profit, cull them, decimate them, eliminate them. You could argue that there are too many of Shakespeare's sonnets. He wrote one hundred and fifty four of them. Far too many, don't you think?

Wouldn't fifty four be enough? Wouldn't the thing to do be to destroy the other hundred? Or take the example of the human race. It is propagating itself faster than the means of subsistence, according to some experts, so wouldn't the thing to do be to start the Third World War and use every means of mass destruction, atom bombs, hydrogen bombs, chemical weapons, the lot. And keep it going for as long as possible! That is the thinking behind the pogrom of the magpies.

"Another thing is this: far from being vile and contemptible the magpie is a really beautiful creature. Indeed if there was such an institution as a Court of Birds a good case could be made to prove that it is the most striking bird we have in Ireland. On your way home after Mass or sometime this evening or tomorrow take a long look at it. Yes, you have seen hundreds of them but have you ever looked, really looked at any one of them?"

"If you do, what will you see? Basically, what you will see is a black-and-white bird. You ladies who are present will know that a black-and-white ensemble never ceases to be elegant. Yes, of course, scarlet or lemon is more spectacular, but if you want to be really chic black-and-white is the combination to wear. Right then, the magpie is elegant in its black-and-white costume. But there is more to it than that, as every woman knows. There are the accessories. Get up close or get behind a pair of binoculars. Look at that long tail, for heaven's sake: it is shot with bronze and green and purple sheens, changing all the time as the bird changes its position. It's a bit like what the car manufacturers call metallic when they want you to pay a few hundred pounds more for a special colour. That is how special the magpie's tail is.

"And when it is in flight, with those white webs on the outside of the rounded wings what does it remind you of? I'll tell you what it reminds me of. It reminds me of a Red Indian medicine man, with hundreds of years of wisdom in his head and a costume of black and white feathers covering his arms and back. And need I remind you that the Red Indians too were eliminated by the gun because they were different and because there were too many of them just like the magpies.

"Well, of course they are not good singers, I'll grant you that. They belong to the crow family and nobody in that family has a good voice. They sound more like machine guns than opera stars, to be honest. But then what about ourselves? Most of us, including myself, are crows too. Not too many of us would pass a test to get into a choir, and when we sing in pubs it is Paddy Flaherty who is doing most of the singing. So don't damn them on that score unless you are a bit of a Pavarotti or a Renata Tebaldi yourself.

"They have a bad reputation as thieves: again I grant you that. If you are gardening and you take off your diamond ring don't leave it on the window sill because if you do the chances are that it will finish up adorning the magpie's nest. Like ourselves they have a weakness for rubies and emeralds! And of course they make the occasional raid on your grain and your seeds, but I like to think of them myself as gleaners rather than as robbers, like Ruth in Bethlehem, the woman without rights, the woman who owned nothing, who gleaned in the fields behind the harvesters to keep herself alive. That's not a crime, surely. You won't miss the few ears, the few seeds, or the few pennies.

And as regards the bounty as they call it, you can live without the two shillings blood money. Do not redden your hands with it. It is , I suppose, worth noting as well that the word they use, that word "bounty', is the very same word that the English used when they were ruling this country and were offering five pounds for a wolf or a priest. The same sum for both. As a successor of the many priests who were hunted like the wolves I can say to you honestly that I am in no way offended at the parity because we humans and the otters and the foxes and the badgers and the magpie are all part of God's plan of creation, and his love shines as truly through their eyes as it does through ours.

I'll tell you something else about them that I have learned, because I have been studying them: they are not selfish; they believe in share and share alike. When I put out some food for them as I often do, one magpie comes into the garden first with that sort of paddling action of the wings as if he were rowing a boat fast with short strokes, and he lands and lifts his tail off the ground and then what does he do? Does he settle down there selfishly and gobble it all up himself? He does not. He picks up a tidbit and away with him sweeping the air with his paddles again. And within a minute he is back with his mate, and the two of them settle down to a shared companionable meal. What do you think of that? Isn't there something we could learn from that: to be less selfish, to share our good fortune with others, to make meals times of companionship? Or do you really think that, in acting like that, the magpies are vile and contemptible?

Well now this sermon, if you can call it that, has gone on long enough, so I'll wind it down with two statements made by the greatest preacher of all time, Our Lord and Saviour Jesus Christ. The first occurs in the sermon on the Mount, the most famous sermon in the history of the world. He said "Look at the birds of the air" — He said "Look at them," He didn't say "shoot them" — "They neither sow nor do they reap nor gather into barns, yet your heavenly Father feeds them." That is in Saint Matthew's gospel, chapter 6, verse 26. And in another sermon later on, a very special sermon for the twelve apostles, quoted in Saint Matthew's gospel, chapter 10, verse 29, he said "Not a bird falls to the ground without your Father knowing of it." So when a bird falls to the ground for any reason God knows about it, and when a bird falls to the ground because it is sliced out of the air by a bullet the heavenly Father knows who pulled the trigger. It is something you should think about before you join in this vermin shoot, as they are calling it.

"Of course you have to make up your own minds about it. Don't let me sway you if you do not want to be swayed, but please do not be swayed by that word "vermin".

"The magpies are not vermin but I think I know who the vermin are".

For the most part sermons never produce anything except aching buttocks and leaden minds, but this one did have results. The farmers ignored the posters, they didn't let the Gun Club on to their lands, and the magpies got a reprieve. In that sense it was probably the only triumph of my homiletic life but in another sense it was a pyrrhic victory because Sergeant Miller never forgave me for my final sentence. I thought it was a great punch line at the time but as events proved the punch turned out to be a boomerang that came back and clobbered myself.

To say that we disliked each other intensely is to falsify the state of emotional play between us. On my side it fell just short of theological hatred: I never did or would wish the man evil, but I supped, breakfasted, lunched and dined on the satisfaction served up to me on the day of the Arab and on the day that followed it that Killer was tracking something he would never find.

On his side, the frustration about the shunted notices, the belittling of his intelligence when I indulged myself in the fanciful flight into heaven of the modern day Mohammed from the Mass rock at the rear of my house and above all the sermon on the magpie and the transfer of the designation 'vermin' from the hunted to the hunter must have stoked the fires of hatred in him to such an extent that sooner or later the chimney itself would go on fire. It was no surprise to me to see the black look on his face from behind the brightness of the monstrance on the Sunday of the procession.

When we were not engaged in hostilities, it was no more than a temporary disengagement of forces; the only question was where and when the next battle would take place.

* * *

The answer came when the whale beached itself on Sandy Cove. It was early winter, the time when the North Atlantic right whales leave the Arctic and travel south to warmer seas off the African coast to reproduce their kind. Some zoologists call them Biscayan whales because they shoulder their way south and north again through the bay of Biscay, but it wasn't the zoologists who gave them the name 'right' but the whalers who classified them by greed rather than by science and concluded they were the right whales to hunt because they didn't have the turn of speed necessary to escape when the pursuit began and because they conveniently stayed afloat to be flensed when they were killed. There was also a right time to kill them: that was when they were making for the Tropics because then they were in peak condition with blubber on them two feet thick.

They have a constantly rotating cycle of life, and the two pedals which drive that wheel are the search for food and the search for love. In no sense would I be flippant about the noble animals, but on the compass of their instincts the direction north points to food and the direction south points to love. In the northern summer they cruise the Arctic waters consuming vast quantities of prawn and shrimp until they are bulging with that fatty layer below the skin which is their insulation against cold and which is known as blubber. Then in the late autumn and into the early winter the mating instinct takes over and they head south for warmer waters and warmer relationships. They winter in the Tropics and there they mate and when that hunger is satisfied and the hunger for crustaceans takes over again the cycle spins anew and they head back north in the spring for the rich feeding of the Arctic.

It was from there that the whales were making their passage in a school of seven or eight when they raised Croghan Point on that Monday in November. But something went wrong with their navigational system because instead of setting their course well out to sea, keeping the Point to port they cut inside it to starboard and surged up Croghan harbour. Later in the day somebody jokingly suggested that perhaps they were trying to take a short cut and the clown might have been wiser than he knew because in the National Library in Dublin once I came upon a Spanish map of Ireland of the year 1580 or thereabouts and on it Croghan harbour as it is now is shown as an open strait. The inference is that Sandy Cove beach at the head of the harbour didn't then exist and the narrow isthmus behind it where the golfers now swing their clubs between sea and sea hadn't then built up dune upon dune. Maybe, just maybe, the North Atlantic right whales were still carrying the charts of the 16th century in their great atavistic heads. Whatever the reason, whether it was ancestral storage or modern blunder, they swept up Croghan harbour headed for disaster.

There was one witness of their progress. That was Paul Carmody. Paul said that they steered a perfect course, not middling the harbour exactly, but nearer to the Kilbroney road than to Croghan pier. There wasn't a harbour master at Croghan but Paul had the eyes and ears of one, even if he didn't have the buttons. He spent all day watching the comings and goings, and even when there was no coming of a yacht or going of a fishing boat he kept his eyes trained on the gulls and the garbage. He had two vantage points: one was on the concrete bollard on the pier — no one could understand why the cold of that seat in the winter time hadn't turned his water into blood — and the other was a high stool inside the window of Davern's bar where he sat with his pint and his elbows resting on the ledge while his eyes ceaselessly ranged over the punts and the puffs of wind.

Daverns hadn't yet opened the morning doors when the whales gave notice of their arrival at the harbour mouth and for that reason Paul was in his pre-pub position on the bollard with a perfect view of the flotilla of Arctic submarines when they showed. First one and then another and then another surfaced and exploded the air through its nostrils in a cloud of smoky mucus. Paul was no fool: he had been a blue water sailor for years and he knew that whales can stay submerged for twenty or thirty minutes at a time, and therefore he was certain that this was a school coming up the harbour not a lone lost pupil: if there had been only one whale there would have been only one explosion of air. What is more, to tamper with Saint Paul's meaning, he wasn't seeing through his glass darkly: nothing had yet moistened his imagination except a cup of Lyons tea.

Paul followed their heading by a sort of bulge that came and went on the surface of the water; it was as if, he said, the harbour was breathing gently in and out. Then as one of the whales came abreast of the pier it broke the surface and shot the spent air of its lungs into the air in the shape of an ornamental tree. It was a signal to the harbour master that all was well, but the harbour master flinched, knowing that a distress signal would have been more to its purpose.

Paul swivelled around on the bollard and gave a quick look at the state of the tide. It was still making an effort to push its mark a few more inches up the slipway but in the opinion of anyone except an astronomer it was full tide, good and proper, which meant that the sands of the Cove were now covered completely right up to the seawall, which in turn meant that the whales would now see only water ahead of them, instead of the tawny arc of danger which they would have seen two, three, four, five or six hours before. Never a harpoon man, Paul would have sent a warning shot across their snouts if he had been able, but all he could do was watch and wait, watch until they had rounded Fraser's Rock in the middle of the harbour and wait for whatever might happen when they swam out of deep water into the shallows.

Fraser's Rock had been compared in its time to everything from a hulk to a barracks, and the effect of its position and its sheer mass was to conceal from view whatever might be happening in its lee. It was as if while a play was still being acted on stage someone pulled down the heavy fire curtain. But while the audience in that situation couldn't see anything they could still hear voices being raised or a door being slammed or a shot being fired, and Paul could hear from a mile and a half away a tremendous threshing of water the sound of which was then relayed from the granite cliffs directly opposite Croghan village. He couldn't see those mighty flukes whacking the water but he could visualise the frenzy of the fearful animals as they tried to fight their way out of the Sandy Cove ambush. Then the frantic thudding ceased and the cliffs went back to the broadcasting of the shrill trumpets of the gulls.

Daverns opened, but Paul postponed the first pint of the day, and paced up and down the pier waiting for the good news that low domes of raised water between Fraser's Rock and himself or another ornamental tree suddenly shooting from a living island would bring him. At last, three quarters of an hour to an hour later, the news he hoped for came when, once again, he noticed that strange camber on the surface of the harbour, and it was confirmed for him when one of the whales passing the Point and heading for the safety of the open sea expelled the last of the Croghan air from its hectic lungs in a cloud of mucus that had no shape but the shape of terror.

He didn't know how many whales had heaved their vast tonnage up the harbour — seven or eight of them, he guessed — or how many had now turned their convulsed tails on the treacherous Cove — seven or eight, he hoped. All he knew as he shuffled to Daverns was that he had seen something which would inch its way slowly down many a pint of Guinness during the day.

Four narrative inches down the first glass, the mail car arrived in Croghan with an epilogue to Paul's story. At every door where the mail car man knocked with a letter the same conversation took place: "There's nothing in that letter, Tom . . . there's nothing in that letter, Dinny . . . there's nothing in that letter, Mary, to match the news I have myself".

"And what news is that, Jimmy?"

"There's a whale washed up in Sandy Cove."

He had no letter for Daverns but he had a great need of a pint and he nearly put his elbow through the glass panel of the door in his rush to get it.

"A Guinness there, Mick," he called to Davern. "My tongue is like a board."

"Too much milk you're drinking, Jimmy".

"Not milk this time, but it's a kind of cream, if you like."

"Cream?"

"Yes, the cream of Monday morning's news".

Jimmy brought the post and the papers from Hilltown every day and he felt it was his daily duty not only to deliver eggs but to hatch them.

"You're the man who'll be interested in this, Paul," he said, turning away from Mick and bringing his pint over to Paul's window. "There's a whale washed up in Sandy Cove."

"Ah, no. Ah, God, no. Don't tell me so, Jimmy."

"I'm telling you, then. There's a whale washed up in Sandy Cove".

Paul let him off with the phrase the first time, but not the second. Blue water sailors are very precise people; otherwise they wouldn't be walking down gangways in Antofagasta or Surabajo or be sitting on bollards at the end of their days.

"Stranded, you mean," he said.

"Do I? What's the difference?"

"A dead whale gets washed up. A living whale gets stranded. The whale you have seen is stranded. I saw him powering up the harbour an hour ago."

"Well, you won't see him powering down again. He looks to me as dead as a rock."

"I'm sorry to hear that," Paul said, pushing the remnants of his pint away from him almost in loathing. "Really sorry. There aren't so many of them left, and to think it should happen here in Croghan of all places. It's too bad." Then after a pause he asked "Whereabouts on the beach is he?"

"Right in the middle and about fifty feet out from the road, I'd say."

"How big?"

"Hard to say. Three times as big as the car. More maybe. He's only half showing. Do you know what he would remind you of? A half tide rock. Black, and the water lapping around it." And with the thought of the water lapping around his brain, he asked, "Is the tide coming in or going out?"

"Ebbing for an hour." Paul used the correct word as always, but it was a hard word to say; the exultation he felt earlier when the whale broached and blew as it left Croghan Point astern was also ebbing fast.

"There will be more and more of him to be seen, so, as the day goes on," Jimmy said excitedly, "but even as things stand he is one mighty fish."

There was an anger building up inside Paul against shelving beaches and the forces of nature and he vented it on Jimmy.

"It's not a fish; it's a mammal," he said.

"It swims: it must be a fish," Jimmy countered.

"We swim; we're not fish. Dogs swim; they're not fish. Whales swim, they're not fish. They're just like us: mammals." Irritation in every word.

"Alright, Paul. Don't get excited. I believe you. You spent longer in school than I did"

"The school of the sea, anyhow," said Paul, mollified, and he smiled. "Yes, just like us. They are warm blooded just like ourselves. They breathe atmospheric air the same as we do. They bear live young, the same as women. They suckle their young, which women hardly do anymore. In many ways they are more highly developed than humans. Do you know, even supposing that the air in here was fresh, which it never is on a Monday morning, that when you breathe in as you are doing now only about 15% of the air in your lungs is replaced; the other 85% is left as it was, stale and unhealthy. It is exactly the opposite with a whale: when a whale comes up to the surface it blows all but 15% of the stale air out of its lungs and all of that 85% is replaced by the cleanest air in the world."

"You have a fierce stock of knowledge about them," Jimmy said. "Did you make a study of them or what?"

"Well, no, but I read up about them one time after a voyage from Brazil to Tasmania. We were outward bound from Rio to Hobart. 'Twas the start of winter time in the southern ocean like it is here now, and one day, I'll never forget it" — he paused until the vision blazed in his eyes again — "one day a blue whale heading for the Tropics crossed our bows. It was a hundred feet long, that blue. A hundred and thirty tons weight. Can you imagine that? A living creature a hundred feet long, weighing one hundred and thirty tons and doing no harm to anybody. Navigating from the Antarctic to French West Africa without any instruments except the brain that God gave it. It was overwhelming, I tell you, Jimmy, the vastness and the power and the motion and the innocence of it. I was never the same man afterwards, I felt so puny and so shallow."

"A hundred feet?"

"A hundred feet."

"A hundred and thirty tons?"

"A hundred and thirty tons."

Jimmy gulped, and it was the astonishment in Paul's figures and not the potency in the last swig of the Guinness that did it to him. Then he asked "Would you like to see it?"

"You mean the whale to the west?"

"Yes. I'll be going back with the post at 2 o'clock. I'll bring you to see it if you'd like."

"No. I wouldn't like. 'Twould be like seeing Christ on the cross."

Jimmy couldn't make anything of that strange talk, so he just said "I'd better be going. I have a lot more mail to deliver and I want to spread the news about the mammal stranded in Sandy Cove." He said 'mammal stranded' with the pride of a youngster who has learnt two new words in school and raps them out as soon as he gets home.

* * *

If I had had any sense at all I wouldn't have gone to Sandy Cove anymore than Paul did because knowing how vulnerable I was in any situation involving animals, living, dead or dying I should have known that there would be a limpet mine attached to the stranded whale. But not only is there "a divinity that shapes our ends" but some of the timber which the Carpenter handles won't lend itself to any other shape.

The weather and the breviary conspired to put me on the Carpenter's bench. It was a remarkable day for early November: far from having our customary Holy Souls weather, as we called it, with fog to the ground like a pall over a coffin — because that is what the parish always was for the first nine days of November, a communal coffin with all the living crowding around all the dead — the day was as clear as an advertisement for holidays and the sun was telling us to beatify out purgatorial faces.

After my lunch I decided to take air and prayer together and I set out for that section of the coast road to Croghan which was cut like a shelf out of the granite cliffs and where on fine days when the wind was around to the north I could walk up and down reading my breviary without a page of it being flipped over except the page I was turning myself. Winter was the best time for "doing the deck," as Paul christened it when he first saw me walking up and down, up and down, up and down the same stretch of road from his perch in Davern's directly across the harbour, because then there wasn't a tourist within fifty miles of us or a distraction of a car in every dozen psalms. So I was able to obey the rubric of 'digne, attente ac devote" — in a worthy, attentive and devout frame of mind — much better in that locale than, for example, on the day at Cotter's corner when I caused the crash.

Looking back now I am struck by the weird fact that the breviary was a major factor in precipitating the change that came about in my life when the ring of revenge finally closed in on me. If it weren't for the breviary and the crash there wouldn't have been all that speculation about the undertaker's speeding hearse and the empty coffin within which led to Gobnait's forming the ring of revenge in the first place. And if it weren't for the breviary on the coast road on the day of the whale that ring wouldn't have become a noose for the ring leader, Sergeant Miller, to draw tighter around my neck. The fact of the matter is that I wouldn't have heard of the whale at all, certainly not on the fateful day, if the sun hadn't shone, if the wind hadn't been light from the north, if the conditions hadn't been just right for reading the breviary along the road that led to the Cove where the whale was stranded.

Most people think that a priest knows everything, either from the whisperings in the confessional, complaints brought to his house, a network of informers as penetrative as the byeroads and divine inspiration, but in fact he is often the very last to pick up a morsel of news such as the swelling of a womb where no swelling should be or the slipping in and out of audacious beds. And on that day I still hadn't heard of the whale's misadventure six hours after it had thrust itself out of its element into the alien grip of the sands.

However I wasn't five minutes on the coastal road with my breviary in my conventional hands when I realised that something very strange was going on. Instead of the distraction of one passing car every dozen psalms my head was being lifted from the book, psalm after puzzled psalm, by a procession of cars speeding to the west or heading back east a deal more slowly. What could it mean? There was neither a wake nor a beer festival in Croghan — sometimes the first oozed into the second! — nor a dispersal sale of milch cows anywhere to the west. There was only one way to find out: shut the breviary and stop a car.

As luck would have it, the next car coming from the west was the Saab of Hugh Kelleher. If anyone could give a Reuter's report, Hugh could. He loved drama on and off the stage: his considerable bulk carried the plays in the local hall. Wherever there were oysters to be eaten in public, a protest by angry farmers or a train off a line Hugh was there. He ran the grocery shop in Kilbroney — he was Bill Driscoll's bete noir, all of Bill's curses so far having failed to put him out of business — but if he heard of an auction of regency furniture eighty miles away he thought nothing of pulling the oil cloth covering over the cash register and driving off to survey the chaise longues.

He had had a good education, which was why he was so showy, so people said. I daresay he was, but then even a small hill is showy in a flat plain. He wore a trim stiff beard with the distinction of a commander who has torpedoed a dozen cargo vessels, and the car he drove, the elegant Saab, had him right out front stage in a parish of untheatrical automobiles. He was a fine talker — indeed the only fear I had on the Day of the Arab was that he would abandon the Bisto tins and come out to accost me — and so he was just the man to tell me what it was that had all the cars racing and chasing.

I waved him down and he stood on the brakes as if a cow had leapt over a ditch in front of him: he was that sort of man. He switched off the engine, his prelude to a long conversation.

"Hugh, what's happening?"

"Gosh, Father Brendan, do you mean you don't know? I thought you would be the first to hear."

"No. Hugh, I don't have the advantage of running a grocery where everybody trades in news as well as money."

"Touché, Father. Well, actually, everything and nothing."

"Meaning?"

"There's a sort of circus going on in Sandy Cove, with a big crowd and just one animal. A whale has been stranded but it has all come to nothing because they have failed to get the unfortunate creature back in the water."

"The crowd, do you mean?"

"Ah, no, no, no. Don't be ridiculous, Father. It is forty feet long and one of the old salts from Croghan reckoned it weighed a ton for every foot."

"How then?"

"Two tractors, Sam Attridge's and Pete Connor's, and you know how big Sam's is : it's a 66, the biggest in the parish; but even the two of them working together couldn't do anything with it. I never before saw a Protestant and a Catholic working so closely together but they needed more than ecumenism to shift that whale. I'd say myself you would need as many tractors as the Yankees have in the cornfields of the Mid West. They tried everything, Sam taking the strain on one flank and Pete on the other; another time Sam pulling by the tail and Pete pushing the snout but if they gained a foot it's as much as they made. Their main problem was that they couldn't get proper purchase anywhere on it except the tail, but anyhow they have slipped the ropes off it now and admitted defeat. Matter over mind."

"Is it still living?"

"Hard to say. I don't reckon so myself. How could it be, high and dry for six hours, since half past nine this morning?"

"Half past nine!"

"Yes. Paul Carmody saw a flotilla of them — leave it to Paul; that's the word he used, flotilla; what's that the French say, the mot juste, isn't it? — well, he saw this flotilla making passage up the harbour at half past nine. They must have thought they were in a fiord, with deep water all the way. Too late they realised their mistake. Or rather too late this one realised its mistake. It got lodged in the sand. The others got away."

"Thank God for that anyway."

"Well, yes. I know how you feel about these things, Father Brendan. The good thing from your point of view is that no one lured it in here, no one exploded a harpoon in it. Providence of God, would you say? I heard you quoting from the gospel the time of the magpies that not one of them falls from the sky without the heavenly Father knowing about it, so I suppose not a whale is stranded without the heavenly Father knowing about it as well."

I couldn't be sure if he was having a sly dig at me or not, so I said nothing.

He continued, "The one thing certain is: it will mean a big clean up job for the County Council. It would take a tug boat at high tide to pull the carcass out into deep water, and they are not going to spend that sort of money. McEntagart will draft in a gang of workers, and they will cut it up and bury it. Wait till you see. And do you know what, we could have the best of oil for Christmas if only we had any lamps left to burn it."

He switched on the engine. His last words were "Go and have a look, Father. As I said, it is like a circus. They never got a crowd like it at Croghan Regatta. Everyone is there, young and old, rich and poor, everyone except the famous Arab," and with that he pulled away in a stench of inflamed rubber, theatrical as always.

Theatre. There was folk theatre at Sandy Cove. The question was: did I want to be part of it? My unfinished breviary said: don't go. My sensibilities said: don't go. All my prior experience involving so-called civilised people on the one hand and wild animals on the other said: don't go. But the pull of the mysterious creature on the sands was almost as great as the pull of that other stranded creature, the sphinx, had been until I had gone to Egypt to see it, and all the don'ts in the western world couldn't counter it. Besides there was the numeral forty. Forty feet. Forty tons. For a man like myself who read a passage of scripture every day there was something mystical about forty. The rain waters that lifted Noah's ark fell on the earth for forty days. The Israelites wandered for forty years in the desert. King David reigned for forty years. Christ fasted for for forty days and forty nights in the wasteland west of Jericho. And for forty days between his resurrection and his ascension he appeared to his friends on northern shores and southern slopes. Forty feet. Forty tons. I crossed to the other side of the road, and I waved down the next car travelling to the west.

"Are you going to see the whale?" I asked.

"The very thing," Batt Ellis answered.

"Would you give me a lift?"

"Sure thing, Father. Sit in."

When Batt and I arrived at Sandy Cove, Sam Attridge was having difficulty getting his tractor back on the road because some fool had parked his car right across the gap leading up from the beach. It wouldn't be too difficult to find him, however, because everyone present was in a shambling circle around the whale, like so many vultures pecking with their hands instead of beaks, and uttering cries not too far removed from the

African plains. In the short time it took to locate him, I had a chance of talking to Sam.

"Thanks, Sam," I shouted up to him. "You are one good man, that's what you are." The shock of getting praise from a priest nearly unseated him inside in his Protestant cab, and he leant across and opened the door. I climbed the steps until our heads were nearly level.

"I'll say this for you Church of Ireland people," I said to him. "You have a reverence for God's creatures that we Catholics do not have. I never heard of a Protestant in this parish violating the Sabbath with guns or hounds. Thanks again for a mighty effort even if it was an unavailing one."

"You're the man with the words, Father" he replied, not to be outdone in the compliments. "And that is the very word I was looking for all day and couldn't think of — unavailing. I'll tell you why. I was doing a few chores in the yard above at about half nine. I don't know what in the wide world made me look down at the Cove, but when I did I saw them at that very instant hitting the beach, one of them very high up. There were five or six of them, all told, I'd say. First I thought they were all in trouble together, all in the same tangle, but then as they kept on butting their heads in and out and whacking the water with their tails I could see that it was how they were trying to get their companion out of the tangle. They tried hard, very hard. But to use your word, Father, it was unavailing. Then the tide began to ebb and they made off down the harbour. I suppose they knew that companionship by itself was no good. Life is tough".

I was moved by what he said. "So that's why ...". I began to say but I never finished the sentence.

"Yes," he said "that's why I brought the tractor down. I only tried to do what they tried to do. I thought if I could move the whale out to the low water mark that when the tide made again and covered it, it could lift and free itself. But no good. It was all unavailing."

The parking fool was found, the car was shifted, Sam went home on his tractor and I walked up along the road that skirted the beach until I was level with the whale. I didn't go down on to the beach; I stayed on the road with my elbows resting on the sea wall not looking anywhere in particular. It was a bit like staying outside on a hospital corridor unable to face the death rattle of someone you love inside in the ward.

What Hugh said about the circus came back to me. I could well believe that when he was present there was more of the circus atmosphere, because the tractors were whining, tow ropes were skiddering off the flanks of the whale, there was much holding of breath, there was an air of expectancy that something could go very wrong and there was the sheer comicality of seeing a blue dinky toy trying to push a heavy black cushion.

Now that the tractors had left, everyone had converged on the whale itself which became the focus of attention for what it was rather than for what might or might not happen to it. To be fair to them most people just walked around it trying to find the space for it in their minds, and there were several men who were stepping out their yard long paces and counting ten, eleven, twelve, thirteen, to measure its astounding length for themselves.

Then a change came about when children on their way home from school in their mothers' cars poured on to the beach and turned the whale into a fairground plaything: one after another they would run at it at full tilt, butt it with their heads and fall back on their joyous buttocks with the impact. Only that their mothers were present I would have kicked their buttocks for them good and hard and inflicted more damage than the sands. My blood began to rise for the first time.

While this fun was at its height two women stepped out of a car which had given them a lift, one in her early twenties, the other in her late fifties, both well known to me for different reasons. The young one was Marie Coleman who was due to be married early in the New Year; I had become accustomed to her hatchet face and her smoker's breath from the pre-marriage instruction I was giving her. The other was an English woman, a settler, a good friend of mine and an eccentric if ever there was one. Maybe that was why we were friends: it could have been a case of one ciaróg recognising another. Her name was Sarah Field.

Marie Coleman swung her legs over the seawall and walked down to the whale. Sarah came and stood alongside me on the road. "Say nothing just yet, Sarah; just look," I said. We both looked at the Marie lassie. Even as I write this, the pen shakes in my hand with vexation. The bitch stood up on the tail — if only those giant flukes could have catapulted her into the harbour! — and walked up along the crest of the whale's back, waving to the crowd as she went, and then slithered down its snout to the sand. I made a very quick but firm resolution: to say not a single evviva in her honour at her wedding feast in January.

"What do you think, Sarah? I asked.

"The animal is more noble dead than she is living", she answered.

And so said I.

Sarah had been a teacher in the secondary school system in Britain for many years until she was dismissed for insubordination or unorthodoxy or some other such reason which would have been consonant with her rare personality. She had a face that had been battered by life but she still carried around in her brain countless packets of knowledge in pristine condition. So I asked her "Is the whale dead?"

"Yes, I think so," she answered. "From what I remember of my zoology class, a whale stranded on the seashore dies fairly quickly of asphyxia from the weight of its own huge body compressing the lungs. Its oxygen must surely be exhausted by now, and if it isn't dead it is in a state of deep unconsciousness from which only something really diabolical could jolt it back to this world of pain."

"Speak of the devil, Sarah," I said, "Look who's coming".

"I met murder on the way;

He had a mask like Castlereagh", she quoted.

Miller was walking up the beach with what I would call the pace of intent. He was dressed in his sergeant's uniform, which meant that he had belted Ireland on to his person along with his jacket. As he got nearer to the whale I could feel my pulse drumming in my ears and the only other time I had that experience was when I had a high fever with flu. When he reached the whale he barked out some instruction or other which neither of us could pick up, and all the spectators fell back from the animal into a much wider circle. Had I got the man all wrong? Had I vilified him unfairly? Was he demanding a respectful distance? Was he setting up a sort of cordon such as one finds in a zoo?

What he did next I remember only as I remember a coup de grace from a surrealist film. Following in the graceless footsteps of Marie Coleman he planted two official boots on the whale's tail and climbed up the sloping back until he reached the blowhole on the top of the head. Then — and again I tremble as I write — he pulled a revolver from his pocket, bent over the animal's head and from a distance of about a foot above the nostrils discharged six bullets, one, two, three, four, five, six in quick succession into the blowhole. The granite cliffs bruited the brute's heroics up and down the harbour.

I cannot remember jumping off the wall but I certainly remember jumping at Killer when he slid down off the whale on to his patch of police-polluted sand.

"You bastard," I shouted. "What do you think you are doing? Think!" I snorted. "The only way you can think is out of the barrel of a gun".

"Pulpit basher," he shouted back. "All you can do is talk. I did the humane thing. I put him out of his agony"

"Humane! All you know about humane is how to spell it, if even that. Out of his agony, I like that. What you did was to jolt him out of a coma into agony. Into agony, not out of it."

"Are you questioning my authority?"

"I am not questioning your authority. I am questioning your intelligence. I am questioning your sanity."

"Sanity, you say. It's you who are insane, insane with passion."

"I'd rather be insane with passion than insane with cruelty. You are the fellow who has charged Sarah over there with cruelty to a donkey. You should be charged yourself with cruelty to this dying animal. You are a disgrace to your uniform and a disgrace to your country."

"You have some right to be talking about uniforms, of all things. I am satisfied in my mind . . . "

"If you have one"

"that you were the fellow who dressed up in the Arab's uniform."

"Prove it. And even if you can, there is a big difference between fun and gun. The Arab was a fun man. You are a gunman. A killer. You kill the living. You kill the dying. You kill the dead. That's all you are, a killer."

He took two menacing steps in my direction. "Laide," he said, "I'll quieten you". The fact that he used my surname isolated in that insulting way showed that the passion which he spoke about was catching.

"You will, with a bullet, I expect," I answered. "But not today. The magazine is spent. You will have to go back to your clubhouse for more supplies."

I was vaguely aware all this slagging time of people moving to the road. I could see out of a small corner of my inflamed eye mothers pulling children away. The shock of hearing the priest and the sergeant berating each other like that wiped the whale off the beach.

"I'll get you," Miller continued. "It won't be with a bullet. It will be a much cleaner job than that. With a summons, that's how."

"For questioning your mighty authority, I suppose".

"No. For slander from the altar. For dangerous driving. For keeping the parish hall open after 2 o'clock. For bathing in the nude. I'll get you. That's sure to you. You'll remember this day."

He was right.

Chapter 5

ECCENTRIC

I walked home to Kilbroney with Sarah. We had much to discuss, and all of it had to do with Miller: Miller past, present and to come, what he had just done to the whale, what he had done on that same beach some years before to the choughs, the threat he posed to myself with those future summonses, and the summons he had recently issued to Sarah to attend the sitting of Hilltown District Court on the 11th of December, barely a month away.

Her offense as stated on the summons was "that on September 23rd in the townland of Knocknashinagh she had grossly overloaded her donkey thereby causing undue suffering and distress to the animal."

That was the most immediate matter of concern on our minds and on our tongues on the way home. It was like a council of war. How could we outflank Miller? Could we hope to defeat him? What tactics should we employ? Should we engage a solicitor? Would I succeed in persuading Connie Con O'Leary to give evidence for us? At no stage in our discussion did I say to her "You should do this, Sarah" or "You should do that." At all times I said "We shall do this" or "We shall do that." We. My name wasn't on the summons but Sarah and I were in the case together.

We were an odd pair. She was twenty years older than I was; her face was what you would call challenging, not attractive; and her clothes looked as if the only wardrobe she had was a duffle bag, so none of the usual elements of an amorous relationship were present. The parishioners reacted to our friendship with surprise rather than alarm, because it was generally believed that I disliked Protestants and hated the English, and Sarah was both. Unhappily for the good of my Christian soul I had read too much history in my time but even in my most intemperate moments I would never have classified Sarah under the categories of rigid Protestants or colonial English.

Although her cottage was so close to the Protestant church that it fell under its shadow when the sun slid to the west, the only time her own shadow fell on that church door was for the harvest festival: she loved the camaraderie of that occasion and she couldn't understand, she told me one time, how a Church as Mediterranean as the Catholic Church had left so fruity a rite to one that originated in gnarled northern climes.

On several occasions she asked me to receive her into the Catholic Church, but I declined. Not that Saint Brona's couldn't have done with another pair of knees at a time when the young were legging it out of the parish in relays for Birmingham and Boston but that she was so argumentative herself and so un-submissive to the arguments of others that I knew there was no chance whatsoever that she would assent to doctrines such as the Immaculate Conception of the Blessed Virgin or the infallibility of the Pope. In fact, I couldn't see Sarah belonging, really belonging to any religious persuasion because frankly no one could persuade her that white was white if she chose to chequer it.

I was thinking of my own mental comfort too! She occasionally came to Mass as a gesture of friendship but almost invariably she put that friendship to the test by coming into the sacristy immediately after Mass to tell me that in my exposition of the origins of Protestantism I had put Henry VIII's wives in the wrong chronological order or that I had misinformed the congregation that it was Dryden who wrote "To err is human, to forgive divine" whereas in fact the line belonged to Alexander Pope. I knew that if I admitted her not only to the pews but to membership it would be no time before she would be striding into the sacristy to correct not me but the Holy Roman Catholic and Apostolic Church!

Her Englishness was very obvious to us Irish but it was discounted by her fellow English settlers in the parish. They reckoned that her habit of tucking her slacks inside her wellington boots, her practice of sitting at wakes to swallow tea and local lore and her use of donkeys as a means of transport rather than as pieces of live sculpture in a garden were proofs of the fact that she had gone native and therefore she was inadmissible at their sherry parties and croquet tournaments. Not that that worried Sarah a lot: the last thing she wanted to be taken for was a new English colonial of the impregnable bungalow variety.

When we were walking home to Kilbroney on that Monday in November we weren't linking arms; what linked us was our love of animals, and what brought her to Saint Brona's was that from time to time I filled the Church with the screams of hares being torn to pieces by greyhounds or with the thud of bullets in the foxbright hills. Reverence for God's creatures was the only doctrine she adhered to and the only church music she wanted to hear was when I launched myself into a tirade against the killers of the Hilltown Gun Club.

The first time I knew her for what she was, a kindred spirit, was the day when I opened "The Irish Times" at the correspondence page and saw a letter which the subeditor had entitled KILLING OF CHOUGHS at the end of which was the startling name and address: Sarah Field, Fuchsia Cottage, Kilbroney.

It was what a letter-to-the-editor should be: well written, uncompromising, accusatory and full of passion. It said:

Sir,

There are people who say that the chough is "only a crow." I am not one of them. And if you have ever seen a male chough in the mating season showing off to a female by dropping out of the sky like a dive bomber and levelling off over the agitated surf at the very last suicidal second you would not say so either.

The chough is not a rare bird in the technical sense that it belongs to an imperilled species, but it is a very rare bird indeed in the sense that it is found nowhere in Northern Europe except Ireland, Wales, Scotland, the Isle of Man and Brittany: it is therefore stridently a Celtic bird. And it is a rare bird also in the sense that it clings to life only in those parts of Ireland where the hardiest of the people also cling to life, that is in the coastal regions of the North West, West, and Southwest where the Atlantic fights its eternal war with the cliffs. Nobody in the genteel parts of Ireland has ever seen this gentle bird before his or her cooked breakfast.

For some years past, a pair of choughs have nested in a tidal cave near Sandy Cove just west of the fishing village of Croghan in the parish of Kilbroney. But never again. They are both dead. They didn't die from being caught unawares by a freak wave, they didn't die from malnutrition, they didn't die from eating diseased oysters or mussels. They died of gunshot wounds.

How does it happen, you may ask, that these two birds, belonging to a protected species, have been shot? If you would turn your eyes for a moment to the North of Ireland where the Nationalist population is also, under the law, a protected species, you will find the answer. The people who are charged with the protecting are the very people who are doing the shooting. Will they be prosecuted, North or South? For answer, give a cynical smirk or alternatively ask yourself a further question: quis custodiet ipsos custodes?

These were gorgeous birds. With their long curved pointed red bills, elegant red legs and glossy black plumage they were nature's fashion creation in le rouge et le noir. The children who came here from all over Ireland for their summer holidays forgot about sun, sand and sea when these birds floated above them and put on their acrobatic acts out of the sheer joy of performing at a height no human acrobat would dare to. What is more, the children did not need to have their handbooks of birds with them: the choughs said tchuff and told them who they were. Never again will the children see them, hear them or marvel at them.

I am not Irish by birth myself, although there have been many times since I came to live here when I wished that I was. But, as I write this letter, I can tell you that not even for an honoured place in Irish history would I want to be the fellow citizen of the Irish man who shot these Irish choughs.

Yours truly,
Sarah Field.

On the day after reading the letter I called to Fuchsia Cottage for the first time. The fuchsia perfectly typified the character of the owner: it was colourful and undisciplined. It had jumped across the gate from both sides, forming a sort of buckling arch and narrowing the space of the entry into a keyhole shape, through which I slid sideways. Somebody, most probably herself, had yanked the knocker off the door; it was still lying on the ground, a reminder that would never be heeded. So I used my knuckles to announce my arrival.

Almost immediately — she must have been watching my navigation through the fuchsia strait — the door opened, and Sarah was standing there saying "How good to see you, Father Laide." She was wearing what I could call a kimono, but perhaps there is a different name for it in English educational circles. She was also wearing the smile which her face often donned and for which, I discovered as the months passed, the dress materials were amusement and cognac in equal measure.

"Thank you, Miss Field".

"O, don't call me that," she said with an unhappy shake of the hand. "It reminds me of a cricketer falling over his flannels on the long leg boundary and dropping a catch."

A great image. She had probably used it before but it made me one of the eleven right away. I got no time to settle in the team, however, because she bowled me a googly immediately. "If you were a woman how would you like it if somebody called you Mislaid?"

It was the first time I ever thought of what my sisters must have endured before they married. She was sharp, this woman, sharp as Abu Ali's dagger.

"Call me Sarah," she said. "It is a good biblical name."

"Thank you. Sarah" I answered, "I shall" and I secretly congratulated myself on getting the first person singular number future tense of the verb "to be" uncharacteristically right.

"May I call you Brendan?" In a day of firsts it was the first time since I was ordained that anybody had asked me that question.

"Yes, sure" I answered, although I wasn't sure of anything just then except that she was setting the pace and it was a fast one. Within three minutes of our first meeting we were on a first name basis.

"Come inside, Brendan," she said, flashing me a smile that was all of it welcome and none of it either amusement or cognac, and adding "But don't be thrown by the chaos in here." It was a well chosen word. The living room, if we were to call it that, because I couldn't imagine how anyone could live in it, had something of the tohu and bohu of the first day of creation about it; everything was present but it was all in a jumble. Her Britannic Majesty's other subjects in Hilltown, Kilbroney and Croghan would not have been amused.

I was hit by so many distractions all at once that I temporarily forgot why I was there. There were books like stepping stones all over the floor, there were chairs heaped with clothes like the overflow of a pawn, there were ziggurats of tanned old newspapers on the table, there were buckets of sea shells in one corner, a dislodged magpie's nest in another and in a third what I took at first glance to be a year's supply of scrawny potatoes but turned out to be a heap of pine cones. But her next question focussed my attention again on the purpose of my visit.

"Have you come to convert me, Brendan?" she asked.

"No, as a matter of fact you and I share the same faith in one most important matter."

"And what is that?"

"The sacredness of life, all life, and more immediately the life of choughs".

"You have read it?"

"Yes, that is why I am here: to congratulate you on a fine bit of work. Le rouge et le noir. The red of anger and the black of ink — the ultimate combination."

"You think so?"

"Yes. Lyrical on the birds."

"I had the bird books."

"That didn't come from bird books; that came from the heart."

"And the rest of it?"

"From the cauldron. The people who are charged with the protecting are the very people who are doing the shooting"

"Will Miller read it?"

"Of course, he'll read it. His comrade-in-arms at the Delicatessen, Maguire, always gets the "Irish Times". You are sure it was Miller, are you?"

"Quite sure. I was talking to Sam Attridge."

"And what did he say?"

"He said the sergeant was shooting crows in the Cove the day before."

"And you are certain the choughs were shot?'

"As certain as I have eyes. I picked them up myself. One was in the dunes, on the third fairway. The other was flapping at the top of the tide, but it was the tide that was doing the flapping. Miller didn't just kill them, you know. He savaged them. Buck shot. I buried them as near as I could to their cave."

"That was good."

"What are we going to do about him?"

"I don't really know. I have bashed his head against the pulpit a few times."

"So I've heard."

"But it hasn't done any good. The choughs are proof of that. Anyway there were only three or four hundred people present to hear me. Your audience was a hundred times bigger than that, and more power to you. Thirty or forty thousand people buy the "Times" and whatever else they don't read, they all read the letters. 'Twas a good day's work. And clever too."

"In what way?"

"Your signpost says 'Garda Station', but that is all. You don't name anybody in particular. But the locals will know which of the custodes is the guilty custos you have in mind. I like your use of the Latin."

"Thanks".

"Miller will be a long time biting on that particular bullet. The ignoramus."

* * *

In the first intoxication of the letter to the editor I had told Sarah I was calling to congratulate her, but the more I thought about it in the soberer days that followed the more I realised I should have called to commiserate with her. The sergeant didn't suffer opponents, all of whom he regarded as fools, gladly. With birds and animals he lived up to the name I gave him, Killer, and he did his killing quickly. With people he lived up to his family name, Miller, and ground them down slowly. Hilltown people who suffered from his vindictiveness said as much when they used the bucolic phrase 'He would make porridge of you for his breakfast'. And perhaps I ought to have told Sarah that the Irish word for her beloved fuchsia was deora Dé, the tears of God. Bloodied tears were Miller's stock-in-trade.

His chance to get even with her came to him on the back of her donkey. Coming from a country where donkeys were regarded with something of the same reverence as vintage cars, one of the ritualistic things many of the English settlers did when they came to Kilbroney was to take pity on some ramshackle donkey still travelling the roads, buy it from its as-tonished owner who up to that point had never entered it in his calculating head under the column Assets, and refurbish it to something approaching its original condition in the cossetting comfort of their Irish acres.

The first I heard of Sarah's donkey or rather that she had joined in the queue for a donkey was one day when I called to Florrie's for petrol: he assuaged the thirst of motor cars outside his premises and the thirst of the motorists inside. Sarah was a regular customer of his for the brandy rather than the benzine, and he saw a lot more of her than I did.

"I thought we would have to send for you yesterday, Father," he said, "on an urgent sick call".

"Did somebody get sick in the bar, Florrie?" I asked.

"Ah, no, no, but we thought that maybe Connie Con would have his skull split open before the day was out." He said it with a smile so I knew that the danger of the murderous intent had passed.

"And who had the hatchet?" I asked.

"Your own Miss Field, then," he answered with a mischievous eye.

"Sarah!" I exclaimed. "With a hatchet! How come?"

So he told me the story of Connie Con's donkey.

"A few months ago Connie Con agreed to sell his donkey to the Banfords for £30. They gave him a £5 deposit and said they would give him the balance when he delivered the donkey to Glenure. Balance is probably not a good word to use about Connie Con when he has a good rattle in his pocket and I have to admit to you that most of the deposit finished up in my till. Anyhow the lads that were drinking with him persuaded him that he had made a bad deal. "You drove that donkey too hard" they said "but you drove the bargain too soft". You will be pleased at this part of it, Father. He is evidently one of your keenest listeners at the 12 o'clock Mass. Do you remember that you preached about the sanctity of Sunday a short while back? Well, away with Connie Con to Glenure not with the donkey but with a plan to reopen the negotiations. "Mr and Mrs Banford", said he, "I regret to inform ye that the deal we made was invalid because it was made on a Sunday and according to our religion a person must abstain from all unnecessary commercial activities on the day of rest". Are you listening to me, Father?"

"If I had ten ears you would have the whole ten of them, Florrie!"

"That being the case" said Connie "we will have to make a new deal because neither you nor I would have any luck buying and selling an animal that was sacred to the Lord on the Lord's Day".

"Better and better", I said, enthralled at the tale and the telling.

"The Banfords couldn't see any fun in it, however, and they ran him from the door. "Keep your donkey" they said, "Sunday, Monday and every other day. And keep the deposit as well. We wouldn't take it back" they said, that is, if you want to believe him …"

"I don't".

"If you gave it back to us in crisp new English notes".

"That's marvellous".

Connie retired from the field battered but beaming because he retained his booty, £5 worth of free beer, and that is where Miss Field came into the picture. Connie still had a donkey to sell and Miss Field took a particular liking to the animal. That was foolish of her because Connie made her pay for her fancy: £35 for the donkey, £30 to be paid right away and the final fiver when the donkey was delivered to Fuchsia Cottage. She gave him the £30 and they fixed on a date for delivery and do you know when that date was? Yesterday!

She was in and out of the bar all day not that she had a bigger thirst than usual but that as hour followed hour she expected to see the donkey tethered to one of the rings on the gable end. No luck. No Connie. No donkey. And the fiver in her hand.

"Look here, Miss Field" said I, the sixth and last time she came in. "And tell me something. What day of the week was it when you made the deal?"

"A Sunday" she said.

"A Sunday!" I exclaimed and everyone in the bar roared laughing. "Are you sure?"

"Of course I'm sure. It was after last Mass. I met him on our way out in the porch. I couldn't possibly forget, because he lowered his hand like a saucer into the stoup and slashed the holy water all over his face. 'Twas probably the only wash he got for the week".

"H'm, I'd say now you are wrong there, Miss Field. What he was doing was washing the deal away in God's name."

"How do you mean?"

"Well, the same man doesn't regard any business done on a Sunday as being valid in the sight of God. It's a sacrilege or something like that. Did you give him the £30?"

"There and then."

"H'm. If you ask me, he will hold on to the money and the donkey too."

"We shall see about that", she said "and it won't be next Sunday. It will be to-day. Right now."

"What will you do?" we all asked her.

She gave us a marvellous answer. Like something you'd hear in a play in the hall, Father. "You see this hand", she said, holding out her left hand to us. "What's in it?" "A fiver", we said. "And you see this other hand", she said, stretching out her right hand, "What's in it?" "Nothing", we said. "Nothing now". she said "but what will be in it when I set out for Connie Con's?"

We shook our heads. "A hatchet", she said. "You can't be serious", we suggested. "Never so serious since I turned down my third offer of marriage", she said. "Either I shall come back from Dunsheen riding on the donkey, or I shall come back leading it, with Connie Con's corpse sprawled across its back like in the cowboy films". "What a woman! The Irish are only lambs compared to a woman like that. Wouldn't you agree, Father?"

I agreed with him. "And what happened? Did she come back riding or walking?"

"Walking, but not, as it happened, with Connie Con's head spurting blood down the donkey's flank. What she put into his skull was the fear of God, not the hatchet. She gave him an ultimatum of twenty four hours. "If you haven't the donkey at my place tomorrow evening" — that's this evening — "at 6 o'clock,

I shall slice your head open like it was a cabbage. I am going to spend twelve of the twenty four hours whetting this hatchet. It isn't nearly sharp enough for the job as it is". Lambs, did I say? The Irish are only worms compared to a woman like that!" . . .

At twenty five minutes past twelve that night I was getting ready for bed, pyjamas on and all when there was a knock at the front door. Sick call, surely. Had Sarah carried out her threat? I hadn't even one leg into my trousers when there was another almighty knock. Urgent sick call, by the frantic sound of it. Run it, Laide. Was there somebody at the door with Connie Con's head on a dish? I went down the twisty staircase as if it was a slalom, and swung the door open. Who was there only Connie Con himself, head on his shoulders, and not a pimple of blood to be seen!

I nearly ate him like the head of cabbage that Sarah said she would slice in two. "What the hell do you mean? . . . at this hour of night . . . the fright you gave me . . . have you any consideration? what the blazes do you want?"

He answered that final question cooly and simply. "A place to sleep for the night, good Father", he said. In my time I had been addressed as reverend Father, dear Father, even holy Father, but never before as good Father. It was the ultimate challenge to my Christianity. "Come in", I said and I shut the door behind him.

I led him into my living room and switched on the light. The cat on the hearth rug opened one protesting eye at this intrusion into her beauty sleep. There was still a lot of rouge on the face of the fire.

"The bed in the spare room is too damp to put you into, Connie", I said, my sudden storm as suddenly ended. "It hasn't been slept in for ages".

"What bed do I want? Sure I'm not the Pope".

"What about the armchair then?"

"Grand." He caught the two arms of the chair and lowered himself into it very gingerly as if he was testing the temperature

of a bath with his bottom. Then he looked up at me and he released his breath contentedly. "Fit for a prince", he said.

I was moving in high society, conversationally, with Popes
and princes, no less, and my mind expanded accordingly. "Put
on more fire, if you want it; there is plenty of coal in the scuttle.
Or is it something to keep your insides warm you would like?"

"Well, I wouldn't say no to your good self" he answered.
That word "good" again. He was some diplomat, was Connie
Con.

"A brandy?"

"There's nothing I'd like better". He tossed off my best
Remy Martin as if it was a raw egg, and then he said, looking all
around him, "Didn't I hit the right place!"

"You did, but not at the right time."

"Well, I'm very sorry about that, Father, but those black-
guards down in Florrie's delayed me and then not one of them
would drive me home to Dunsheen".

"But I thought you had your own transport, Connie", I said,
drawing him out.

"So I had, but I have it no longer. I sold my faithful friend,
my Jack o'Lantern today".

"You did! To whom?"

"To that Englishwoman who lives down near the Protestant
Church. I'm sure you know her. She comes to Mass some
Sundays to hear yourself".

"And would that make her a good judge of a donkey, do you
think?" I was warming to the conversation and I stretched out
my hand for the bottle to give him another throw.

"Well, I don't know about that, Father, but she sure has got a
good one in Jack o'Lantern. By the way, did I ever tell you why
I called him that? He is kind of hard to pin down to any one
place, but he is a bright spirit and when she is on his back he
will be as obedient as one of your altarboys."

"Hold out your glass there". He did. "Maybe you will drink
to her health".

"I will not, then. She has the health of a shark as it is. She has a mouth on her that would make ribbons of you".

"She has?"

"She is one tough woman, I'm telling you. If ever ye have women priests she will make a fierce missioner. She would put the fear of God in you".

I poured him the second brandy. "Your health, Father", he said, "and may you stay with us for as long as there are donkeys on the road!" It wasn't exactly a felicitous compliment but I hoped I knew what he meant. On this occasion he eased back the drink with an appreciative closing of both eyes, and he handed me back the glass, saying "If there is ever a thing in the whole wide world that I can do for you, just you ask me".

"Well, Connie, all I am asking you at the moment is don't walk on my cat. She is there on the rug".

"Why would I do a thing like that? Haven't I seven cats myself?" And Fan An jumped up on his lap to show he was no menace at all. And there I left them.

* * *

When Miller's summons was delivered to Sarah, there was indeed something that Connie Con could do for me and it didn't lie in the vague wide world that he was thinking of when he made his offer but in the specific narrow world of Hilltown and Kilbroney. A character witness like myself could, at best, only put a bit of a gloss on the donkey's back. What Sarah needed was a material witness who would blow the prosecution case away and Connie was that witness. Approaching him wasn't easy: it was like asking someone who has been attacked by a shark — his image for her! — to go to its rescue when it has been ensnared in a net. But the memory of the armchair and the brandy cancelled the memory of the hatchet and the cabbage, and he agreed to appear as a witness for the defence.

The case attracted a lot of interest in the peninsula, not only because of the novelty of having an English person before the court on the unprecedented charge of cruelty to animals, but because in the minds of most people the donkey was a phantom and the reality was the feud between Sarah and the sergeant. I never gave him credit for subtlety but in so far as he could be subtle he was subtle in this instance: what he was doing was taking her on with her own choice-of-weapon. It was the equivalent of accusing the Pope of heresy or a schoolteacher of not knowing his five times tables. In effect his contention was that she hadn't practised on the donkey what she had preached on the choughs.

The Hilltown Parish Hall became the Hilltown District Courthouse on the second Tuesday of each month. Normally the court sat in a large room that was used for such activities as children's dancing classes, ping pong nights and meetings of such groups as the Gun Club but on Tuesday morning the 11th of December when Sarah's case was due to be called so many people had already gathered for the duel half an hour before the court was due to rise that the sergeant, the courtclerk and the caretaker put their apprehensive heads together and changed the location to the main hall. It was only the third time that that had happened since the Land War!

So I was present to see the furniture being arranged at the top of the hall, the table for the judge and court clerk being positioned in the centre facing down, and two tables being placed at right angles to it, facing across at each other, one for the members of the Gardai who would be prosecuting in the various cases and the other for the defending solicitors and the accused. The judicial area therefore took on the shape of what we used to call in our Greek classes the dining triclinium, thus ⌐ ⌐ , the shape between the three tables being left open in classical times for entertainers and it was for entertainment not for justice that most of the Kilbroney contingent were present. Prominent among them were the regulars in Florrie's who had sacrificed a lie in bed, a day's fishing or the chance to change their books in the Tuesday mobile library van for the joy of anticipating a Greek symposium in Florrie's that very evening at Sarah's expense, if she won.

At three minutes to eleven when Garda Moriarty walked up between the seats to inform the court clerk that the Judge's car had arrived outside, the hall was as full as it would be for a concert. On his way down again he told three English women who were sitting together to take their hats off. I presumed that they were there as observers on behalf of the settler class and the first observation forced on them was that while they found it difficult to keep their hair on in the presence of Sarah they couldn't keep their hats on in the presence of her judge.

There was a chuckle at the door. I looked around to see who was making it. It was Judge Crowley, thanks be to God, he and no other. As a barrister he had been involved in amateur dramatics and it was often said of him that he carried the greasepaint with him when he put on the judge's wig. I had the happy feeling that the setting would not be lost on him when the drama of Knocknashinagh unfolded.

He walked up the central aisle like the chief actor in an experimental production who enters from the auditorium rather than from the stage, and the audience fell silent. He had a face as round and lips as upturned as a child would have in a drawing: it was another good omen. He placed his brief case on the table and nodded to the court clerk. The clerk said "The court will rise". We all stood up and the judge at the other, the weighty end, of the seesaw sat down. Then the clerk said "The court will sit" and we all settled into our places for the rising of the curtain.

There was bound to be a bad omen too and it arrived when the court clerk announced that the first six cases would be prosecuted by Sergeant Miller, and he listed them in order, one to six. Sarah's was third in the schedule. It was a well known fact that Miller presented his cases in order of ease: he did his smooth sailing first and kept the choppy waters for later. It seemed that all he had to do with Sarah was sail out the course, unimpeded, and his facile win in the first two cases gave credence to that view.

Paddy McCarthy was charged with having four bald tyres at Kealinga on the 18th of September. Miller testified that they were as smooth as banana skins, and although Paddy's solicitor contended that Paddy demonstrated four new tyres on the car at the Garda Station in Hilltown on the 19th, Judge Crowley reminded him that the offence had taken place on the 18th not the 19th and that it was no use picking up banana skins after somebody broke a leg, and he fined his client £10.

Jerry McCarthy, no relation, was charged with having his milk churns in an unhygienic condition at Shanacloon on the 10th of September, and when the sergeant was asked what he meant by unhygienic he said that there was a sort of fur growing on the inside. Jerry's solicitor stated that the water supply in Shanacloon was polluted from other people's slurry and that it was more dangerous to wash the churns than to leave them in their natural state. Once again the Judge found in favour of the sergeant, and he imposed a fine of £20 suggesting that perhaps the best thing for Paddy to do was either to sell the cows or buy new churns. The balanced stage diction was coming down to the audience but as yet there was no titter of comedy.

Then the clerk called Sarah's case.

"Is the defendant in court?" Judge Crowley asked.

Sarah stood up and answered from her chair next to mine "Yes, I am, your Honour". For most people in the hall what had gone before were only supporting items; this was the main feature.

Sarah strode up the hall. There is nothing wrong about striding, but it looks better in slacks than in a dress. She lived in slacks, but for the big day she was wearing a dress which she might have worn to a garden fete twenty years before. It was reeking of moth balls, and the waist was at odds with Sarah's, and with her cropped head and lengthy stride she looked much less a woman than a man dressed up as a woman. She was carrying a plastic bag which completed the ungainly picture; nobody but myself knew what was in it.

For the first time that morning Judge Crowley took off his reading glasses and very nearly swallowed her with his eyes as she approached the defendant's chair. I could see from where I was that he was putting a mental sash across her that blazoned the word "Eccentric". Good. Eccentrics make for drama. The Judge loved drama.

"Are you professionally represented?" he asked her.

"No. I intend to defend myself".

Miller looked up in alarm. Professionals he could deal with: they were as predictable as gun dogs. Amateurs were different; they were like cocker spaniels: you never knew what line they might take.

"And I would ask your indulgence" she added "to allow me to call this witness later". She put a slip of paper with the name "Cornelius O'Leary" on the table in front of the clerk.

"I shall in all my best facilitate you, madam", the judge said with a smile.

"Hamlet Act 1, scene 2". Sarah responded, "with your own emendation, of course".

"Of course," the judge repeated, smiling again.

Miller looked at one and then the other; there was some sort of literary chemistry going on between them which he had no way of gauging. It was as if the local radio station which he was listening to suddenly switched from English to Chinese. Sarah was riding on a comber; Miller was under the curl of it. Our side was a goal up before the referee even blew the whistle for centre off.

The sergeant got first possession of the ball, and this is how he played it:– "Your honour, on the 23rd of September I was in the townland of Knocknashinagh on the road that comes up from the beach of Tránagloch. I was proceeding in that general direction at the time. Approximately 200 yards distance from the side road which comes out of the state forest I met the accused, Miss Sarah Field. She was riding a donkey, and across the donkey's back in front of her she had a heavy quality hessian sack, filled to its fullest extent. I signalled to her to stop and when she did I asked her what she had in the sack. Stones, she replied. I would like to explain to your Lordship that quite a number of people go to Tránagloch with cars and trailers to take away the smooth gobs that are to be found there, which they use for their pathways. Until that day I had never seen anybody use a donkey for that purpose. In my opinion that weight of stones would have been sufficient almost to break the donkey's back, and when it was combined with her own weight it constituted a degree of cruelty which can only be termed extreme. I told her that I would be summonsing her to a sitting of this court on that charge. I had my notebook and pencil with me and I warned her that anything she said could be used in evidence against her. She made no response of any kind. In fact the only word she spoke from beginning to end was the word 'stones'. She gave no indication whatsoever of any remorse. Indeed she continued her journey as before to Kilbroney and that in my opinion aggravated the offence and showed a complete disregard for the animal's welfare".

It was a damning statement, but, strangely, Sarah sat as upright as a marble bishop throughout, and many people remarked later that the judge appeared to be more worried than she was when he turned to her and asked, "Would you like to respond, Miss Field?"

"Yes, I would, my Lord", she answered and when the court clerk presented the Bible to her she said in a steady voice "I, Sarah Field, do solemnly swear that I shall tell the truth, the whole truth and nothing but the truth. So help me God".

Most people present felt she would need all the help that God could provide, but she started off in confident fashion.

"I readily admit, my Lord", she said, "that many of the statements made by Sergeant Miller are true: I admit that I was in the townland of Knocknashinagh on the 23rd of September. I admit that he met me on the road that comes up from Tránagloch. I admit that I was riding a donkey. I admit that I had a heavy quality jute sack in front of me on the donkey's back. I admit that I answered "stones" when he asked me what the sack contained and I admit that I continued my journey to Kilbroney without taking either myself or the load off the donkey. However, two of his inferences are entirely at variance with the facts: one, that I had been to Tránagloch and two, that I had a consignment of stones on the donkey's back. The truth is that I was nowhere near Tránagloch on that day. As you know well, my Lord, one could be on the road from Paris to Le Mans, at Chartres, say, without having been in Paris. In fact where I was that day was deep in the state forest collecting pine cones. Actually I had just emerged from the forest when the sergeant came along in his car. What I had in the sack were pine cones and nothing else. They are bulky, but extremely light. I would hazard a guess that a similar sack tightly packed with feathers would weigh more. I therefore totally deny that the donkey was overloaded or a victim of cruelty".

The judge intervened at this point, saying "I must remind you, Miss Field, that you are on oath, and ask you two questions: one, did you tell the sergeant a lie? And, two, if you did, how can I be sure that you aren't telling another lie now?"

"No, I did not tell a lie, as such" she answered. "In fact I was using a mental reservation. What I was saying to him was:– 'In so far as you are concerned what I have in the sack are stones, but what I really have is my own business and no one else's. I am not infringing any law and you have no right to accost me' As regards your second question, my Lord, I was brought up in the strict High Anglican Communion and I fully understand and respect the sanctity of the oath."

Did I, out of the corner of my otherwise very focussed eye see the heads of the three English settlers go down when Sarah mentioned the High Anglicans? For they were known to me as members of the lowest of the low church in Hilltown.

"Very well", said the judge and then he picked up a sheet of notepaper he had been scribbling on, "I have one further question for you. No, two. Why did you bring back a sackful of pine cones to your house? What use do you make of them?"

"I can answer the two questions with one exhibit" Sarah said triumphantly, bending for the plastic bag which she had placed on the floor near her chair. "I make things with them. I'm not sure if one would designate them objets d'art but such as they are, they are mine" and with that she produced an artefact about 18 inches by 12 constructed entirely out of pinecones. She placed it on the judge's table. "I call this one 'The temple of the golden pagodas'" she said.

Judge Crowley raised it to eye level, looked at it for the longest half minute of the day so far, and delivered his judgment. "Very elegant", he declared.

Miller's goose was cooked. It only remained for Connie Con to pour his steaming sauce all over it.

"Cornelius O'Leary", the clerk called.

Everyone looked around at where Connie was seated, three rows from the back. No budge out of Connie.

"Cornelius O'Leary!" the clerk called again, much more forcibly this time. Someone in the row behind Connie gave him four knuckles in the back, and he shot up. He was a tall man but the western gales had hunched him like the few ash trees on his holding and he walked up the hall like a man who was watching his step on a mucky boreen.

"You are Cornelius O'Leary?" the judge asked him when he reached the space between the three tables.

"I am, your honour".

"Did I detect a certain hesitation on your part to come up here?"

"O no, your honour. Tis just that everybody calls me Connie. When I hear Cornelius I think they are talking about someone else".

Judge Crowley's lips opened in a smile like the moon on its back. He was being handed a script for a rural drama and he knew it. The audience – because audience it was now, not an attendance at a court – knew it as well, and they laughed.

"You are here to give evidence for Miss Sarah Field?" the judge enquired of him.

"Well, not exactly, your honour. I am here to give evidence for the donkey."

The judge joined in the laughter.

"And how is that?"

"Well, 'twas I owned him before the Englishwoman. I reared him from a foal. And 'twas I gave him his name."

"O, he has a name?"

"He has indeed, your honour. Jack o'Lantern."

"Jack o'Lantern!" spluttered the judge." That is a very original name for a donkey. You must have had a reason for that."

"I had indeed, your honour. You see, if I went out to the haggart of a winter's night and shone the torch all around to see where he was, his two eyes would be beaming at me from the hayshed like a motor car. If I went out again a half an hour later they would only be the size of cats' eyes away west of the well. And if I went out a third time he would be up north in the bog like two stars. He wouldn't be steady anywhere but he would be shining everywhere. A real Jack o'Lantern".

The judge was impressed. The words were singing like Synge. "And tell me now", he said. "Apart from his grand name has he any other quality to recommend him?"

"That's what I want to tell you, your honour" said Connie, tossing out his left hand, as he always did, but looking surprised to find no pipe in it. "He is what I would call a very self-respecting donkey."

"A very self-respecting donkey", the judge repeated, giving the cue for another laugh. "What do you mean by that, Connie?" It was another score for our side; Connie was Connie, not Cornelius or Mr O'Leary.

"Well, he is very particular about what he will carry on his back. He will carry wrack after a storm. He will carry furze for the open fire. He will carry baróid from the bog. He will even carry a new mattress for the Stations. But there is one thing he will not carry."

"And what is that?" asked the judge.

"Stones", answered Connie.

"Stones!" exclaimed the judge.

"Stones", chanted a dozen people caught up in the drama, like extras.

"Stones", Connie confirmed solemnly. And he continued. "Three times, four times, maybe even five times I tried to get him to carry stones from Tránagloch but he became a stone himself. A big stone, I mean. A rock. He wouldn't budge an inch until I took the load off. One time I tried him with a soft rope basket that a child could carry, with all kinds of coloured stones in it that I thought would look nice on top of the pillars, but no, he must have smelled them. Pulling him, pushing him, beating him, coaxing him, 'twas all the same: he wouldn't stir from where he was."

"If they were precious stones, now, Connie", said the judge, lured on stage, "things like rubies and sapphires and emeralds, would he carry them, do you think?"

"He would not then. He must have made up his mind as a foal that he wouldn't carry any sort of stones for anyone. I don't think it's the dead weight of them either. I think it has to do with the stones themselves being dead. And do you know another thing that I think?"

"No, but I'd love to hear it", said Judge Crowley with his hands in front of him and his fingers lightly tapping against each other in anticipation.

"I'd say that if Jack o'Lantern was there at the birth of our Saviour and if Joseph put a few stones from Bethlehem into their baggage to carry away with them as souvenirs on their flight into Egypt he wouldn't stir a foot".

"No?" the judge asked, ready to burst.

"No", answered Connie, "not even if Herod's soldiers were coming up the street".

The judge clapped his hand to his mouth, but in spite of that a sound came out like a multiple hee-haw, and the audience collapsed in laughter. The chuckling, chortling and giggling continued for half a minute. Even the Holy Family would have been amused.

Judge Crowley may have found it difficult to resume his official role, but from his days as a stage manager he knew exactly when to bring the curtain down.

"Case dismissed", he said.

* * *

It was Sarah's greatest triumph. The "Western Orb" carried a word for word account of the proceedings and it outsold the comics that week, but it was flawed in one respect: where it noted that "Miss Sarah Field conducted her own defence" it should have inserted "Instructed by Fr. Brendan Laide C.C.". It was I who provided her with the jesuitical escape route via the mental reservation. In that sense it was my greatest triumph too.

But our combined joy was short lived. Within five months, from that December to the following May, the fuchsias at the Cottage had turned into tears of blood. Something that I cannot define got into Sarah. It began with impishness and developed into recklessness. Eccentricity teetered on the edge of instability. Some people said that the triumph over Miller went to her head; a more likely explanation is that too much alcohol went into her blood stream. She spent far too much time and far too much money in Florrie's and without realising it she became the unpaid entertainer at the hoolies. The plastic bags contained a lot more in the way of liquids than of solids on their way from the village to the Cottage and as a result her clothes, never fashionable, took on the appearance of famine.

Most people in the parish regarded poetry as something to be shouted under duress in a schoolroom not something to be shouted with delight along a country road, and they were shocked out of their unpoetic minds when they heard Wordsworth or Betjeman coming around the next corner before they saw Sarah.

She bought a second donkey, which was a huge mistake. His was a free spirit, much like her own, and she spent hours, even days, searching for him. She didn't name him for the first few weeks until she had time to study his character, but she told me that she would continue the theme of light which Connie Con initiated with Jack o'Lantern. Eventually she hit on the name Comet for him because of his exploratory head, his streaky tail, his long disappearances from view and his desire to be moving, moving, moving. The wit was unmistakeable but the wisdom was lacking. Jack o'Lantern tired of being unemployed and probably of being unfed as well, and he followed Comet's lead into the unknown worlds of Tinniscert and Knocknaferry in the hills above Croghan harbour. Then people got tired of looking for the donkeys on her behalf and they got tired of bringing them back to her. In the long run they simply took off like tangents from the vicious circle of the comings and goings of Comet and Jack o'Lantern.

She had a great desire to go crab fishing with Pad Murray, but in reply to her endless requests he gave her endless excuses: he went to sea too early; he returned too late; he never made plans until the dawn; his boat was too filthy for a lady, and he had nowhere for a lady to go when she had to go. Sarah was too intelligent not to read his excuses as refusals and she short circuited his resistance by stowing away in the forward cubby of his boat long before dawn one fine morning. Pad was pulling his first string of pots on the Falls o'Garry reef three miles out from shore when she made her exit from the cubby giving him the biggest fright of his life since a basking shark erupted under his bow twenty years before and damn nearly capsized him. The report that Connie Con had called her a shark wasn't lost on him. Pad was a bachelor, and Sarah gave him buttered scones with sliced banana for lunch which he had never had before, but soon after that he told her that the fishing was awful slack and he made for shore earlier than he had ever done before.

She was observed several times in late April and early May swimming with all her clothes on in Cuasgorm just underneath her cottage, and that caused more comment than if she had been swimming with no clothes on at all. The most articulate of the observers was Hugh Kelleher, shopkeeper, Saab owner and Shakespeare reader, and he told me, rightly or wrongly, that she was singing on the day when he spotted her and he wasn't at all sure whether he was looking at reality or at a sensational production of "Hamlet" at the point where Ophelia

> fell in the weeping brook; her clothes spread wide
> and mermaid-like awhile they bore her up
> which time she chanted snatches of old lauds
> or like a creature native and indued
> unto that element!

One Sunday she snored loudly during Mass and most of the congregation stared accusingly at me not at her. It was after that "sacrilege", as one old pious petticoat called it, that a number of people came to my house and said I should do something about her. What could I do? I advised her to give up the drink, I advised her to give up the donkeys, I even advised her to give up being herself, but she equated advice with interference and, rich in cricketing terms, she hit me for six every time.

Then there was the affair of the windcharger. One of the new rich down from Dublin, name of Cusack, rich especially in novelties, erected a windcharger on the skull of the bare cliff below his bungalow, just east of the village. He had no planning permission that anybody knew of, but many people objected to what they saw as a piece of cheap Woolworths jewellery on a noble face. However, none of them submitted a formal complaint: laying information against another was not part of their tradition. The loudest of the objections were made in Florrie's and Sarah's voice soared overall. "Maybe you will get out the hatchet again", they said to her, "the one you sharpened for Connie Con".

One morning after a stormy night, the windcharger was flat on its broken back. But examination of the wreckage showed that the guy cables on the windward side had been cut: therefore the storm had had an accessory before the fact. Had Sarah cut through them? I never believed it: she hadn't the strength of solid food in her to do it, and, besides, a hatchet would only have bounced off thick cable such as the Dubliner's. However, give a dog a bad name ... and Sarah's was so bad just before the episode of the goat that even if a plane fell out of the skies over Kilbroney she would have been accused of planting a bomb on it.

May day came and with it the goat, and the goat was her final undoing. The man who persuaded her to get the second donkey told her that donkeys need the company of their own kind so she provided Jack o'Lantern with the company of Comet but far from making him more content with the pasture of Fuchsia Cottage it gave him a severe dose of wanderlust. So then her advisor told her that the company of a goat would sedate them both, and she bought the goat.

It solved nothing. In fact, after two weeks of utter loneliness the goat sickened and died. Sarah told me that the goat was sick but sadly she didn't tell me that it had died. Perhaps, if she had done so, I could have solved the situation, but she didn't and a gale of complaints about her erratic behaviour blew up, all but one of the complaints howling in the direction of Doctor Morgan, and the one that came to me was three days too late.

What happened during those three days was that, on the first, she tried to bury the goat but, try as she might, she hadn't the strength to push the spade into the soil let alone dig a grave. She then tried doing it on her hands and knees with a kitchen shovel, but only the clang of frustration came back to her from the stones that the shovel hit. She gave it up; she would try cremation instead. It was on the second day that the passersby concluded she was out of her mind. They could see her ringing the dead goat with bits of kindling and turf, building up a sort of scaffolding of wood around it and then attempting to ignite the lot with fire lighters. She spent the most of two days at that, but all she succeeded in doing was to roast a few small areas of the flesh and to create upward swirls and outward squiggles of stinking smoke.

It was on the evening of the third day that I heard of her plight and I drove to Fuchsia Cottage. "Brendan, I am so glad that you have come", she said. She looked the scruffiest I had ever seen her — no wonder — and near to tears; if I had shed even one she would have cried her sick heart out. But I steeled myself, and she came up with a joke, the last I ever heard from her. "I have bitten off more than I can chew here", she said.

"Ah, why didn't you tell me, Sarah," I said, "I would have chucked it over Faill an Phréacháin for you".

"That is why", she answered. "The sea is living. Nothing dead should go into the sea".

I was struck by her answer then. I still am. I see genius in it, not the madness to which genius is near allied.

I looked at the shambles. For the first time in my life the literal meaning of the word assailed me, and I said "We will have to start all over again".

"We?"

"Yes, you and I, Sarah".

I am not the most practical of men but I was the only man I had and I devised a rough-and-ready plan to cremate the goat.

"We shall have to build a bit of a pyre" I said, "fetch some petrol and pray for a breeze of wind." Almost immediately the evening breeze that Pad Murray, her reluctant fisherman, always called a "fresh" streamed in from the south east. "That is a good start" I said, "God is with us".

"I don't often hear you speaking about God", she said reflectively "except in your sermons."

"Well, I am speaking about Him now", I said. "We need His help, and if anyone can kindle a holocaust, He can".

I went home for some dozed floorboards that I had in the garage and some limbs of an ash that had fallen down during the winter. I jammed them into the boot of the car the best way I could. There was a lot more of them protruding from the boot than was clamped inside, and if Miller had arrived on the scene he would have had me up for dangerous driving, but desperate cases require desperate remedies and I set off on the return journey to Fuchsia Cottage, stopping on the way for a gallon of petrol at Florrie's.

He looked at my load of timber, questioningly. "Tis too early yet for Bonfire Night, Father," he remarked.

"Not where I'm going", I said. "Give me a gallon of petrol in the can and listen for an explosion later."

"It's the goat, isn't it?"

"I know whom I'd like to be burning", I said for transmission to his customers later on, "the man who told her to get the goat".

When I arrived at Sarah's, I built up a criss cross structure with the ash limbs, making sure a good draught from Pad Murray's fresh was running through them. Then I placed the beautifully rotten planks on top of them in a sort of platform and I lifted the charred goat with a garden fork on top of that. 'Twas the hardest work I did in years, harder than keeping "Lú na Lon" pointing to windward in a force 5. Then I got the petrol, and poured it all over the ash, the planks and the goat itself. Just in time I remembered something vital and I halted the slashing about of the fuel.

"Have you any old sock inside, Sarah" I asked, "one that you won't need again?"

"Yes, sure", she said and went to fetch it.

"That is the very colour I was hoping for", I said, when she brought it, "the colour of flame". I picked up a stone and dropped it into the sock. Then I doused the foot of the sock in petrol.

"Matches", I said. She gave them to me.

"Now stand well back, Sarah".

I lit a match, put it to the foot of the sock and threw it flaming underarm into the heart of the pyre. There was a whoosh, then a bang that could be heard in three townlands, and the pyre bloomed with huge petals of flame. The heat was so intense that we had to retreat further and further from it. The goat sizzled like a steam engine. Then gradually the planks collapsed on the limbs of ash sending sparks higher than the roof of the Protestant church, and at the end there wasn't as much of the goat to be seen as if it was a dead mouse we had put to the flames. For the second time in a short while I learned the literal meaning of a word: this time the word was 'holocaust', from the Greek, 'holos' — whole and 'kaustos' — burnt.

"Would you do one thing more for me, Brendan?"

"Not burn the Protestant church down, I hope!" I said, trying to break the tension that I could see she was experiencing.

"No; just get rid of that baulk of wrack for me", she said, pointing to what looked like the butt of a telephone pole near her original pyre. "For two days I have been trying to set fire to it, but it wouldn't burn".

"It is sodden", I said, examining it. "Too soon out of the water to burn. I'll chuck it back in".

"No, you won't", she said. "Remember what I told you. Nothing dead must go into the sea".

"I know what", I said. I was looking in the direction of the Protestant graveyard next door. "Dead to the dead."

I picked up the piece of wrack. It was heavy. It was soggy. It was reeking. It was covered in sooty fur. I stumbled with it through her garden to the churchyard wall and tossed it over.

"They say I'm crazy", Sarah said. "But you are worse".

She could be right.

* * *

Three or four days later there was a knocking, a repeated strident knocking at my door which indicated panic. The thought that occurred to me was that somebody was enclosed in a coffin and he or she was frantically trying to get out. I ran to open the coffin, I mean the door. Sarah was standing there. Her hands were trembling and her eyes were bulging with fright.

"What's wrong, Sarah? Come in".

It took a long while for her to tell me her story. Panic has a way of fazing focus and of destroying syntax, but the gist of it was that Dr. Morgan had visited her, he had told her that he was very concerned about her present state of mental health and he was in the process of making arrangements for her to have treatment.

"And what did you say, Sarah?"

"Not very much. The man frightens me. He is a bully. I am afraid of bullies."

"Well, I am not afraid of bullies", I said, "not even bullies with stethoscopes. I'll go over and talk to him. Will you wait for me here?"

"No, I shall go home and lie down. I feel weary, my mind especially, very weary."

I realise now that I went to see the doctor in a totally wrong frame of mind. There are no diplomats in my genes. I was steaming with anger. I turned my head into a boxing glove, and you don't win an argument with a boxing glove.

The doctor's bell said 'Press' and I did just that; I nearly drove my thumb through it. He came to the door himself and asked the same question that I had asked Sarah, "What's wrong?"

"There isn't anything wrong with me, Doctor, except my temper. I want to talk to you about Sarah Field".

"O, yes." he said with a placid, professional smile. How do these people do it? Have they some sort of electronic body vest that keeps them cool?

He strode towards his surgery in front of me. He was a big man in his early thirties. Looking at his shoulders, I got the feeling that I was following him through a tunnel in a rugby stadium before a match, and in fact he had played rugby for his university as a back row forward where his job was to push and push and push. He was the latest in a series of young G.P.s who came and went every two years or so. Kilbroney meant no more to them than a springboard to a bigger pool. It had the advantage, admittedly, that they brought the most up-to-date medical knowledge with them in their bags, but that is where their knowledge ended: they knew nothing of people.

"Sit down, Father", he began, but he stayed standing himself in front of his rolltop desk.

"No, thank you, I'll stand". I had no intention of being dominated by his muscular presence.

"As you please. You were saying . . ."

"I was saying that I am in a temper. I am fit to be tied, in fact, in which case I could be directed like Sarah to the asylum".

"Oh, now, Father, hang on there. St. Clare's is not an asylum; it is a psychiatric hospital. She needs treatment".

"On what grounds?"

"On the grounds of acting very strangely".

"Have you seen her acting strangely, as you call it?"

"Well, no, but lots and lots of people whose evidence I trust have approached me."

"Evidence of what, may I ask?"

"Well, the most recent aberration was the burning of the goat."

"Burning of the goat! 'Twas I burnt the goat. She failed. I succeeded. We had different methods, that's all. Did they complain me too?"

"Nobody complained about you, Father."

"Well, I am complaining about them. They are the people with the real problem. She needed help but they didn't give it. She had a problem with a dead goat. They have a problem with a dead religion".

"I am prepared to listen to you about religion at Mass, but not here. Here we discuss medicine."

"Medicine. Do you mean rows of bottles?"

"I do not mean rows of bottles and you know it. I mean the treatment of a person who is sick."

"She isn't sick. She simply doesn't fit into your conventional box, so she is a witch."

"Who said anything about her being a witch?"

"Your informants, probably".

"Nonsense, but I'll tell you confidentially what she is. A manic depressive".

"What qualifications do you have to enable you to come to that conclusion?"

"It has nothing to do with qualifications. It has to do with facts".

"Facts, indeed! What facts?"

"She has highs. She has lows. Highs, like swimming at her ease in her clothes when another woman would be drowning; at the same time singing at the top of her voice when another woman would be shouting. And lows, like these last few days when she couldn't even dig a shallow hole."

"That's where I directly challenge you. That isn't manic depressive behaviour. That is eccentric behaviour. The English are the classic eccentrics in the social history of the world. She is one of them. I know her better than anybody."

"Just so. You have stated your problem. You are emotionally involved. You can't stand back from her far enough to see what her trouble is."

"And you can, I suppose. The iceberg can see the 'Titanic' coming."

"I don't know what you mean by that. Let us get back to facts. The woman is sick. As a doctor I know she is sick. And as the medical officer of health in this parish I have made the decision about how she can get better."

"By shifting her to St. Clare's where she will be reduced to a chemical zombie, like the rest."

"That is an outrageous statement."

"This is an outrageous situation. I have been there many times and I have seen it."

There was a pause. I was getting nowhere except higher on the blood pressure gauge.

We looked at each other through combative eyes.

He put the shove on again. "It is my responsibility", he said. "Mine. No one else's. I am sending her to St. Clare's because I believe it is the right course of action to take."

I was being outshoved in the pack. "When?" I asked weakly.

"Probably on Friday."

"And how?"

"I was hoping that you . . ."

"You can do your own dirty work, Doctor. I won't do it for you."

"That is a highly insulting statement."

"Sorry. What I mean to say is that I will not be party to what I see as a completely unbalanced view of Sarah. You can see only one side of her. There is the other side."

"Unfortunately the other side is not the side that is causing the problem."

"Problem. Problem. Everything is a problem. The problem with you people is that you see people as problems."

I deserved a knee in the groin, and I got one. "You are ranting again," he said. "I understand your loyalty, but I resent your language."

"Sorry about the language, Doctor, but out of loyalty I won't drive her." I calmed a bit and then I asked, "If I won't, who will?"

"The State," he answered.

"Meaning what?"

"A Garda car from Hilltown."

As soon as I heard that, the scrummage got rottweiler rough again.

"Does that mean she is being committed?"

"Yes and no".

"With people's freedom it can't be yes and no. Are you or aren't you committing her?"

"I am".

"Well, at least we know now where we stand."

"How do you mean?"

"I mean I am standing here and you are standing there and . . ."

"And?"

"I don't think I need to complete the sentence."

For the first time since the argument began he looked perturbed, because the most important relationship that a doctor has in a rural parish is with the curate. I turned my back on him, but a face stopped me before I got to the door: it was the face of Miller. I turned around again. "Do me this final favour, Doctor." I said. "No, on second thoughts do yourself a favour. Get in touch with Sergeant Miller. Tell him not to be the one that will come for her, because if he does I won't be responsible for what will happen. You will."

What I was thinking on my way home was that I had run in a few good tries, but the powerful forwards on the other team had pulverised me in the end.

That was on a Wednesday. I spent the rest of that day and the most of Thursday in and out to her. I put the house in the best sort of order I could. I got her to eat a little. I promised to get Jack o'Lantern back to Connie Con in Dunsheen where he got his name from his practice of projecting his light with a different intensity from the haggart, the well and the bog. I promised further that I would put the Comet back into his original orbit. On one of my visits I took her Siamese cat away to my own house and I told her that I would try and compensate for my failure to receive herself into the Church by making a good Catholic of the King of Siam, as she called him.

Dr Morgan called on the Thursday, but I avoided further conflict by hiding out in the no man's land of the scullery. What he did to her during that visit was little short of criminal: he gave her an injection which deadened her eyes, slurred her speech and turned her militant self into pale acquiescence. After that there was nothing to do except wait for the Garda car to arrive on the Friday.

I guessed that Miller's priority for that day would be to shift Sarah from the cliffs and choughs of Kilbroney as early as he could, and I guessed correctly. Immediately after saying Mass I drove to Fuchsia Cottage and I was there less than half an hour when the Garda car drew up outside. I looked out. The doctor had heeded my warning. It was tall Garda Moriarty who ducked his head to get under the fuchsia arch and used his knuckles to noise the door. I opened up.

"Is Miss Field here, Father?"

"She is, Garda."

"Is she ready, Father?"

"She is, Garda."

"Will she come out so, Father?"

"She will, Garda."

"Will I bring her bags, Father?"

"No, I'll do that, Garda. Thank you all the same."

Sarah walked down the path rather unsteadily and got into the rear of the car without ever looking back at the red tears of the fuchsias. I put her luggage into the boot.

Garda Moriarty was a decent man, fair dues to him. He had laughed heartily with the rest of us on the day of the donkey trial. Now he walked fifty paces up the road pretending to be looking at the Protestant church.

I opened the rear door of the car, leaned in and gave Sarah a kiss. How I regret now that it was the first and only time that I had done so. Then I said "Sarah, we will beat them yet, the bastards", but I didn't really believe what I said and I knew by the look in her eyes that she didn't believe it either.

Chapter 6

FIRST UNHOLY COMMUNION

I don't know much about rugby types, not having been educated in one of those snobbish boot camps which the snobbish religious orders run for the benefit of the snobbish upper middle classes. However I had observed on television how the rugby players of the Five Nations stamped on each other's ribs and rammed elbows into each other's faces in what they blithely called a maul and then, when the referee blew an end to the legitimised mayhem, they threw their arms around each other's shoulders to show that it was all just a bit of patriotic fun. So I figured that as time ticked away, to use a phrase beloved of sports commentators, Adrian Morgan, back row forward and general practitioner, would forgive me for the insults I had uttered in the heat of the contest and throw me a manly word.

However, as there are two halves to a rugby match, so there are two halves to a marriage, and Adrian's other half, Alice, was his most fervent supporter, and supporters are notoriously more unforgiving than players. Still I hoped that as time would pass, on the big clock of weeks rather than on the small watch of days, even she might soften her face, but I had the misfortune, straight away after the Sarah encounter, to walk on her superior toe. It was unintentional on my part, but that counted for nothing; like a child she bawled exaggeratedly at the hurt.

I admit it was an error of judgment, although it seemed to me as a priest that it was the right thing to do at the time. Who could imagine that one could get into an unholy row about holy communion? I had plenty of experience in administering the sacraments, and I knew from my training in theology on the one hand and my knowledge of human nature on the other that sacraments are for the unredeemed. The mistake I made was to give too much thought to the sacrament and not enough to the unredeemed.

I can think of a perfect image for the situation now, but as always with a bright image it comes too late when I am seeing stars. The image is this: one is driving a wide car into a narrow garage. One must not drive the car too much to the left or one will hit the wall on that side, or too much to the right or one will tear the right hand side of the car. One must steer the car exactly half way between the two. I didn't. I aimed for the sacramental side of things and I finished up with a wreck.

Even the unholiest of us priests will testify that the day of the First Holy Communion in the parish is the most blessed day of his year. It is the feast of innocence. The eyes that look up at one do not really belong in those sockets. It is the real Christmas Day: when the first communicant holds out her hands or his hands the shape they take is the shape of a manger and the Child of Bethlehem lies there wrapped in the swaddling clothes of faith. There is no other moment like it in life: the children know it, the teachers know it, the priest knows it. I just wonder if the parents know it.

The trouble about Kilbroney is that there were two First Communions. When I was going to school Jim Kelly impressed upon my young mind that you couldn't have two firsts: the first two runners could cross the line in a race, but not two firsts. But in this as in so many other things the parish of Kilbroney was different: it had two Firsts.

It derived from the fact that there were two national schools in the parish, Kilbroney in the west and Moulabranna in the east, and never that twain did meet except in rivalry. The practice had grown up that each of the two schools had its own First Communion Day on consecutive Saturdays in June, and if it rained on one lot of children it was taken to mean that God favoured the other. I heartily disapproved of the practice because it seemed to me to be a contradiction of the very word 'communion', a coming together in union. I simply could not understand how the two sides of the parish could be allowed to take the body of Christ every June and divide it in two not for the purpose of sharing but as a symbol of disunity.

Moreover, it had become, improperly in my view of things, a school function rather than a parochial function. Granted, the children would not have been prepared at all if it were not for the dedication of the teachers, but that is where the schoolgate should have been shut on it. After that, the children should have been seen as all coming together in their parish church as fully practising members of the Catholic faith for the first time, and not as pupils of one school or the other.

Then came the year of Sarah and the doctor and myself and it seemed that Providence was showing all of us which way we should go; well, either Providence or a very unusual pattern of births seven years previously. The situation was that there were nine children for the First Holy Communion in Moulabranna N.S. but only one in Kilbroney N.S. Even from a mathematical point of view the obvious solution was to bring all ten children together in one ceremony and that is what I proposed to do.

I went first to Peter Kinsella the principal at Moulabranna to ask him if he would have any objection to taking a lone lamb from the west into his flock for the one day, and he looked surprised that I even asked him the question: men do not have mental blocks about such things. He said the child would be more than welcome.

Then I approached Rose Feehan the principal at Kilbroney to see if I could twist what I thought might be a stiffer arm, but it proved to be much more pliant than I anticipated. She was a weekday as well as a Sunday Catholic and she had been to a seminar on worship at Glenstal Abbey, so first of all I put the liturgical argument to her that union, unity, communion and community were four peas in the same sacred pod and that nothing would please the Infant Lord more than to arrive east and west on the same day. Then because she loved balance and good order in the procession of the children with their gifts at the offertory of the Mass and again in their approach to receive Holy Communion, I pointed out to her that an even number of ten would be much more manageable than an odd number of nine or one. It was when I said 'one' in the context of the procession that the weight of my argument fell heavily on her shepherding mind: how would her lone lamb find its companionless way with bouquets to statues, with gifts to the altar and with herself to the Lord? Rose offered no counter arguments when she heard that one, and she readily agreed that from every point of view, organisational, liturgical and parochial, bringing all ten of the children together for one ceremony was the right thing to do.

But there was one snag and it was strong enough to wrench the oar out of my hands. The snag was that the solitary child in Kilbroney national school was little Gretta, the daughter of Dr. and Mrs Alice Morgan; to be more precise, the little lamb, as we called her, had no timid ewe as her dam.

Rose Feehan sent a note to the mother in the child's lunch box to the effect that Fr. Laide had decided to have only one First Holy Communion Mass, due to the fact that Gretta was the only one for communion in Kilbroney and that the combined ceremony would take place on Saturday the 11th of June.

Alice's response was immediate and forceful. That very evening she stormed through Gobnait's papershop – Gobnait reckoned from the quick glance she had of her face that the intensity was at least force 8 on the human Beaufort scale – and up the stairs to Rose's flat. She berated her for kowtowing to my wishes and demanded that she reopen the case and re-establish the principle of one school, one Communion, even if there was only one for Communion.

There were several slates off the roof of Rose's head when she left.

When she came downstairs again, Gobnait was conveniently placed across her tracks to get the final lick of the storm.

"What sort of a teacher is that you have under your roof?" she wanted to know.

"She surely didn't slap little Gretta", Gobnait said, hoping that the suggestion would throw petrol on the fire.

"No, not that, although when I come to think about it, that is what she did do . . . give us all a slap in the face".

"What do you mean, Alice?"

"I mean Fr Laide told her he didn't want Kilbroney to have First Communion on its own this year, and she agreed. He wants to throw Gretta in with the kids from Moulabranna."

"O, well, everyone knows that Moulabranna are his favourites." This from Gobnait. An outrageous lie, but a useful extra little noggin of petrol for the flames.

"It is an insult to Kilbroney. Imagine: setting aside a long standing custom, just like that. After all the years and all the pupils, no First Communion. But he won't get away with it; I'll see to that."

"And you would be right. He is so long in charge now, with Fr. Mac sick, that he thinks he is actually the parish priest."

"Parish Priest! Pope you mean. Telling everybody their business. What a cheek! He even tried to tell Adrian what to do."

"He did!?"

"Yes, he tried to stop Adrian sending Sarah Field away."

"Good Lord, you wouldn't need to be a fine doctor like your husband to know that she was completely off her rocker."

"He failed with Adrian and he will fail with me. The lady upstairs had better get him to change his mind or we will change it for him." And away she went, the wind still gusting, and Gobnait rubbed her hands together as though she had sold every magazine on the rack in one almighty clearance.

The lady upstairs, as Alice called her, wasn't long about coming downstairs. Where Gobnait was concerned, Rose consistently kept to her upper level both structurally and personally until something happened to bring her down to the lower level of Gobnait's kitchen and Gobnait's company. When she found herself in bits, Gobnait got the job of helping her to pick up the pieces, even if Gobnait's methods had the finesse of a mechanical shovel.

When Rose appeared Gobnait wasted no time posturing. She got into the cab of the mechanical shovel right away. "You don't have to tell me what happened," she said. "I know. Alice told me. Soon everyone will know: she has her loud mouth on her." Kettle and pot, but Rose had to consider her tenure of the flat and didn't call attention to the proverb.

"What do you think I should do?" Rose asked.

"Well, there are two things to consider: the school and yourself. When the parents hear that you have put the curate before the school they will have you for supper, and some of them have sharper teeth than Alice. And when it comes to deciding between the curate and the doctor, I would go for the doctor, if I were you. I can't see Brendan Laide curing your migraine for you".

"No, but I'm sure he means well. He said our parish is one parish, not two; and the whole point of Communion is to show we are one, not two or ten or a hundred".

"Ah, yes, his usual style: blinding the people with flashy talk. But in the long run it all comes down to power, interference, sticking his big nose in, knocking people off ladders, telling girls whom they shouldn't marry, taking on the sergeant. That's right: power, the power he has assumed since Fr. Mac got sick. He is now trying it on the school and on yourself."

"Do you think so?" Rose asked weakly.

"I don't think so. I know so", Gobnait answered. It was one of her favourite phrases. "You would be a damn fool to give in to him, and I'll tell you why. Fr. Mac is very bad. I'm sure you know that."

"Yes, I do. I was to see him last week."

"He could be dead in days, and when he goes, Laide's power will go with him. The new P.P. will put him in his box and shut the lid on him. Tell him you have changed your mind. You have nothing to lose except Laide, and God send you no greater loss."

But Rose held her fire for two days and by that stage I had become happy with the ground I had gained and I had no notion of conceding it again. I tried to calm her the best way I could. "You have nothing to worry about, Rose", I said when she called. "Storms pass and this one will pass as well. We have done the right thing, you and I. It is the sacrament that matters, not the swank. That's what Mrs Doctor is interested in, the swank of having a First Communion all to herself. Like the royals in England. Prestige and all that. And as for a long-standing custom, what does she know about that? She hasn't been here for two years yet, and the child wasn't even born in the parish. Don't get involved with her. Let it to me. Tell her you tried, which you did, and if she isn't satisfied with that she can phone me and come and talk to me directly."

Which is what the unsedated Alice did, very directly indeed. She did most of the talking, which is what she came to do, and I let her talk away. There was nothing very new in what she had to say: I had heard most of it already at second hand from Rose. But I now had to bare my chest rather than my back to her charges about breaching long standing custom, insulting Kilbroney and defying tradition.

The first palpable shock I got was when she said to me "You are acting ultra vires" and the jolt came not so much from the charge as from the phrase. Most of her education had derived from being abroad on cheap package holidays, so I concluded that the doctor had primed her with that particular bit of ammunition.

"Meaning what?" I asked, my gorge rising at last.

"Well, you know Latin, so you should know."

"O, I know Latin, madam. The question is: Do you?"

It was very ungracious of me, but I had learned from experience that graciousness is interpreted as weakness by the unlettered. She was good enough for me, however; the doctor had obviously schooled her in the meaning. "You are acting beyond the powers you have as a curate," she said.

"O, is that it? Much as your husband acted as a G.P. when he blundered into the science of psychotherapy".

She was stung, but she wasn't sure where. "Leave my husband out of it", was all she could say.

"Your husband is in it, my dear woman. Where else did you get ultra vires?"

It was now in danger of becoming a cat fight, not an argument, so I quickly said "We aren't getting anywhere. I have to tell you that I am not going to change my mind."

"In that case there is something I have to tell you, Father", and she said 'Father' in the same sarcastic tone that I had used with 'madam' and 'my dear woman'. "Gretta will not be making her First Communion with Moulabranna. That is definite. I shall keep her back until next year."

"Your decision entirely. It is your right as a parent to present her or not, this year or next, as you please. I just thought you might put the child's privilege above your own pique".

Surprisingly I got in the last word, but of course it was she who got in the last shot.

* * *

Two days later Fr. Mac died and all thoughts of First Communion were buried under a mound of work and worry as I made preparations for his funeral. I filled a page of an A4 pad with things to be thought of and things to be done: a coffin to be selected, a grave to be lined with concrete blocks, a church to be shampooed, a choir to be mustered, altarboys to be put through the rubrical manoeuvres, seats to be reserved, ushers to be chosen for their gentility, car park marshals to be chosen for their obduracy, bidding prayers to be composed, a homily to be shaped, a sanctuary chair large enough to accommodate the episcopal bottom to be borrowed, a dinner for the twelve apostles to be planned around the bishop's known culinary preferences, several good women to be dragooned into cooking it, the parish hall to be converted into a vast refectory for the hundreds of disciples who would have to be satisfied with tea and buns, and St. Francis de Sales's prayer for patience to be said every hour on the hour. There was no room for Alice or Gobnait or Rose or Gretta to get in among that lot.

Anyway, although I was moving up and down among the living like a conductor on a crowded train, my mind wasn't riding with them; my mind was in the puzzling darkness with Father Mac. He was my beau ideal among Parish Priests. He didn't bawl at anybody, he equally enjoyed the cup of tea in the cottage and the glass of port in the rear-admiral's, his church never became a counting house either of heads or of pounds, he loved a joke, he wasn't worried about the shiny elbows of his jacket, he cried whenever he saw a baby's coffin, and he was the world's worst book-keeper. The only thing he wouldn't tolerate was talking at a graveside. If he said any prayers at all he said them where only God would notice, and he didn't run the parish as a secret society from which he excluded the curate. I mourned him as I would mourn my own father and for the three days of his lying in repose, the removal of his remains and his requiem and burial there was no way that Alice or Gobnait or Rose or Gretta could come between me and my memories of him.

Towards the end of the funeral Mass Bishop Irwin addressed the congregation on what be termed a few practical matters. He began by thanking all those who had helped with the liturgy, using a prompt card which he had asked me to prepare for him, and then, to my great astonishment, because bishops are not noted for thanking their priests, either in private or in public, he thanked myself. "I wish to thank Fr. Laide", he said "for doing two priests' work without demur over the long period of seventeen months while Fr. McCarthy was ill, and in particular for his capable work as administrator of the parish during that time." It was the first I had heard of my promotion to administrator: my postfactum appointment amused me, as it did one of the two priests flanking me — a 'cute bastard' he called him. What I would love to have seen was the look in the eyes of Gobnait O'Brien and Alice Morgan when they heard the news that they hadn't been dealing with a mere curate all those fractious months.

What the bishop said next was quite unusual, and, in so far as I was concerned, momentous. "My dear people of Kilbroney parish", he said, "due to the sad circumstances of Fr. McCarthy's prolonged illness you have been without a parish priest for an unprecedented length of time. For that reason I do not propose to delay the appointment of a new parish priest until the autumn, as I usually would. He will be with you in a matter of a week or two, and I am certain that you will find him a conscientious and pious priest."

"That reduces the field," the wag on my left commented.

Later, when the bishop had finished his sumptuous dinner — all I managed to get myself as butler and communicator between dining room and kitchen was a gull's mouthful now and then as I made frantic pecks at my plate — he called me aside and astonished me for the second time that day.

"Fr. Laide", he said, "two things. One, I want you and Fr. Burke who is, I understand, the executor to contact Fr. McCarthy's people right away, and between you to remove all his furniture and effects to the auction rooms in Hilltown as quickly as possible, so that the house will be ready for occupancy from next weekend. You heard me saying that I intend to send you a new parish priest without delay?"

"O, yes, my Lord" I said, "if I had been as dead as Fr. Mac, that would have jolted me back to life."

He was thrown, I think, by the familiarity of my diction and he almost forgot no. 2 as a result.

"I shall see about the furniture right away, my Lord." I said, and then I gave him the prompt. "And the second thing you were going to tell me?"

"O, yes. I normally do not do this, but because of the rushed nature of the appointment I want to tell you that Fr. Michael O'Donnell will be coming here as the new parish priest. I informed him to that effect yesterday. I need hardly remind you that you will treat this information with the utmost secrecy and not divulge it to anyone until the announcement appears on the paper."

I thanked him for his courtesy in telling me the news, but not, deep in my heart, for the news itself. I wouldn't be ringing the bells of St. Brona's with a joyful clangour to convey a happy mood to the village; on the contrary, a resumption of the funeral feeling with one ponderous thump every minute would be more appropriate.

The only thing I knew about O'Donnell was that he had a reputation for holiness, and that didn't put my hand reaching for the rope of the tenor bell. The received wisdom of the clergy was that holy priests were good only for themselves and God, but they were impossible to live with. Fr. Mac, who was my mentor in the ways of men and holymarys, told me one time, "If you ever meet a priest who walks up and down the church with a great rosary beads dangling from him like a holy pendulum, take flight, because he will cut your throat when he gets to the 'Hail Holy Queen'. Beware of holy priests: they tell lies, they are unscrupulous, they are self centred and they are crafty."

Well, I would have to wait and see if Fr. Mac's words were true, but I didn't have long to wait to see the new incumbent. About an hour after the bishop's entourage had left, there was what I would call a cagey knock at my door. I opened up, and who was standing there but Fr. O'Donnell. I had never seen him close up before, because we moved along different clerical orbits, but what struck me straightaway was that he wasn't standing frontally, facing the door, facing the house, facing myself; he was standing sideways on, his face in profile, his eyes on the eternal hills. I thought it was damn odd.

I very nearly said "Congratulations, Father", but that would have been a big mistake. Had I done so, I would have missed my first lesson in getting to know my new parish priest. I knew that he knew he was Michael O Donnell P.P. Kilbroney; the question was did he know that I knew? I checked myself just in time and instead asked him inside, "although to tell you the truth", I added, "it is more chaos than house at the moment."

"No, thanks" he said, addressing my escallonia. "You have had a very busy day. What I really want are the keys to the parochial house, if you will be good enough to trust me with them".

Again I nearly made the mistake of leaping before I looked, and saying "No one has a better right to the keys than yourself" but again something on that detached face checked me.

"The word is out," he said — lovely personal phrase that was, "the word is out" — "that Fr. McCarthy's furniture, books and so on are to be conveyed to Hilltown in the next day or two, and what I want to do before that happens is to recover a book of mine that I believe he had. It is volume 2 of Philip Hughes's 'History of the Church'. I lent it to Fr. Markey one time, and, you know how it is with books, he lent it to Fr. McCarthy."

Of course I knew how it was with books, having, in spite of Polonius's good advice, both a borrower and a lender been, but I also knew how it was with devious clerics who won't look you straight in the eye. I asked him in again but again he declined, so I simply said "Right. I'll get you the keys. It might take you a while to track that book down. The spare bedroom is full of books. Take as long as you need."

When he was out of earshot I addressed him again but I had rather a different message for him as he receded into his world of deceit. "You can take from now till midnight, but you won't find that book, because it isn't there. I have been up and down every bookspine and there's no Philip Hughes there, I can tell you that. Anyway I doubt that you lent it to Fr. Markey. As a matter of fact, I doubt that you ever owned the book at all, because Philip Hughes volume 2 is the one that has the story of Marozia, the woman who bedded a Pope, who mothered a Pope and who smothered a Pope: not your sort of spiritual reading! I don't believe you are going to waste even one minute looking for the book. You are going to do what your housekeeper told you to do: you are going to measure the windows for curtains, pace out the rooms to see if your carpets will fit, and count the shelves and cupboards in the kitchen. And while you are at it, you are going to figure out which direction is south and pick the southfacing bedroom for yourself. Philip Hughes, my arse! Who do you think you are fooling, Michael O Donnell?"

The search for the book took a long long time; I knew it would. He didn't find it; I knew he couldn't. Fr O Donnell came back to my door empty handed, but I reckoned that his pockets were stuffed with notes about length, breadth, height and thickness. He didn't look at all disappointed which confirmed my surmise about the "missing" book. For the third time I invited him to come in, but for the third time he declined. His excuse was that he had an interview with a lady scheduled for teatime, but my hunch was that the lady in question was his housekeeper and that the interview would be about the dimensions of the living room, the awkwardness of the bay window, the alterations that would be necessary in their curtains and the number of power points in the kitchen.

Once again I was involved in the phenomenon of talking to somebody at right angles, because instead of standing foursquare and facing myself he stood sideways on and faced the pink blossoms of the escallonia. I do not doubt that the blossoms were more handsome than I was, but I very much doubt that he was making a statement on aesthetics. The strangest feature of his stance was that once or twice, although he didn't alter his position at all, his left eye, which was the one nearer to myself, seemed to turn ninety degrees in its socket and focus directly and hugely on my unease.

He gave me the keys and left. I went inside and asked myself two questions. Question 1: where did I meet anyone like him before? Answer: nowhere. Question 2: where did I see a face like that before, entirely in profile except for one frontal eye? I considered it for a long time: not in the world of living people, for sure, so it had to be in the domain of art. And then it came to me in a flash of yellows, greens and reds, with a grimace of grotesque face modelling. Answer: in a painting by Picasso in the Museum of Modern Art in New York. At least he gave me that much satisfaction: I was able to do what some philosopher said was the most important work of the imagination, that is, make connections.

Exactly a week later the announcement of his appointment appeared on the "Western Orb" and that evening he was back at my door for the keys. My puzzlement grew. He made no reference of any sort, good or bad, jocose or apologetic, to his previous call. I thought he would at the very least make a joke of the charade and tell me that Mollie would have starved him for the week if he hadn't brought back some facts and figures about the house, or else if his mental wheels did not run on such levity that he would say straight out that he had been bound to secrecy and that he couldn't in conscience tell me his good news on that reticent occasion. But no, he came for the keys, not for a chat, not for a laugh, not for a parley. It was unreal; it was as though he had left for home straight after Fr. Mac's funeral that day and had never contemplated the escallonias at all.

I could think of only two possible explanations — I thought a lot about him after he took away the keys to claim his emptied house not his imaginary copy of Philip Hughes — and they both had to do with piety. Either his holiness had rendered him totally insensitive, like the Celtic monks of old who used to stand naked in icy rivers to rid themselves of concupiscence, or else it had miraculously blotted out all unhappy memories in the way that the grace of the sacrament wipes out all our wretched sins. Insensitivity or amnesia or both? I had no way of knowing for sure, because unlike Fr. O'Donnell I had no practical experience of holiness.

* * *

In the week that followed I threw in all the cards in my priestly hand and I left the table entirely to O'Donnell. The rhythms of Hopkins's "Glory be to God for dappled things" which I said every morning and Lyte's "Abide with me" which

I said every evening resonated less with me as I contracted a severe dose of John Masefield's sea fever:–

I must go down to the seas again, to the lonely sea and the sky,
And all I ask is a tall ship and a star to steer her by;
And the wheel's kick and the wind's song and the white sails shaking,
And the grey mist on the sea's face, and a grey dawn breaking.

I must go down to the seas again, for the call of the running tide
Is a wild call and a clear call that may not be denied;
And all I ask is a windy day with the white clouds flying,
And the flung spray and the blown spume and the seagulls crying.

I didn't have a tall ship: the mast was only twenty-two feet high; I didn't have a wheel: I moved a humble tiller to ease or to incite her; and I didn't expect to be steering by a star except by mischance. But everything else in Masefield was raising my temperature — the wind's song, the white sails, the flung spray, the blown spume — and quite definitely the call of the running tide was a wild call and a clear call that could no longer be denied. All the previous summer, the joy of my life "Lú na Lon" was sitting on her trailer in the garden, rigid and dry as a cactus because I was on duty twenty-four hours a day seven days a week. But now that O'Donnell, the burning and the shining light, was in position as a beacon to guide the storm tossed souls of the parish into the heavenhaven of their desire, it was time for me to get back to some real living.

So in the days when they were busy in the Parochial house hanging curtains, fitting carpets, posing chairs and ringing the walls with a pantheon of cheap-print saints I stripped the weatherproofs off "Lú na Lon" and exposed her to the sun and air. I propped the stepladder against the transom to get into the cockpit, opened up the cabin, spread out the sails on the lawn, got suds and sponges to wipe the smudge of two winters off the hull and then spent hour after semi-narcotic hour smearing anti-fouling paint on the keel. I forgot all about housecalls, the humouring of teachers, the foliating of family trees for Yankees, the unopened correspondence on my desk and the arrangements for First Holy Communion. The boat wasn't yet afloat but I was in my element and the cats knew it. They bounced up the stepladder into the boat; the King of Siam, as became his high station, sat regally upright in the stern, and Fan-An lay down chin to heat on the foredeck and every now and then she exchanged winks with the skipper.

But I ran into a problem. I was examining the rigging and I met with a bottlescrew that wouldn't unwind. I tried to coax the stubborn thing with a drink of three-in-one but it wouldn't budge. There was only one thing for it and that was to teach it manners with a vicegrips. I knew where I could find one, handily enough; I wasn't likely to forget its whereabouts after the opening of Stephen Burke's coffin.

Using the church as a shortcut to the boilerhouse wasn't something I should ever have done; I did it that day and I was promptly punished for it. I thrust my way through the swing doors of Saint Brona's but that was as far as I got, because there in front of me was Fr. Mac's nightmare: a priest walking down the centre aisle towards me with a great rosary beads dangling from him like a holy pendulum. The priest was Fr. O'Donnell, the beads were large enough to drape over the shoulders of a Celtic Cross in the graveyard, and the heavy cross on the beads was swinging like a pendulum on a grandfather clock. Fr. Mac's advice was "Take flight" but it was as if there were magnets on the soles of my shoes and they clung me to the tiles just inside the door. He approached.

"Good day, Father," he said, addressing, as near as made no difference, the seventh station of the cross on the wall.

I Fathered him back: clearly, first name familiarity would not be allowed to bridge the chasm between a parish priest and a curate.

"These are very fine days now, Father," he stated.

"Yes," I said "very suitable for what I am at. I am overhauling my boat."

"Indeed?"

And then he said "O, by the way", and he paused. It was a phrase that I became very familiar with in the weeks that followed: it always prefaced the announcement of a dirty trick, either planned or perfected. "O, by the way, there will be two First Holy Communions as usual. The doctor's wife paid me a visit in connection with the matter the night before last, and I agreed to her request. I think it best that I should officiate at that ceremony myself".

"He will cut your throat," Fr. Mac said. He did, as deftly as if he had Abu Ali's dagger.

Chapter 7

A FIGHT TOO MANY

If I had had the vicegrips in my hand at the time, I think I would probably have taken O'Donnell by the nose and twisted his head around into a frontal position and then threatened him saying "Now repeat what you said, while you are looking me straight in the eyes". Even if I had broken his nose in the process it would have been, in my view, justifiable retaliation for his act of war, because act of war it was. We were now, the two of us, whether he realised it or not, in a state of war. No declaration was necessary. When the Germans invaded Poland at dawn on the 1st of September 1939 they didn't declare war: they delivered it. And when O'Donnell cut my throat at the back of the church on that unsuspecting June afternoon he didn't declare war either: he delivered it.

The gospel sets out the guiding principle very simply: it says "He who is not with me is against me". Any parish priest worth his brotherly salt will defend his curate in a parochial dispute, but what had happened two nights before was that, far from defending me, he didn't even give me the opportunity of defending myself. Judgment was given on the evidence of the prosecution case only. Amongst us priests, disloyalty to our fellow priests is seen as taking off the chasuble and putting on the gaberdine of Judas.

I do not deny that he had a perfect right to establish himself as the new ruler in the eyes of his subjects, and if the cry "The king is dead, long live the king" wasn't coming back to him straightaway with the intensity that he desired, all he had to do, as history had shown, was to be patient for a few months and it would. I feel he was looking for instant clamour but that isn't as easy to induce as instant coffee.

I understood his predicament far better than he gave me credit for. I appreciated the fact that he had arrived after an interregnum of a year and a half and that he would have to find a way of telling the regent that his administration was at an end. He viewed clerical life in terms of competition and therefore it cannot have been a happy experience for him to see himself starting a race when another man was already a lap and a half in front of him.

Besides, it was the beginning of the new era of lay involvement in church affairs: the five thousand on the hillside were now every bit as important as the twelve apostles who were delivering the bread, and arguably Michael O'Driscoll had decided to sit on the grass with the five thousand rather than give a supporting arm to one of the basket carriers. All of that I knew, but I still regarded it as a serious error of judgment on his part to see me as a challenge rather than as a curate, a rival rather than as a right hand man. He ought to have been able to see that the worst way to begin his command of the ship was to tick off the first mate in the hearing of the crew on the very first occasion when he visited the bridge.

John the Baptist said one time "He must increase and I must decrease" and I was quite prepared to place that as my scriptural motto above my bed, and sleep on it. O'Donnell's methods of translating motto into reality were crude at best and belligerent at worst, but that is not to say that my own reactions were not at times like those of a chidden child.

Enough of this preamble. Back to the story. In practice there were variations from parish to parish, but in Kilbroney the curate's theatre of operations had always included teaching catechism in the two schools every week and doing all the regular monthly communion calls to "the sick, aged and housebound" — a phrase famous for its exceptions because there were always people who figured on the list who were neither sick, aged nor housebound! The second time I heard "O, by the way" from O'Donnell was when he informed me that in future he himself would take responsibility for Kilbroney national school leaving me to guard against juvenile heresy in Moulabranna, and further that he would do the communion calls in the western half of the parish, leaving me to bang wheel hubs against the stone walls of the boreens in the east. From a lazy man's point of view that was all good news, but from a strategist's point of view it was a reminder to me that we were in a sort of a twilight war and what General O'Donnell was doing was driving two deep salients into my traditional territory.

Much worse followed. Shortly before the day of the Moulabranna First Communion I spent hours working in the church grounds, as I did every fine Friday or Saturday during the summer months. Usually what I did could be dismissed as a mere lowering of the grass in the squares, rectangles and one diamond that surround the church, but what I did for the nine smoothfaced children could only be described as shaving it to their own nicety: only linoleum would have been smoother, and the groundsman who looked after the croquet lawns at Rear Admiral Bright's could hardly have done better.

Later that day I was walking down to the village and I looked in the church gate to admire my handiwork. What I saw gave me the creeps instead. O'Donnell was slowly pacing along the outside of the geometrical shapes pouring some sort of concoction out of a can on to the grass. "What the hell are you doing to my lawn?" were the words that shaped themselves in my yelping mind, but my guardian angel reminded me that it belonged to O'Donnell much more than it belonged to me. All the same I resented what I saw as outside interference. I had worked so many manhours on it over the years, I had rotted so many shirts on its behalf, I had spent so much money on petrol for the Stiga to keep it trimmed and I had raced my heartbeat to such dangerous levels trying to restart the recalcitrant engine that I felt I had established some sort of a prescriptive right to that grass. The sight of the oversize crow with the clipped wings shuffling along the margins gave me such a nasty shock that I forgot what I was going to the village for.

I got a much more painful shock on the following Wednesday when the weedkiller showed what it could do. All around my beautiful lawn, on every side of the geometrical shapes of squares, rectangles and one diamond ran a streak of horrible plaguey yellow. It was no longer a lawn with admiring pathways crossing through it; it was reduced to a group of monotone cubist pictures sitting in vulgar yellow frames. I was furious.

My guardian angel counselled caution. "It is only a bit of grass," he said. "Hardly enough to fill a cow for one day. It will be green again in a few months' time. Ignore the provocation. Don't make bad worse. And, remember, you can hardly preach about neighbours squabbling if you are squabbling yourself with the parish priest." My guardian angel was a gutless pacifist, and I rejected his advice.

On Friday I propelled the Stiga mower down the hill, as if it was a Centurion tank. I steered it through the church gate and along through the yellow peril to the parish priest's house. I rang the bell. Mollie appeared. "Come in", she said, "Father was anxious to see you. I think he has something to ask you about the First Communion tomorrow".

"No, Mollie", I said. "I can't, unless I can bring the lawn mower in with me. There is something I want to discuss with Fr. O'Donnell about it, so maybe you would ask him to come out".

I have never seen a sheep smiling, but if it ever does, that was the sort of smile he had on his face when he came to the door.

"What's this about the mower?" he asked, addressing the church. I took two little skips to the left such as a footballer takes when he is shaping up to kick a placed ball. The stratagem worked: I had him looking straight at me!

"You are conducting the strictly private ceremony of First Communion tomorrow" I said to him, "so I thought you might like to cut the grass for the special occasion. There won't be as much of it to cut as usual because your weedkiller has gnawed a lot of it away. If you decide not to, I'll call back for it tomorrow to cut the grass for the Sunday Masses. On the other hand, you might like to take over the grass cutting responsibilities altogether. If so, there's the mower; it is parish property".

There was no smile on his face now, sheepish or other-creatured.

"There is something biting you"? he asked.

"There sure is", I answered "When I came to the parish, the church grounds were cut by a scythe a few times a year. I turned the hayfield into a lawn. But you have vandalised it, yes," I repeated, "vandalised it, you and your weedkiller".

Fair dues to the man, he counterattacked fiercely. "You are boasting about the care you have given to the grounds", he said, "but what you don't seem to have noticed is that the grass is encroaching on the tarmacadam. In another while the people will either be walking single file on the paths or walking on the grass everywhere. That is why I had to put a check on it."

"I grant you that", I said, "but there's a right way and a wrong way of doing everything. A garden spade would be the right way; weedkiller was the wrong way".

"Two years ago was the time for the spade; now was the time for the paraquat."

He didn't divert me with the word 'paraquat.' "Weedkiller is weedkiller", I snapped, "it kills weeds. That is what it was processed for, but not for grass. It doesn't just kill grass; it massacres it. For God's sake, will you look at it," and I pointed an accusing finger at the horrible straggly yellow border.

"What's wrong with it? I can't see anything wrong with it."

"Well I can. It looks as though a giant puked his guts on top of it."

I was afraid that that repulsive image might provoke him into using the argument from authority, as we used to call it in Maynooth, and it did.

"I make the decisions in this parish now", he said, with what he thought was the tone of finality, but he wasn't finished with me yet. There was only one thing in my head that I really wanted to say when I came down from my house and now was the time to say it.

"As it is you who make the decisions, Father" I said, "maybe you would make another one, and that is to get a few bucketfuls of white-wash from Finn Twomey next week when he is liming the walls for the procession. What you could do with it would be to pour it over the middle of the lawn. Then you would have green, white and yellow, and any aircraft that had lost its way and its radio would know it was over Ireland!"

* * *

The parish priest picked the next arena, and it was a clever choice. We went indoors from the church lawn to the parish hall.

For even longer than I was caring for the grounds I was managing the hall. It was the first job that Fr. Mac gave me when I arrived in the parish. It involved looking after the fabric, putting on a concert for St. Patrick's night, making it available for the meetings of all the local associations, except the Hilltown Gun Club from whom I wouldn't accept a booking even if they gave me a hundred pounds, providing new cues for aggressive billiard players, paying a fleeting visit to the whist players on the Sunday nights of winter — they liked attention, but not distraction, so fleeting it had to be — and, most difficult of all, supervising the tourist crammed dances on the Sunday nights of summer.

I really abominated the job of dance marshal and it very nearly made me into a split personality, because I was at once an impresario and a sort of policeman. If there was no bounce in the dancing I had to circulate like a hornet trying to sting people into action, and if there was two much fire on the floor I had to equip myself with a waterhose.

Dealing with the forces who charged my defences after Florrie's pub closed for the night was often a big problem. One of the few operating rules I got from Fr. Mac stated that no one in a drunken condition should be admitted, but as time went on I bent that rule until it was looking like a horse shoe, because I discovered that the definitive drunks sat down quietly and went to sleep apart from the occasional hurroo which they uttered when the siege of Ennis was at its clamorous height whereas the fellows who had half their senses went totally crazy on the strength of the other half.

It was all a great learning experience in the school of human nature, but the draughts from the open door, casual conversation with my neighbour which sounded like a shouting war in order to be heard above the racket, and which led to many a raw throat, the stink of cigarette smoke which my clothes inhaled and didn't exhale until Thursday, and the thought that I was supposed to be doing all this so that Jesus Christ might be glorified made my Monday mornings very bleak experiences indeed. I think there was only one period that I enjoyed and that was when the ditty "One day at a time, sweet Jesus" was in vogue. Many of our clientele were pious ladies in their sixties who never danced but came along for a tinge of excitement by proxy, and whenever the vocalist intoned the words 'sweet Jesus' they all bowed their heads in reverence together as if it was a meeting of the confraternity of the Sacred Heart they were attending. It was a moment I always savoured but it scarcely balanced out the wretched hours of the remainder of the night.

I am not suggesting I did it all singlehanded. We were a two-man team, the other member being Bernard Lowry the caretaker, who did the opening and shutting, the lighting of a fire before meetings and the sweeping away of the jetsam on the mornings after the night before. I thought we were providing a good service, considering that he was being paid in pennies and I was being paid mostly in abuse, but it wasn't good enough for a lot of people who thought we should be doing much more. What they had in mind were discos for teenagers, keep fit sessions for the women, boxing for the men, indoor training for the footballers and a soft drinks centre in opposition to Florrie's bar with tables and chairs and TV and newspapers where all and sundry could spend their nights for the price of one Coca Cola. I didn't dance any jig when I heard those tunes being played. I had two reasons for my immobility: first of all I had no intention of taking Bernard away from his family five nights a week and I had no notion of changing my mode of address from Father Laide to Mr. Entertainer.

The chief protagonist for a new deal in hall affairs was Mark Sheerin. He regarded himself as the catalyst for change in our backward parish. He had worked for some years in England and when he returned he believed he could lift the bustling Irish centre from Kilburn and put it down on the edge of Kilbroney. He never gave his tongue a rest but loquacious though he was he never actually conversed with anybody: he delivered person-to-person lectures in his daily circuit of the parish. He was a knowall whose knowledge was based on 6th Standard in the primary school and much commuting on the London Underground.

His chief claim to fame so far was in the provision of public toilets. He badgered Fr. Mac into building one behind the church, and — all credit to him — he shamed the County Council into providing an alternative to the rushes and stonewalls at Sandy Cove. Encouraged by his cloacal successes he thereafter set his upgrading eyes on the hall. But so far as I was concerned he hadn't an empty box's chance in a typhoon of being allowed even to secure a loose slate on the roof.

However, when the news of how Fr. O'Donnell had vetoed my decision on the First Communions made the rounds of the gossips, he surely realised that his hour had come and although I didn't actually see him going into the parochial house to deliver his lecture on the present regrettable state of the hall I knew in my heart that sooner or later he would follow in the footsteps of Alice Morgan.

My surmise was correct. On the Saturday evening before the procession when O'Donnell and I met in the sacristy to decide who was going to do what, his ominous phrase "O, by the way" rattled my ears again. "O, by the way" he said "I am thinking of calling a general meeting in the hall next week". He didn't tell me why so I didn't give him the satisfaction of asking the question "What about?" All was revealed on the following morning when I glanced at the notice book before going out to begin Mass.

One item switched the procession, the flower strewers, the rosary reciters, the cars along the route, the dawdling choir and everything else in my suddenly pounding head off the mainline on to a sidetrack. It said:– "A public meeting will be held in the hall on Tuesday evening at 9 o'clock to elect a committee to help with the running of the hall. A large attendance is requested." I felt like the Trojans when the Greeks dropped through the belly of the wooden horse; he had found the weak point in my defences and gone right through them.

To get back from Homer to home, what could I do to harry him? It was the worst possible preparation for a recollected Mass, but in the few minutes before the clock struck the hour I realised that I was now in the position of a junior partner in a coalition government who hasn't been told by the senior partner about an important change of policy; therefore, as the politicians say, I had to consider my position as a matter of urgency. And so when it came to reading the notices I made three slight but significant changes in the wording of his announcement. I said: "Fr. O'Donnell is calling a public meeting which will be held in the hall on Tuesday evening at 9 o'clock. The purpose of the meeting is to elect a committee which will run the hall in future. A large attendance is requested."

His request was granted and a large attendance turned up. Among the number I saw Mark, his wife, his three children, his brother, his sister-in-law, his two sisters and their husbands all "ably supported," as provincial newspapers say about the more prominent footballers on a team, by their neighbours, relatives and friends. The hall may not have been jampacked, but it was a packed audience.

At 25 minutes past 9, Greenwich Mean Time, that is 9 o'clock local time — everything in Kilbroney, except Mass, started twenty five minutes late — Fr. O'Donnell stood up and called the meeting to order. He asked if anyone would like to chair the meeting and in the absence of any volunteer and in spite of much shaking of the head and much wobbling of the hands he allowed himself to be directed to the chair which Bernard had placed behind a table at the top of the hall.

He thanked us all for coming, remarking that the big attendance denoted a big interest in the matter-in-hand. He said that the hall had a great potential, and an expansion of activities was desirable but that two people couldn't possibly be expected to do more than they were doing already, hence the need for a committee. He then outlined his ideas about the composition of the committee. He thought it should consist of twelve members, three ex officio and nine elected. First he had thought of ten elected members but that would have resulted in a committee of thirteen and he thought that would be tempting fate. (Big laugh for the parish priest's joke). The three ex officio members would be himself as P.P., the reverend manager and the caretaker, and among the nine elected members he thought it desirable to have three ladies.

Then, before proceeding to the election, he threw the meeting open to the audience for comments, suggestions or reservations. Mark was first on his feet. He said that a closed hall was as bad as a closed factory; it had to be open all the time in order to be productive and profitable or words to that effect. He advocated the introduction of judo, table tennis, carpentry, badminton, boxing, seashell varnishing, slimming exercises, flower arranging and First Aid. He supported everything the parish priest said except the brief allusion to the reverend manager and he sat down to prolonged applause. Various other speakers mentioned the neglect of youth, the desirability of a minerals' bar and the impossibility of gaining access to the billiard room when Bernard was at work and the reverend manager was away. I got an occasional nod of praise, but no salaam. One kind soul did aver that Bernard and I had done Trojan work over the years but with all the slings and arrows of outrageous comments that were winging my way the only Trojan feature

I could think of was the Horse as more and more Greeks dropped out of his belly.

The general impression created by the speakers was that the Turk had done his work and the Turk could go, which wasn't very comforting in view of all the chills I got sitting at the door between the hectic heat inside and the keen air outside, but just the incentive I needed for what I had in mind.

Then the elections took place and I wasn't sure whether I was in Kilbroney hall or Tammany Hall. The Sheerin caucus proposed, seconded, and carried seven of the nine members, and the chairman wasn't familiar enough with the clan system in the parish to know he was being hoodwinked. Not surprisingly, among those seven were Mark himself, his wife and a partner of his with whom he operated an agricultural machinery venture.

Fr. O'Donnell brought the public meeting to a close by stating that it was a good night's work, a remark that was greeted with applause by the Sheerin supporters, and then he surprised everybody by saying there would be a very short private meeting of the new committee to follow after a five minutes' break. It was, in a very different sense, just the break I needed.

During the interval I raced down home to grab hold of a dossier of material which I had put together during the day, so when I returned to the hall I was the only one of the twelve who gave a business like impression for the first meeting of the Kilbroney Hall Committee.

Once again the parish priest gave a very poor actor's performance as a person who was unwilling to have greatness thrust upon him — Hugh Kelleher certainly wouldn't have him in his local drama group — but once again he was loudly persuaded to take the chair. The rest of us sat in the front seats facing him. He said there were just two things to consider briefly: 1. to fix a date for the first full working meeting and 2. to draw up a very rough agenda for that meeting. "What do you think are the top three priorities?" he asked.

I broke my silence for the first time that night. "The top priority for me" I said, trying to keep the words at a slower rate than my heartbeat, "is to explain my position vis-a-vis the new committee. First of all, Fr. O'Donnell stated that I am an ex officio member. The question is: ex quo officio? from what office? The only official position I have in the parish is that of curate, and when the bishop wrote his letter of appointment and set out my duties he made no mention of manager of the hall. Therefore I cannot be a member of the committee by virtue of my curacy.

"The second point is this: the only reason why I was manager at all was that Fr. McCarthy, not the bishop, appointed me. But Fr. McCarthy is dead, more is the pity" — I was getting cheeky — "and therefore my appointment has been terminated by his death."

O'Donnell had his mouth open, and he was about to say that he was reappointing me but I didn't give him the chance. I forged ahead. "Whether or which", I said, "I am now formally tendering my resignation from the position of manager to you, very reverend Chairman and to you, members of the committee. I was never a committee type of person myself and I should hate to block the good work that I know ye will do by being an unwilling or an uncomfortable member. The only apologia I will make for my style of running the hall is to say that basically I am a Frank Sinatra type and I did things my way."

That remark brought a smile or two, but there was no rush of voices seeking to dissuade me. I think that perhaps after the light fare that had gone before they were unable to handle the unexpected melodrama.

Villain that I am, and looking at the ten in the seats I continued, "You will have the perfect replacement in the person of Fr. O'Donnell. As parish priest he will have the authority that I never had when there were arguments at the door and disturbances in the body of the hall. And, of course, it will be a very valuable experience for himself because he will meet people at that same door whom otherwise he would never have the opportunity of meeting at all!" There were several broader smiles at this as some of the ten let their minds rest for a moment on the likes of Connie Con of Dunsheen and the harbour master of Croghan.

O'Donnell's face was now a study to behold. The ham acting phase was over and in its place there was a look of unfeigned horror on his countenance as he considered the awful prospect of being out of his bed until two o'clock in the morning listening to the woes of the rhinestone cowboy on a continent far from Kilbroney, and the praises of the wild colonial boy on a continent even farther away.

Then, suiting the action to the word and the word to the action — I do believe that Hugh Kelleher would have given me an audition on the strength of it — I took my dossier, walked to the table, and placed various items, one by one, solemnly, on the tabletop in front of the very reverend Chairman. "First of all", I said, "those are the keys, the symbol of my high office. Next, you have the cheque book, with the present healthy credit balance on the back of the stub. Thirdly, there is the legal correspondence about the dance licence. And fourthly," I said as I put a bulging foolscap package on the table, "in there you have everything from the regulations about the copyright of plays to the wholesale prices of Dettol antiseptic."

I then turned around to face the ten and ignoring O'Donnell completely I said "I should very much like at this parting of the ways to pay tribute to Bernard. I have been referred to tonight as the reverend manager. I am certain that on countless occasions I have been given far less complimentary epithets than "reverend", but the fact of the matter is that the real manager here was Bernard. Not only did he open the hall, but he kept the hall open. Not only did he close the hall but he closed the door to a lot of trouble. If I managed the hall, Bernard managed the crises. In the broadest sense I couldn't have managed without him. Thank you, Bernard. Anything I know, he knows, so he will help you to establish yourselves. And if perchance there is something that he doesn't know I shall be very happy to help you in any way I can. Thank you all for your attention."

And without even a nod to O'Donnell I walked down Bernard's beautifully crystalled maple dance floor and out the awful draughty door for the last time.

I felt chuffed.

I had taken quite a battering in the first nine rounds, but I had landed a few solid punches in the tenth and final round.

* * *

Sooner or later in every story, money gets in the way of people, and halfway through the month of July it came between O'Donnell and myself like an unoccupied trench that we fought over.

No matter how often a priest tells his people from the pulpit that they cannot serve God and Mammon, and no matter how often he quotes Paul's words to his protegé Timothy to the effect that the love of money is the root of all evils, as soon as he gets down out of the pulpit there are half a dozen men trawling the church for money and as soon as he leaves the altar there are people visiting him in the sacristy with offerings for this, that and the other.

A priest has to pay for his petrol the same as everyone else, and if he favours a grapefruit for his breakfast he cannot get it to grow on his apple tree. Therefore he likes to have a jingle in his pocket the same as another man or, better still, a bulge in his wallet, and it was precisely on that issue of jingle or bulge that the next battle was fought.

Up to that point we had fought three engagements. The first on the question of Holy Communion was a pre-emptive strike on his part, and my base was blown to pieces before I could get a fighter into the air. I picked the site of the second clash and I won the battle of the grass. Following which, he picked the location of the third tussle and he won the battle of the hall, even though it was somewhat of a pyrrhic victory for him. Neither of us picked the next battlefield: we simply blundered into each other like O'Neill and Mountjoy at the Battle of Kinsale. Who could have guessed that a few packets of loose coin would blow up into a major engagement, and become the turning point of the war?

The parish priest phoned me and asked me to call to his house. He didn't use his introductory phrase "O, by the way . . ." so there was no reason to suspect a booby trap. In fact it sounded like good news. "I have some money here", he said "and I think we should have a divide." That word 'divide' is one that a priest learns very quickly in his glossary of special terms when he is appointed to his first curacy. The irony of it is that far from dividing the priests of a parish it unites them as nothing else in jollity and good will.

What happens is that at intervals throughout the year — it could be anything from a month to three months depending on how much money is to hand — the parish priest convenes a meeting of his priests at which the money they have received for such things as weddings, baptisms and dues since the last such meeting is pooled and divided. A formula similar to that used on salmon yawls and small fishing boats is employed to apportion each priest's proper share. If there are two in a yawl, the skipper gets two shares to his mate's one. If there are three in a smack the skipper gets two shares and his mates one each. In much the same way where there are three priests in a parish the parish priest gets half the divisible revenue and the curates a quarter each, and in a parish such as ours in Kilbroney the parish priest got two thirds and the curate a third.

During the year and a half when Fr. Mac was away, all the moneys intended for the upkeep of the priests came into my hands but, of course, they didn't stay in my hands: Fr. Mac was still the parish priest and whenever I got down to the financial fractions I lodged his two thirds share in his bank account and kept a hard earned third for myself. In other words I continued to follow the system of the divide. Now that a new parish priest was installed, it was up to him to get out the division tables and to say "one for you, two for me". That was what he had in mind when he rang me to say "I have some moneys here; I think we should have a divide."

I gathered up the money that had come my way since Fr. Mac's death. It was mostly what we called petrol money, a collection taken up in different parts of the parish during the summertime to help keep our thirsty cars supplied with drink. The total came to £257.70. Much of it arrived in broken money but as I didn't think it fitting to bring a scatter of coins with me to the parish priest's table I walked down to Florrie's pub to change all I could of it into notes. Florrie was always looking for coin so it suited both of us to exchange metal for paper. Then with only £2.70 in coins and the remainder in becoming notes I walked back up the hill, through the cubist exhibition now at its nauseating height, and along to the parochial house.

Mollie answered the bell and let me in. She had her official face on, the one to accord with the parish priest's current estimation of the caller and it was severe and unfriendly. I followed her to the teller's. It was the first time I was inside the house since I had packed up Fr. Mac's furniture and the fancies of a lifetime for the auction. It was a visit I am never likely to forget, nor is Michael O'Donnell.

He was rather stiff — I couldn't blame him for that — but he was courteous and he directed me to a chair at one end of his counting table while he sat himself at the other. The first thing I noticed was the advanced state of his preparations for the momentous divide. In a row along the table to his right and my left were slim wads of £20 notes, £10 notes and £5 notes as well as reclining A.I.B. bags of £1 coins, 50p coins, 20p coins and 10p coins.

He wasted no time on pleasantries. Fr. Mac always produced a bottle of Benedictine and a bottle of brandy, a mixture to which he was partial, saying it was highly medicinal and neglecting to say it was also highly intoxicating!

"How much do you have, Father?" O'Donnell asked.

"£257.70", I answered like a schoolboy in a maths class. I produced the sum from my coat pocket and put it down in front of him, the £255 in a rubber banded roll, and the £2.70 in coin. Like the authentic teller that he was, he slipped the rubber band off the notes and placed them on top of his own, counting as he went . . . "£130 . . . £175 . . . £200 . . . £220 . . . £250 . . . £255". He then dropped the two pound coins into an open lipped A.I.B. bag amending the figure on the bag with a black marker and he slipped the 50p and the two 10p coins into two other open bags. It was all very methodical and very detached.

"I have £322.44" he then announced. "It's all there to the side of you. I have checked it and double checked it. You may, if you so please, check it again."

"No, there's no need", I answered. "I presume you can count, although it would appear as though you doubt if I can", my blood beginning to rise from tepid to hot.

He ignored the sarcasm — he had a longer fuse than I had — and said "All we have to do now is to add the two figures and divide the total by three." I just couldn't rid myself of the memory of the hated maths class of my youth.

He went to work on a yellow memo pad — the very colour of it was disgusting — and came up with the figure of £580.14. That divided by 3 would give him the share that I was entitled to, and he worked it out aloud like a kid in the national school. "Three into five, once and two over. Three into twenty-eight, nine and one over. Three into ten, three and one over. Three into eleven, three and two over. Three into twenty-four, eight exactly." Then lifting his head from the memo pad and looking sideways at his bookcase — I followed his glance and I wondered if he had Philip Hughes, volume 2 there — he announced "£193.38."

What he did next astounded me, and turned what was always in Fr. Mac's time an occasion for reminiscence, mild bishop-bashing, speculation on the latest betting on the promotion stakes and the slow savouring of the beloved B. and B. into a purely banking operation. He gathered up £150 in assorted notes from his bundles and then picked up five bags of coin — I watched mesmerised while his fingers nimbly hopped from bag to bag — one £10 bag of 50p pieces, two £10 bags of 20p pieces and two £5 bags of 10p pieces and set them all out in front of me saying "There's £190".

It was only when he began to rummage in the open bags for the balance of £3.38 that the shock registered, and I got my voice back.

"Are you not going to give me a cheque?" I said incredulously.

"No," he said. "I am giving you cash. What is wrong with that?"

"There is nothing wrong with it. It just isn't customary, that's all."

"Customs vary from place to place".

"Not here in Kilbroney. Fr. McCarthy always lodged the entire sum and paid me my share by cheque."

"Well, I am not Fr. McCarthy, more is the pity, as you said in the hall". Good. He wasn't as thick skinned as I thought. The barbed shaft had penetrated and had stuck there. He continued, "What Fr. McCarthy didn't seem to realise was that in lodging the entire sum, not just his own share, in his account he was making himself liable to extra tax. I have no intention of doing that."

"Ah, but that is ridiculous, Father. The tax people can only get access to your bank account on foot of a court order, and they will only get that if they believe you are involved in drug trafficking. Are you?" The blood was rising from hot to near-boiling.

O'Donnell had the £3.38 in his hand by this and he shot it across the table at me like enraged dollars and quarters in a western saloon. His blood was up too.

"I insist on being paid by cheque" I said, pushing the whole lot, notes, bags of coins and loose change back across the table. "Paying me in these bits and scraps is degrading."

He immediately shoved the money right back across the table to me and he said "You can take it or leave it. It's up to you". At which he stood up from his chair and started to walk in my direction around the table towards the door.

I mentioned earlier about my very short fuse and it was this action of his, concluding the discussion with such insulting finality, that lit it. I don't know what got into me but whatever it was, it was irrepressible. I picked up a bag of 20p coins and let it fly at him as he was passing, no more than ten feet away. He was looking, as usual, the wrong way and he didn't see it coming. It caught him with full force at the side of the temple and he let a roar out of him to equal Goliath's in the valley of Elah. In the door came Mollie; so fast, she must have been clung to it on the other side, ear, shoulder blade and arm, listening to what was going on. It would have made great comedy for Hugh Kelleher's drama group in the parish hall as she led him away to the kitchen with her hand to his forehead. I have no way of knowing what she applied to the bump, but if she had consulted me I would have told her that there was no better cure for it than to apply a cold coin, and the injured man had an abundance of those on the table.

"Take it or leave it," was what he said. I did both; I took the notes and left the coin. Out the door with me as fast as I could, leaving behind me a quarter of my pay and three quarters of my reputation.

* * *

I guessed that O'Donnell would call on Big Brother for assistance, and he didn't waste any time about it. As near as I can remember I gave him his financial migraine on a Monday. On the following Friday I picked up a letter in my hallway and I only had to glance at the neat, regular, immediately recognisable handwriting on the envelope to know that within there would be a summons to headquarters.

It read:–

Dear Father Laide,

A serious breach of clerical discipline has been brought to my notice concerning you. I am accordingly requesting you to present yourself at my house next Tuesday 23rd July at 11 a.m. in connection with the matter.

In Christo.

Yours truly,

† Andrew Irwin,

Bishop of Demly.

I spent the next few days rehearsing my defence such as it was. In soccer terms I knew what I would have to do when he centred off and made straight for my goal area but as things turned out he didn't take the direct route to goal at all, but attacked first down along one wing and then down along the other, leaving my defence in total disarray.

Bishops have to be given credit for cleverness, and in truth Bishop Irwin was a clever man. He was a professor of sociology in Maynooth before being appointed to Demly, and if professorial texts are ever a preparation for the business of living amongst unprofessorial people his books would have been a help to him because he succeeded to a diocese which had every type of structure in human society: a crowded city, small sparsely inhabited islands such as Inishnagaunogue, market towns like Hilltown which were the hub of great sweeps of agricultural country around them and lizard-shaped peninsular parishes such as Kilbroney where the native population was on the ebb and the settlers on the flood.

Bishop Irwin was one of the old school, rather stern in appearance and distant in manner. What I and most of my fellow priests liked about him was that he was able to draw on his own light to clarify a problem unlike many another bishop who surrounded himself with satellites from whom he hoped to draw light in darkness. For satellites, read advisors, directors and experts. He had a massive mahogany table but no cabinet sitting around it.

He seated me at that table at 11 o'clock on the Tuesday morning, having opened the door of the house to me himself. He was that sort of bishop: he wrote his own letters, he composed his own pastorals, he drove his own car, he managed his own accounts and he made up his own mind.

"You know, of course, why I have summoned you here", he began.

"Yes, my Lord. You stated the reason in your letter."

"Did I? I thought I left it vague, deliberately vague. One never knows whose knife will open a letter".

"You mentioned a serious breach of clerical discipline, my Lord."

"Ah yes. That is what I mean by vague. We shall take that up later. But first there are two other serious complaints against you which I have to deal with".

I was too flabbergasted even to ask "What about?"

He got up from his chair, produced a bunch of keys from his soutane and walked to a filing cabinet. He released the locking mechanism and pulled out a drawer where, I presume, all the black sheep are penned. He came back to the table with two letters.

"These two letters", he said "arrived quite some time ago. I did not act on them at the time because Fr. McCarthy was ill and you were fully extended in Kilbroney, so I merely acknowledged them and put them on file for further reference. I might indeed have disregarded them altogether, if it were not for this latest aberration, but now I am forced to act."

His measured prose would have been enough by itself to render me mute but, in addition to that, the two envelopes that he was turning hither and over in his hands and squinting at to figure out the postmarks were mesmerising not only my eyes but my tongue.

"Yes", he said, discarding one of the envelopes for the time being, and removing the letter from the other. "This one was the first to reach me. It is from a Mrs Catherine Burke".

The voice of the bishop was now only a voice over; the telling sounds in the room were the sounds of nails being driven in my coffin.

"It says here", he continued, "that you opened her husband's coffin without authorisation, causing her grave embarrassment. Is that true?"

"Well, you see, my Lord . . ."

"I don't see anything. Did you or didn't you?"

"Yes, but . . ."

Again he cut me off. "Facts first", he said, "possible extenuation later. Did you or did you not open Stephen Burke's coffin without authorisation?"

"I did, my Lord".

"You remind me of a schoolboy, Father, you are so niggardly with your admissions."

"Meaning no offence, I feel like a schoolboy, my Lord".

Did I or did I not see just the beginning of a smile at the edge of his lips?

"Very well. What explanation do you offer for your strange behaviour?"

"Stephen Burke was a big hefty man, my Lord. But there wasn't the weight of a mouse in his coffin." The words were coming at last. That suggestion of a smile had encouraged me. "And I wanted to find out why that was so."

"In plain English you were motivated by pure curiosity, is that it?"

"Yes and no, my Lord. By interest, more than by curiosity".

"Interest . . . Interest in what?"

"Interest in finding out if Mrs Burke was making a fool of us all, my Lord. She was trying to give the impression that her husband's corpse was in the coffin, but in fact there was only a bag of ashes in there."

"You have no warrant to judge the lady's motives which is what you are doing now. Stay with the facts."

"Well the fact is, my Lord, that she forced me to say the requiem for when a corpse is present, whereas I should have been saying the requiem for when only the ashes are present."

It was a blunder. Bishop Irwin was never interested in the niceties of rubrics and he responded with one word, "Trivia". That threw me. "The central issue here isn't what was in the coffin but what was in the best interests of Mrs Burke to whom the coffin belonged. Those best interests would have been served only by respecting the private nature, indeed I may say the sacred nature of the coffin. I do not go so far as to say that your action was sacrilegious, although undoubtedly that is how this unfortunate woman regards it, but I do say that it was a serious breach of the trust that she placed in you. You failed in your duty to show respect for the dead and concern for the living and in so doing you damaged the cloth, not yours only but mine also and the priesthood generally. I am therefore issuing a grave reprimand to you, Father, for what I consider a most unworthy action,"

With every sentence he uttered I could see Gobnait O' Brien standing behind him and giving him a congratulatory pat on the back. I had come to the bishop's house, I thought, to answer a charge that I had thrown a bag of money at O' Donnell but in fact what was happening was that a stone from David's pouch which she had been carrying all those months from February of the year before had hit me right on the forehead and stunned me.

"O, my prophetic soul," Hamlet said when his suspicions about his uncle became established facts, and my soul too was prophetic. The bishop opened the second envelope.

"This next complaint," he began, "is of an even stranger nature, and it comes from a Miss Gobnait O' Brien" — O, my prophetic soul, indeed. I waited for the worst, and it came. "She states in her letter, which I may say is very well written, that you terrorised the village of Kilbroney while dressed as an

Arab, that you wielded a knife and that as a result she fell from
a ladder and suffered a serious sprain of her right ankle."

I know one doesn't subject a bishop to a sliding tackle but
in soccer parlance it was critical to get in a strong tackle at this
juncture; otherwise I would be completely overrun.

"That is largely fabrication, my Lord," I protested. "I did
indeed dress up as an Arab and the dagger was part of the costume, but there was no question of the village being terrorised.
Miss O' Brien fell off the ladder not because she saw a dagger
but because she saw an Arab and in common with many people
she regards all Arabs as terrorists." At this point I thought that
the tackling was perhaps too vigorous and I finished less vehe-
mently with "It was only a bit of fun, my Lord."

"A schoolboy prank, would you say?"

"I would, my Lord."

I thought it was an escape route, but it was a trap door.

"How old are you, Father?"

"Forty, my Lord".

"Forty! Time to grow up, Father. If you were married you
would have the family half reared by now."

If I said nothing, he punished me. If I counter attacked he
caught me on the break and punished me even more. The score
was rising.

"You said just now that she fell off a ladder." He was mount-
ing another attack. "Do you deny that she suffered a badly
sprained ankle?"

"No. I don't."

"Do you feel responsible for her injury?"

"No, I don't."

"No?"

"No."

"Do you admit that if you were not dressed up as an Arab
she would not have fallen off the ladder?"

"I do, my Lord."

"Then you are responsible for her injury, Father."

As the popular sportswriters say, he was running the show and I was getting the runaround.

He asked a loaded question next. "What directed you to dress up in the first instance?"

"I can't honestly say, my Lord. Something got into me. I get these urges from time to time. A rush of blood to the head. That sort of thing." An own goal, every statement. Then, while his head was lowered, probably considering his verdict, I got an inspiration. "It started out as a bit of fun, as I said, but very quickly it became a serious experiment."

The bishop lifted his head. "A serious experiment.? Experiment in what?"

"In sociology".

He laughed.

"It is true, my Lord. As I moved from door to door, from a building site to a bar, from a person running in terror to a person falling off a ladder, I realised that what I was looking at was the unfeigned reaction of a simple community to what they perceived as a threat."

"Yes?" said his Lordship, really listening to me for the first time.

"Yes. The Arab was no threat to anybody but they let their imaginations run away with them. It was West against East. Christian against Moslem. Native against stranger. It was racism pure and simple." That was his sort of language and I knew it. It was the first time all morning I had shown any skill on the ball. "Did she say in her letter that a man came after me to batter in my skull with a crowbar?"

"No, she didn't."

"Well, that was the only instance of terrorism that day."

"Very interesting, Father. Very interesting indeed." I could actually hear the turboshaft in his mind being thrown into reverse. "I must caution you against ever doing anything like that again," was all he said. It was the first time in my life, I think, that I literally got off with a caution, but it was only a respite in the near gale and the real storm had not hit me yet.

"I see a connection", he said, "between what you did on the Day of the Arab" — I have borrowed his descriptive phrase for a chapter title of this book — "and what you did in Fr. O'Donnell's house, and it is a very dangerous connection indeed, one that I view with the gravest alarm." Sudden rise up the Beaufort scale.

"You had a knife on the day you dressed up?"

"Yes. I had a dagger. A Jordanian dagger."

"I see. Now could I ask you if you would have thrown the dagger, the Jordanian dagger, at Fr. O'Donnell last week if you had had it to hand instead of a bag of coins?"

"Of course not, my Lord."

"I am not so sure. Fr O'Donnell stated in his letter, and I have no reason whatsoever to doubt his word, that you displayed unrestrained violence. Those are his very words. 'Unrestrained violence'. A man who is unrestrainedly violent will use any weapon that he can get his hands on. Lucky for Fr O'Donnell and lucky for you that the weapon was a bag of money and not, as you call it, a Jordanian dagger."

I was being mauled. Only snatches of my rehearsed speech would come to me. "I felt degraded," I said, "put down, debased, humiliated. I thought it was a really demeaning way for a parish priest to deal with his curate, to pay him his dues in bits and scraps of coins."

"And what would you say about the curate's way of dealing with his parish priest? Demeaning, would you call it? Or dangerous?"

"Dangerous," I admitted, "but he provoked me."

"That is what murderers say. Look here, Father, I don't care what the provocation is or was. No priest of mine is going to be allowed to raise his hand against another priest. Do you realise at all the seriousness of what you did? It was a criminal assault. You could go to jail for that."

I wanted to say that O'Donnell would be swept out of any court in the country on gusts of laughter if he brought a case, but I was afraid.

The bishop continued, "I have heard of priests shouting at each other. I have heard of priests ostracising each other. I have heard of a priest who smashed another priest's golf club. I have heard of a priest trampling on another priest's flower bed. I have heard of a priest ballyragging another priest during the holy sacrifice of the Mass, but this is the first time in my long life that I have heard of one priest actually assaulting another."

He stopped to take breath and I think that I was breathing even more heavily than he was. Then he said, quite astonishingly, "I am prepared to be lenient with you in view of the great work you did in the parish all the time that Fr. McCarthy was ill, but only on one condition, that when you return to Kilbroney you go to the parish priest's house and offer him a humble apology."

I said I would.

"As for the future, I am warning you now, in the most serious manner that I can manifest, that if there is any further complaint against you, of any kind, I shall remove you forthwith. Furthermore, I shall demote you. Do you understand, Father?"

I said I did.

I followed him to his front door, followed myself every step of the way by the sword of Damocles.

Chapter 8

SEA AND MOUNTAIN

When I was growing up, I was given a simple — simple, not easy — plan for avoiding sin, and that was to avoid all occasions of sin. So, if I didn't play cards, I wouldn't learn to cheat; if I didn't go to a dance hall, I wouldn't meet a temptress; if I didn't enter a shop where the owner was half blind, I wouldn't steal, and if I didn't attend a football match, I wouldn't pick up bad language.

My instructions now were to avoid trouble and to avoid trouble I had to avoid the occasions of trouble, and the occasions of trouble were the times and places where I might meet people who would make trouble for me or more likely whose very faces would torment me into making trouble for myself.

So, I had to be out of a house where I had a sick call to attend to before Dr. Morgan arrived, lest I be tempted to ask him if the parish priest would be providing a private Sunday Mass for himself, Alice, and the first communicant. I had to gave up calling to Gobnait O'Briens for the "Western Orb," because the danger was that I would ask her when her compensation case for a sprained ankle against the United Arab Republic would be heard in court. I dared not walk on the western cliffs lest I find evidence of Sergeant Miller's marksmanship rotting on the screaming rocks. I couldn't call to compliment Catherine Burke on her luxurious new bungalow because if I saw a vase on the mantelpiece I might ask "Is that an urn, by any chance?" Mark Sheerin was just about everywhere delivering one-to-one lectures on the newstyle parochial hall so I had to avoid just about everywhere. And having duly submitted to the Bishop's directive that I apologise to Fr. O'Donnell, I kept well clear of his prayer orbit lest he hand me one of the money bags I left on his table.

Perhaps the biggest danger I faced was that I might become paranoiac and I decided that the best way to rid myself of any delusions was to get a sailing breeze to sweep through my mind. So I took "Lú na Lon" to sea at every opportunity: out there I was in no danger from anybody or anything except from my big genoa, up and straining in a force 6 from the north west.

Out of sight, out of mind, they say, and the dangerous half dozen people were well out of sight and completely out of mind when I was sailing my boat. There was one period at the end of July and the beginning of August when I pulled the burgee to the top of the mast every day for seven days, something I had never done before, either for fear of what the elements might do or for fear of what the parishioners might say.

Whenever I went sailing I wrote up a sort of a log afterwards, and my log for those seven days reads like this: —

Saturday 27 July. After the 12 o'clock confessions I said to myself that I needed some soul–healing too but there was no point in going down to the pier because the bay was as flat as the top of a table and I would only be sailing like a haystack. So I sat in the garden for an hour reading Lawrence Durrell; then all of a sudden the escallonias started to chatter and to mock at my bad judgement, and out I went. I did a really fast leg to windward as far as Carraig Dhiarmada, but at that stage the wind tired of its efforts, and it took me forty minutes from there to the raucous rocks at Tower Point. I got around Sam's Island, but so slowly I could have painted it. I was unable to decide if a white form on the Derryregan shore was a bleached rock or a brazen bather, but the wind decided at Ballymackus point that it would do no more work for me, so I came home on the engine. Then when I had stored all my gear away, a fresh came up from the southeast, the best breeze of the day, and it mocked me till nightfall.

Sunday 28 July. At twenty minutes to three, twenty minutes before the time we had settled on for the christening, Pat

O'Keeffe and his wife Geraldine were waiting at the church door with their baby daughter Nuala. "Ye are very prompt," I said, as I arrived.

"It's this way" said Pat. "It's a lovely sunny day. There's a grand breeze. When we were leaving Ballymackus there were two yachts out in the bay and we knew you would want to join them as soon as possible!" The yachts were gone when I got out there, but not the sunshine or the breeze. I goosewinged for an hour as far as Sam's Island — I expect I shall have pains in my arms for a week as a result. Then a beat right in close to Ballymackus strand with a dozen tacks to give the tourists something to photograph other than swimsuits; a close reach to the Falls o'Garry; and then an all–action, swishing, spraybulleting, headlong buck into the freshening westerly as far as the Emperor before slackening off for the final leg to Kilbroney. While I was stowing away my gear, a man came down to the pier and asked me if I was cruising around Ireland. When I told him I was the local curate he said "I thought you were a mini millionaire!"

Monday. 29 July. It was no day to be out in a small boat really. The sun came out after dinner and it is difficult to be rational about the sea when the sun is shining. The gusts that swept down off Reenrour were determined fellows, not the usual bluffers that you get in a north westerly. Even with my mainsail reefed to the first batten, and a storm jib, they were pushing her over too far for a middleaged man's comfort. What killed me completely was that a big beefy man and a slip of a crew were sailing a dinghy upright most of the time when I was leaning over at a photographic angle, and a lone swallow came over from the direction of Inishnagaunogue making a lake out of the sea and a puff out of the gale.

Tuesday 30 July. Completely different from yesterday. There wasn't enough wind to fill a cellophane bag. I thought if I went out to sea far enough on the engine that I would pick up a breeze. But what came in to meet me as I noised my way out wasn't a breeze but fog. I don't know of any other situation where you get the impression that you are at the very centre of the world: you can see nothing and so there are no distractions to your own importance! I got a quick compass bearing on Kilbroney, and then I waited for the fog to lift and the wind to descend. Things were so dead for a while that the guillemots must have thought the boat was a rock: scores of them came near me. The young ones squealed "Mammy!" and the mother birds said "Hush!" Then I heard voices, and a big red yacht sailed out of a grey wall. What happened next wasn't as solemn as that; it was more like something out of "Dublin Opinion." I could read the name "Arabesque." I could count six puzzled heads. Then came a baffled voice "Could you tell us where we are?" I couldn't resist the crack: "You are a long way from Arabia anyhow!"

Wednesday 31 July. The forecasters said the drizzle would clear, the cloud would disperse, the sun would shine and the wind would go northeast by mid afternoon. I went out in an act of great faith or sheer madness into thick drizzle, little or no wind, and a rotten short heave spawned by yesterday's fog. After half an hour I decided that punishment was not another word for pleasure and I was about to certify myself a lunatic and go home when inside ten wonderful minutes everything the forecasters predicted happened. It was like something in Walt Disney. A big yacht came bowling out of a clearance south of Tower Head with a blue and orange spinnaker indecently distended. There was wind over there to the north east and it was coming my way. It was a flyer when it arrived. I sailed from the Falls o'Garry, or as near to it as Tim Cronin's lobster pots would let me, to Seal Island, or as near to it as Pad Murray's lobster pots would let me, in twenty five minutes, on a broad reach in a tumbling sea, half fearful that the wind would hit me a wallop when I was falling sideways off a wave. It was the most water I ever covered in twenty five minutes. Only a lone swallow who was switchbacking was having more fun than I was.

Thursday, 1 August. I sailed to Carraig Aonair and back. Well, to be honest, I sailed to Carraig Aonair and half way back, motoring the rest of the way, because the wind which was westerly on my outward trip went in north and lightened and the choice was either noise for an hour or sea for the night. It was a wonderful outward leg. A porpoise tumbled like a halfmoon. A flight of gannets went by so close they stirred the sails in their yellow headed dash. I had some bad moments going through the crayfish grounds: there were so many red buoys it was like a turnip farm. At the Carraig itself there was a formidable swell: "Lú na Lon" climbed up and up, and then from the cockpit as we went down and down the swell climbed up and up the side of the lighthouse. Awesome.

Friday 2 August. "Any wind out there?" I asked Pad Murray at the pier as he came in from pulling his pots. "Very little, then, very little indeed" was the answer, so I changed from the working jib to the huge genoa, hoping to amplify that little into a lot. I shouldn't have, because a mist swept in from the south west bringing a very lively cool of wind with it and there I was, all 9 stone 7 of me holding on in a mental state halfway between terror and delight while the boat demonstrated with all that yardage on her just how far she could go over without going over altogether! After half an hour of that, everything changed again: the mist lifted, the wind lost its edge, the sun returned and the express train became a ghost.

Just as well for the bumble bee. As I was heading back for the pier in puffs that would scarcely redden embers and on a surface as flat and glossy as a photograph what should I see on the starboard side but a bumble bee floating past. I immediately stretched out my right hand and scooped him up. I left him down gently into the cockpit not sure if he was drowned or only dripping. Dripping, it proved to be: in about two minutes

he was crawling along the tail of the mainsheet. Good. All he
needed now was sunshine. So I lifted him up on the stern where
the sun was shining warmly. In ten minutes he flexed his wings
and soared off noisily into the quiet evening.

* * *

I am not sure — there is no mention of it in my log — but
it could be that it was during those seven days that I first noticed the boy at the pier. If it wasn't then it was during the settled August days that followed. I use the word 'noticed' but it
isn't a strong enough word for the sort of presence he exuded.
Whenever I drove to the pier, I noticed if Pad Murray's boat
was in or out, or if any young prankster had left air out of my
inflatable. I noticed such things as the scales of herrings, the
skeletons of crabs, the remnants of a picnic or an abandoned
sandal. But this boy wasn't so much an object to be noticed like
a bollard or a boat; he was more like an obstruction. It wasn't
a case of my noticing him; it was a case of his situating himself
where he would have to be noticed.

The inflatable which I employed to get out to 'Lú na Lon"
is a good example. I used to tether it to the sloping rock at the
landward side of the pier. One day, as soon as I parked my car,
he jumped up from where he was sitting at the edge of the pier
and skipped across to the inflatable. " Will I untie it for you?"
he asked me in an English accent.

"Ah, no, it's o.k.. There's a knack to it."

"I know the knack. I have been watching you doing it." He
had the knots undone, the rope pulled through the staples in
the rock and the inflatable flat on the ground before I could say
another "Ah no, it's o.k."

He then knelt on the air tank at one side of it exactly as I
did myself. "It is a bit soft," he said, and I could see by the in-
dent his knees were making in it that it was indeed a bit spongy.
Afterwards I wondered if he had left the air out of it himself,
after the manner of a schoolboy who sabotages one of the mas-

ter's tyres and then rushes into the class hall saying, "Sir, Sir, your tyre is flat and will I go down to tell Timmy the garage to fix it?"

"Will I blow it up for you?," the English boy asked.

"Ah no, it's o.k. It only has myself to carry. Anyhow, there's a knack to it."

"I know the knack, I watched you doing it."

There was nothing for it but to get the foot pump, tube and nozzle out of the car boot and let him at it. While I would have been figuring out for the hundredth uncertain time which end of the tube was which, he had the tube stuck into the open gob of the pump, the nozzle screwed into the valve of the dinghy and his right heel pounding the inflating board with the rapidity of an Irish stepdancer.

Just to say "Thanks, lad" seemed like a rather limp way of rewarding him, when I guessed he had a more seaworthy craft than the inflatable in his head, but I had a rule of many years' standing that I sailed alone, without voices or vexations, and I had no notion of relaxing it for anyone of either sex, young or old.

In the days that followed he was always there on the pier, invariably when I was going out, and occasionally when I was coming back as well, with his list of questions, "Will I untie it for you? Will I bring it down the steps for you? Will I hold it while you are getting in? Will I hold it while you are getting out? Will I bring it up the steps for you? Will I tie it up for you?"

He wasn't charming in a photogenic sort of way but for a twelve year old he had great skill as a manipulator. It was he who handled the formal business of introductions, for instance.

"You are Fr. Laide, aren't you?"

"Yes, I am".

"My name is Kevin. Kevin Warren.'

"Pleased to meet you, Kevin." But was I? He was getting between me and the flung spray and the blown spume. "Are you here on your holidays, Kevin?"

"Yes, till the end of August."

"That's good."

What wasn't good was when I paddled out in the inflatable to "Lú na Lon" which was moored in the middle of the creek and got aboard. He then resumed his surveillance position at the edge of the pier, legs dangling in disappointment. That was when we were physically at the greatest distance from each other, but strangely it was the time when I felt his obstructive presence most. Adjectives such as mean, stingy, miserly and selfish jumped into the cockpit like frogs and wherever I went, to bow or stern, to lockers or mast the frogs croaked their unpleasant truth about me. I never looked at the pier, except when I went into the cabin to fetch the sails and peered through the salted window without any danger of our eyes meeting, but I knew he was staring at every move I made as I got the boat ready for sea.

The feelings I experienced were exactly the same as when I sat down to a plate of sea trout or cod for my dinner and Fan–An jumped up on a chair three feet from me and watched me longingly and reproachfully as forkful after forkful of the fish travelled the exciting arc from plate to mouth. I tried not to look at the cat, but sooner or later her intense stare got the better of my studied disregard and I dropped a remorseful morsel on the floor for her, and then another and another.

So day followed day as under Kevin's gaze I paddled to the yacht and unlocked the cabin and bent the mainsail to the boom and unleashed the tiller and ran up the wind direction burgee and did the other dozen odds and ends of rigging jobs which mean that in elapsed time it is almost a dead heat between getting a yacht ready for sea and a woman ready for a dance. When all was ship shape, I let go of the mooring rope and headed seawards, and it was only then that I looked across at the figure on the pier and gave a farewell wave. At first I got an animated wave in reply but as disappointment followed disappointment what I got was a gesture more like that of a disgruntled emperor in the Colosseum and finally the response to my wave was a limp raising of his hand barely nine inches above the dejected pier.

That was the ultimate reproach. The next day wasn't intended to bring about any change in the plot but when I got to the pier one element in the play was very different. The face was still the face of Kevin but, as he opened the door of my car, the eyes were the eyes of Fan–An. Without thinking, I dropped a morsel to the floor.

"Would you like to go for a sail?' I asked.

"O, I'd love to," he said with a smile that gave him back his own eyes, and he ran to untie the inflatable.

"Not so fast, Kevin," I called after him, and got out of my car. "You will have to get permission." I caught up with him at the inflatable. "I don't want to be reported to the bishop for kidnapping," I said. "Who are you staying with?"

"My aunt Catherine. She is my grand aunt, really, but I call her my aunt."

"I see. And what is the rest of her name?"

"Burke."

"Burke?!"

"Yes, Burke. Catherine Burke."

If the butterfly that came floating towards us had lost its navigational aids and brushed against me, I would have fallen over. The plot had gone berserk.

"Run up," I said, "and ask her if you may go sailing with me. Tell her I have a buoyancy jacket in the boat."

"Yes, right".

"And if she says yes, change into jeans and bring a sweater."

"Yes, right" he said again and ran off to the village as if a tidal wave was after him.

I didn't expect him back in sweater and jeans. As sure as the plastic bag was in the coffin, as sure as aunt Catherine's letter was on file in the bishop's house she would say no. I had mixed feelings about that, disappointment for the boy but relief for myself: I could continue on my solitary track with a clear conscience.

I lugged the dinghy down the steps at the side of the pier and plopped it into the water; then I sat on one of the upper steps to wait for Catherine Burke's decision. It was on or about low tide.

A Dublin man by the name of Breslin who stayed in Gobnait O' Brien's guesthouse every summer and who knew my weakness for sailing came down the pier road towards me.

"Thinking of going sailing, Father?" he called.

"Yes. I am, Mr Breslin. I'm just waiting at present."

"For the tide to come in, is it?"

"Ah no, there is plenty depth where my boat is. I suppose I could say I am waiting for one or other of two things: either a boy running down the road or a coffin floating down the creek."

His head flew back as if something a million times heavier than a Red Admiral hit him.

"A coffin floating down the creek?"

"A very light coffin", I explained.

"A very light coffin", he repeated incredulously.

"Are you a betting man, Mr Breslin?"

"Well, yes, I have a flutter from time to time."

"I'll give you five to one on the boy, but only even money on the coffin."

"Even money on the coffin," he parroted.

"Is that what you are going to take?"

"No. No. No. I was just repeating what you said."

"I see."

I could imagine the construction that he would put on this conversation when he got back to Gobnait's: a definite visit to Florrie's would figure largely in the interpretation!

He gave me a sideways glance that spelled a well known brand of whiskey. He walked to the edge of the pier and then turned to go back up the road again. As he passed, he said, humouring my tipsy condition, "There is no sign of either yet, that I can see." Lord, how I love starting hares. I smiled happily to myself as he stalked away to find Gobnait.

He was the sorry man, was Mr. Breslin. He could have made the price of a good many drinks in Florrie's, if he had put a fiver on the boy. At the turn of the road, from where he had a view that I hadn't he swivelled and called loudly, "There's a boy running."

"No coffin floating?" I enquired at the top of my voice.

"No coffin floating," he shouted back decisively.

I stood up. A minute later, Kevin came into view around the corner and he waved the sweater in triumph over his head. It is possible, I told myself, to be infinitely happy in this life, whatever the theologians might say!

In another minute he was at the top of the steps, smiling like his face was one huge blister of joy.

"She said I could!"

"Good. Did she say anything else?"

"She said to take no chances, that boats are dangerous."

"Just like women," I said, putting a shot intended for Catherine over his head. I led the way down the steps. "And the smaller they are, the more dangerous they are", I said over my shoulder.

"The boats or the women?" The lad was sharp, thank God. A dullard in a boat is worse than scurvy.

"The boats," I answered, "especially this one." The inflatable spun like a child's toy in a running bath when I unhitched it. "In you get. Sit dead centre. Another time I'll show you how to row."

"Does that mean you will take me again?" Did I say that boy was sharp?

"That all depends on whether you obey the captain's orders."

"Aye, aye, sir," he responded with real fervour. It was much closer to film than to reality and the first reel was a lark. In his own mind he joined ship as crew, not as a passenger. Orders he craved, so orders I gave when we got into the cockpit of "Lú na Lon."

"What is the first thing you have seen me doing when I come aboard?"

"You open up the cabin."

"Right. And then?"

"You lower that steel thing over our heads."

"The boom."

"You lower the boom so that you can push the bottom of the sail. . . ."

"So that I can thread the foot of the mainsail along the groove"

"So that you can thread the foot of the mainsail along the groove."

"Right. That is your first job, Kevin. Lower the boom. What is holding it up?"

"A rope from the end of the boom to the top of the mast."

"Do you notice anything different about it from the other ropes?"

"It's much thinner."

"Right. Get up there on the deck to where the mast is stepped. See where I mean? Look for a fitting called a cleat."

"A cleat."

"It has two horns on it like a buffalo's. A very tiny buffalo, of course."

"Of course." He smiled.

"There are ropes of all kinds made fast around it. They are called halyards."

"Halyards."

"Finger around for the thinnest one. That's the one you are looking for. It is the halyard for the topping lift."

"The halyard. The topping lift. The cleat. The boom. The groove. This is like the first day in school."

"It is the first day in school, the oldest school in the world. And the best. So you find that halyard. Loosen it. Lower the boom nice and gently. And make the halyard fast again just as you found it. Right?"

"Aye, aye, sir".

Needless to say I would have done it in a tenth of the time myself. However, speed isn't what matters in school, but interest, zest, an enthusiastic pupil and I daresay a teacher who is keen to impart his knowledge. I could feel sap that had been buried in my sailing roots for years flowing up to the tip of my tongue.

I gave him some other jobs to do as well on that first day, jobs that didn't involve him too much in further lessons on technical terms, such as pulling the sails out of the sailbags, fitting the battens into the pockets of the mainsail — "so she will have a flat tummy on her, Kevin" — connecting the fuel tank to the outboard engine and fixing the compass to the bracket. Then when I had the inflatable attached to the mooring buoy and the mainsail hoisted and flapping furiously with frustration, I said to him "I am eager to go, Kevin. You are eager to go. And the boat is simply bursting to go. So what is stopping us?"

"The mooring rope."

"Right. It is like a prison officer. It has the boat in jail. Would you like to be the one to release it from jail and set it free?"

"I sure would, Captain."

"Right, then. Get up on the foredeck. Untie the rope from the big steel cleat. Do you remember that word?"

"I do."

"But hold on to the rope. Lift it up out of the fitting at the bow, called the fairlead."

"The fairlead."

"But hold on to the rope. Then when you hear me saying 'Let go, for'ard', let go."

"Aye, aye, sir."

He had a little trouble with my assurance-double-sure knots at the cleat but no problem with the fairlead. Then he angled his body like a one-man tug-of-war team as he took the strain of the boat and the wind.

"All set for'ard?"

"Aye, aye, sir."

'Let go for'ard." I called.

"Let gone, sir," he responded which was a nautical expression never heard before in creek, haven, harbour or ocean, and he tossed the rope into the air like something you would see in the Highland games. That is what I always lacked on that boat up to that moment, a touch of theatre.

I put the helm hard over, let the mainsheets run and turned her stern to wind and to village.

"Come on down to the cockpit now, Kevin, but he careful how you tread."

He sat beside me and asked an obvious question but he asked it with such cheeky familiarity that clearly all the ice on his side of the basin had been broken. "The cockpit, Captain. Is this where we fight?"

"Any fighting," I answered "is mutiny, and the mutineer goes overboard without his buoyancy jacket."

"You're gas," he said, which was the nicest compliment I had received all year.

We sailed down the creek with the arrogance of a summer swan and the image must have put poetry into my mind because the next thing I found myself doing was quoting out loud from my favourite poem.

"I must go down to the seas again, to the lonely sea and the sky."

"And all I ask," the lad next to me chimed in and I nearly gybed the boat with the shock,

"is a tall ship and a star to steer her by."

My line next. "And the wheel's kick and the wind's song and the white sails shaking"

And he finished it. "And the grey mist on the sea's face and a grey dawn breaking."

"Gosh, Kevin. Where did you learn that?"

"In school in Bedford."

'And do you know who wrote it?"

"I do. He was John Masefield. He was the poet laureate."

It was a meeting of minds.

I looked shorewards to see where precisely we were so as to marry the moment with a landmark, and we were passing Cláirseach, a cliff face that was given that name a thousand years before because it was shaped like a harp. No other accompaniment could have been so fitting for the duet.

During the next fortnight, if I got my work done in the mornings and if the afternoons celebrated the fact with sun and breeze we went to sea together. He learnt to row and for the first time in my boating life I really did feel like a skipper as I stretched in the stern of the inflatable and he sat high and took the paddles. He got faster at the preparatory jobs aboard "Lú na Lon" and so I gradually added to his schedule and I remember one day in particular when I let him bend on the mainsail all by himself and he turned to me and said "It's not so long since I could hardly say 'thread the foot of the mainsail along the groove of the boom' and now I have actually done it." That added the satisfied feeling of a teacher in front of a class to the cosy feeling of a skipper at the tail of a dinghy.

Day by day I was throwing overboard into the creek items of bitter baggage such as his grandaunt's letter of complaint about me on file in the bishop's house, and the look in Sarah's doctor-drugged eyes as she sat in the back of the Garda car, and the night Gobnait called me a hypocrite and the day Killer emptied his pistol into the blowhole of the whale and the plastic bags of small change on O'Donnell's insulting table.

Out at sea I advanced his cadetship from handling the jib to handling the mainsail and from handling the mainsail to handling jib and main together. The next bit of headway after that was when he took the tiller for the first time while I managed the sails: it was a moment I shall never forget.

"Take the tiller, Kevin."

"Are you sure, Captain?"

"Yes, I'm sure, Kevin."

He plunged his hands quickly over the side into the lustral water, rubbed them up and down the legs of his jeans and looked at them appraisingly. Satisfied, he took the tiller with both hands.

'Steady as she goes, Captain," I told him.

"O, wow," he exclaimed. Whoever said that a slangword cannot be poetic?

The moment reminded me of the first time I took a chalice in both of my hands and I had his very feelings of doubt, unworthiness, desire and awe.

The apogee of his sailing excitement, when he was at the furthest from this dull terrestrial world, was reached on Tuesday 20th of August. It is recorded in the log as follows: —

Tuesday 20th August. "There's no wind out there, is there, Father?" Tom the Traveller said to me at the pier.

"No," I answered, "but I'll tell you what. When I get out there, I shall pray for some, and if God doesn't oblige, I shall try the give-us-game."

"The give-us-game. What's that?"

"Ah, it's a secret formula known only to a few like myself and Kevin here. It never fails."

When we got out into the bay, the sea had a gumsy look about it: no teeth at all. We went down along the Ballyanglin shore at the rate of about 1 knot. The clothes on McDermott's line were as lifeless as if the sky was sketching paper and the clothes were spots of paint on it. We prayed. No response from the Lord of the winds. "We will have to play the give-us-game, Kevin," I said.

"Give us a one, a one, a one, a one," we shouted. "Give as a two, a two, a two, a two." "Give us a three, a three, a three, a three." A force one would be a relief. A force two would be a gift. A force three would be a miracle. We did it again and again and again and again. The McDermott children came running to the backdoor, followed by their mother. I guessed what she was thinking: that priest is gone completely out of his mind. It didn't worry me what she thought: we continued with the give-us-game and we hit the jackpot. We got a one, a two, and a three.

The McDermott washing began to dance like Russians, the cloud cover rolled back as quickly as the sunroof of a car and the bay changed colour to a deep blue.

We headed for the Derryregan shore, cutting between Ballymackus Point and Carraig Dhiarmada; then a run to Sam's Island. At the eastern tip there was a seal like a harbour master watching us nervously; finally he lost his nerve when he decided that this chattering white monster was coming to get him, and he slid into the water to safety.

From there it was a broad reach to the Emperor, four miles of open water in a wind that should have been bottled, it was so delicious.

"Now, Kevin," I said, "let's see what you're made of. Take the tiller. Take the jib sheets. Take the main. Take the boat. One eye ahead for the Emperor. The other up aloft for the bend of the sail."

He took my place and began to sail "Lú na Lon" impeccably by the flutter of the burgee and the curl of the tongue protruding between his teeth. Then, as I sat in the lee of the cabin from where I could give no help but encouragement I saw out of the corner of my eye Bryce's yacht rounding Ballymackus Point with a great red and white spinnaker like bubble gum in its mouth. She too was heading for the Emperor by the looks of it. She was a flyer, everybody said.

"Do you see the 'Topaz', Kevin?"

"Yes, I do," he answered with a quick swivel of his head.

"Beat her to the Emperor and I'll crown you Emperor Kevin the First", I said. "Go, man, go."

We had a good headstart, of course, but Bryce's boat had ten feet on the waterline more than we had and he had a spinnaker pulling her like a tug boat. All we had were a priest's prayers and a boy's pounding heart. They pushed us — how they pushed us, as they began to close: they knew they were in a race as well — but we crossed the gorgeous imaginary line between the Emperor Rock and Seal Island one minute and fifty three seconds ahead of them.

"O, wow!" he hollered and he hit the tiller a mighty whack on the back.

"You're one hell of a sailor, Kevin", I said leaving my post, and, knowing that his back wasn't as tough as larch, I gave him a gentler pat on the back. "And you did it all by yourself."

That is where the entry in the log ends; I only wish to add that I have never seen a photograph of Sir Francis Chichester, aged twelve, at the tiller of his uncle's boat but if one was taken, then he must have looked in it the way Kevin looked when we crossed the finish line.

It was an astonishing business, really, this partnership of ours. It was as if a stray cat came to the back door and found it locked in his face time after time; then he was let into the kitchen for a saucer of milk; then he stretched himself in the hall between the kitchen and the living room; and he finished up sitting in the fireside chair.

* * *

The following is a true account of what happened on the mountain. It is, literally, the whole truth and nothing but the truth.

Wednesday was flat calm: there wasn't enough wind to stir a balloon. Thursday was flat calm: Liam Barrett, home on holidays from Wonthaggi, Victoria, a man who would have reshaped the first article of the Creed to make it read "I believe in Fishing, my God almighty" came in from the fishing grounds west of Carraig Aonair and said he had never seen flatter water between there and Australia. Friday was flat calm: if you chanted "give us a one, a one, a one, a one," "give us a two, a two, a two, a two" all the way to "give us a million, a million, a million, a million" you wouldn't have got even one of the letters of a zephyr in response.

The truth is that Ireland was steaming in the trough of a heatwave; temperatures were in the mid twenties; and nobody could understand how June could have leapt backwards on the calendar to the end of August or how Spain could have leapt twenty degrees northwards to fifty five degrees of latitude.

On Wednesday I told Kevin that it would be pointless to go out sailing that day. On Thursday I told him that it would be pointless to go out sailing any day until the foreign weather, the high pressure area which was stationary over Ireland, left our shores and allowed our native weather to come back in from the Atlantic. On Friday I woke up to another sea as smooth as a coffeetable book and I said to myself "I'll go and climb Slieve Mhuire."

Why it was called Mary's Mountain nobody was ever able to explain to me. Mary hadn't appeared there, and, more to the point, no mountebank ever came down the mountain claiming to have seen her in her blue mantle drifting along its slopes in a holy haze. It may have had something to do with its statue-like appearance: from the foot, as you looked up, it had the shape, very roughly speaking, of the chest and head of a human being; half way up, the two sides angled inwards and levelled off in a plateau like shoulders, and out of this plateau rose the summit in the shape of a veiled head. An icon of Our Lady in rock, grass and heather.

The older people called it August mountain because the tradition, when they were growing up, was to climb it during the month of August, especially around the feast of the Assumption. I had done the climb once but I hadn't met any fellow pilgrims; perhaps their spirit was willing but the weather was weak. But in the sort of weather we were now having, pleasure would pull the penitential rags off any pilgrim's back and it would be, in the encouraging words of the local guidebook, "a gentle stroll to the top." Slieve Mhuire it must be in the afternoon.

With enough done throughout the morning to solve a priest-climber's conscience, I rooted out my rucksack after lunch and I tossed a pair of sunglasses, binoculars, a towel, an orange and a tube of sunblock cream into it. Then I sat into my car and I drove to the village, intending to turn left at Gobnait O' Brien's corner and motor towards Hilltown from where I would pick up a byroad that would come to a sudden death in a collision with Mary's mountain.

At the very last moment I decided to go down to the pier to make sure that Kevin wasn't waiting for a breeze that would never blow. It was a fatal decision. There he was, sitting on the top step, wearing a thick sailing sweater and jeans on the warmest day of the year, and probably half way on the count to the million. He came to the open window of the car.

"Kevin! What are you doing here?"

"I thought there might be a change."

"Ah, no. The fellow on the 1 o'clock news said it would be flat calm in all sea areas with temperatures soaring to 26. You would be a lot better off to get your auntie's bike and go to Sandy Cove for a swim."

"I suppose so. Where are you going yourself, Father?"

"I am heading for Slieve Mhuire. That's Irish for Mary's Mountain."

"Where's that?"

"It's in the neighbouring parish, about six miles to the north of Hilltown in very wild country."

"Sounds exciting."

"Ah no, not really. A lot of hard work getting up and some tricky work getting down. I don't think it would appeal to you. There's no one for you to race up there."

"Except yourself, Father."

"Does that mean you want to come?"

"Would you have me?"

"O, I'd have you alright. I just don't want you to fall into a hole marked "Boredom" half way up, because I really want to get up to the summit. It's a very old custom in these parts for people to climb up there during August to honour Our Lady."

"Oh! Would I have to say a lot of prayers?"

"No, no. When you'd get up there you would be just under the ceiling of heaven and that would be a prayer in itself."

"Sounds good to me. When do we start?"

"Now, right away. But you will have to get your auntie's permission."

"Not again, surely".

"Yes again, surely. There's a world of difference between sea and mountain".

"All right so, I'll ask her." He sat in and I shot up the road to the village and parked outside the bungalow with the new brass plate saying "Chicago."

"What's the name of it again?"

"Slieve Mhuire."

"Slieve Mhuire."

"That's right. I bet she was up there herself when she was young."

"Auntie Catherine on top of a mountain! You must be joking."

"When she was young, I said, when she was young." He went into the Windy City chuckling like a transcontinental express.

I had never been in there myself since she took up residence: my policy with salmon nets was to avoid them, because if you got entangled in them you could get dismasted. She probably thought that my befriending of her grandnephew was a bit of scaffolding from which I hoped to dismantle her hostility, but it wasn't. It was a small sailing shed that was off limits to her, no more.

Kevin came out of the house minus the sweater but wearing a smile. "She said yes." I stopped the car again outside Hugh Kelleher's shop and gave him some money to buy whatever he thought his mouth might need for the climb, only reminding him, "Don't get anything that will melt" and he returned with a bag of crisps, a packet of biscuits and a can of Coke. When these items joined my mountain aids in the rucksack we were ready for road.

About forty minutes later we were at the foot of Slieve Mhuire, not sure whether what we were about to do was a pilgrimage, a poor substitute for a sail or sheer lunacy in that heat. Away with us anyhow, myself the less burdened of the two because Kevin insisted on strapping the rucksack on himself in the belief that it conferred mountaineer status on him.

Two things happened on the way up that now take precedence in my mind over the stops "to admire the scenery"; over the rhino that turned out to be a rock; over the "watch out below" calls when whoever was leading dislodged some sounding shale; and over the kestrel who was building an eleven arch bridge with quick sweeps of arches and a steady hovering of piers in his hunt for mice and beetles.

The first of the two was the last thing I wanted to hear on the mountain; it was the snap of gunshots. We both stopped in our stride as if the bullets had whistled over our own heads. There were two shots in quick succession; I hoped that that meant that the gunman had missed with the first and fired wildly with the second. If the mountain was a place of pilgrimage, then the shooting was an act of sacrilege. I felt a heat inside my head more intense than the heat of the sun on my back.

"Get out the binoculars, Kevin." He handed me the Nikon and I swept the flanks of the mountain with it right and left, but, because of the abundant cover at that lower level and because the echoes were leading my eyes astray in a half dozen different directions, I couldn't pick out the man who, I felt certain, had pulled the trigger. It had to be Killer himself: who else would throw blood at the August sun?

Kevin noticed my agitation. "What's wrong, Father?"

"The presence of that gunman," I answered. "That's what's wrong. I love animals and birds. I hate killers, and I'm inclined to think that the man with the gun up there, down there, or wherever he is lurking is the killer I hate the most."

"Do I know him?"

"No, you don't and I hope you never will."

"What's his name?"

"His name is Miller. He is the Garda sergeant in Hilltown."

"I know him!"

"You do?"

"Yes. I have met him in Auntie Catherine's house twice since I arrived for my holidays." "Well, I hope he didn't invite you to Slieve Mhuire to shoot foxes."

"No, he didn't".

"I'm glad. That man's only pleasure in life is in taking life. To him hares and rabbits and seals and magpies are only targets on a range finder." I paused, "Don't laugh now, Kevin, but I am in his sights as well."

"You?"

"I don't mean he will shoot me like a fox or a pheasant, but he is definitely out to get me. He told me as much."

"Why is that?"

"Because I oppose him every way I can. Here," I said handing him the binoculars, "your eyes are sharper than mine. See if you can spot a man with a gun picking his steps, or picking his next target or picking up the body of his last target."

"No," he said, after sweeping the entire area, east and west. "I can't see anything at all, on the ground, or in the air, either. Do you suppose he shot at the kestrel?"

"He could have. It's an easy target. Stationary. Wings spread."

"He wouldn't though, as a sergeant, would he? I mean hawks are protected, aren't they?"

"Choughs are protected as well, and he shot them. That man would shoot at the angel Gabriel hovering over Nazareth."

"There's no sign of the kestrel now, anyhow. There's nothing moving that I can see except the stream."

We put Miller out of our mids and we started moving again ourselves. There were no more shots, no more blood on the sun's face, but there was a lot of perspiration on our two faces as we tackled the steepest part of the climb, just short of the plateau and parallel to the cascade of water. Kevin was the first to get over the ridge, and from fifty or sixty feet below I could hear his joyous exclamation, "O, wow!"

The object of his excitement was the tarn in the hollow where the plateau ended and the final ascent began. There are lakes that are beautiful because of the trees that cushion the shore line, and there are lakes that are beautiful because of the islands that turtle the surface, but this little lake was beautiful in the very essence of its being: it was a stretch of untreed, un-islanded, untrammelled, utterly focussed water. Nowhere was it more than six feet deep; its gravel bed was laid like a mosaic; where it filled, there was a tumble of water; where it emptied, there was a slide; and it was as clear as it was on the day of creation. If water could be changed into music, this water would be Schubert.

But boys aren't interested in mosaics, Genesis, or Schubert and when Kevin saw the tarn he saw only one thing: a means of cooling off. He wriggled out of the rucksack, letting it slide to the ground, and there was a stain on his shirt that would have done credit to a tv explorer.

"Can I go in?" he asked.

"How do you mean?"

"For a swim."

"Ah, I don't know, Kevin."

"Please!"

'You're too hot; you could get a chill".

"The way I am now I could explode".

"No, I think we should carry on. If we make a long halt here, we just won't get the drive back. You want to make the summit, don't you?"

"O yes, I do".

"If you go kicking your legs in the lake they certainly won't carry you to the top. You know that."

"Alright, so," he said, but the only cloud in the entire day moved over his face.

"Maybe on the way down, if we come down the same way."

I slipped on the rucksack and he made no effort to dispossess me, and so with myself leading we made it up the shiny veil on Our Lady's head until we stood where the halo should have been.

He recovered his good humour quickly, I am glad to say — pouters do not make for pleasant company — especially as he swivelled in every direction taking in lower hills, higher mountains, glens as small as open boats, boats as small as waterbugs, smudges of towns near and far, and the sea like a huge silver rim around the wheel of the world.

I pointed him, and he pointed the binoculars at our sailing area. The stretch of countryside between us and it swallowed up some of our tacking targets and some of our reaching marks, but Sam's Island was still an island and Carraig Aonair was very explicit about the meaning of its Irish name. My own fingers got fidgety, and I wondered out loud why he was so long looking so steadily at one stretch of sea. The explanation when it came was what Shakespeare had in mind when he spoke about boy eternal: Kevin said "I am looking at the finishing line between the Emperor and Seal Island!"

However, for much of the mountain top time he kept looking directly below him at the tarn rather than outwards at the "panoramic view," to use our local auctioneer's favourite marketing phrase.

"Has it a name?" he asked.

"I suppose it has," I answered. "Everything in Ireland has a name. I can look it up for you in the ordnance map."

"No, don't", he said. "We shall give it a name ourselves."

"What do you suggest? What does it look like?"

"From here it looks like. . . . it looks like. . . . it looks like. . . . an eye!"

"Yes, it does. But whose eye?"

"Mary's eye!"

Brilliant. I agreed to blot out the name on my ordnance map and write in his instead. Then he asked, "What's that in Irish?" Thank heavens, he didn't set me a sterner test, because my Irish was getting rustier by the winter.

"Súil Mhuire," I said.

"Súil Mhuire," he repeated. "That's it."

We had a little difficulty about the theological implications of Mary in heaven after her assumption with only one eye, but I solved it by saying to my own and to his untheological satisfaction that she left one eye on earth looking up for mercy and she had the other one in heaven looking down in love.

That question settled, I asked him would he now have his crisps, biscuits and hot Coke, but he said he wouldn't: he didn't like hot Coke but he knew how to cool it.

"How?"

"By putting it under the little waterfall at Súil Mhuire lake."

"Ah, but, Kevin," I said, "there's a much easier way down than that way."

"No," he answered. "I want to christen the lake. . . . please!"

I hesitated. It was the most vital moment of the day. There was a gap in time while I scrabbled about in my brain for an incontestable reason for not going down the way we had come up, and he went through the gap with the weirdest, most irrelevant, most Lewis Carrollish argument I had ever heard.

"You should do the same as the Duke of York," he contended.

"What did the Duke of York do, for heaven's sake?"

"He led his army up the hill
and then he led them down again!"

My defenses crumbled in the laughter, and before I could change my mind he went slithering down the slope as fast as the cascade, the rucksack swinging merrily in the air.

When I got down to the tarn, trying to figure out with every heel I planted on the way down how it was I had been outmanoeuvred, he was on his face and hands placing his can of Coke into the cooler."Did you christen it yet?" I asked.

"No, not yet. I was waiting for you."

"Go ahead, so."

He came around to where I was standing on the bank, and bent down with his right hand hollowed in a ladle shape. He scooped up a fill of water in it, and said aloud, "Súil Mhuire, I baptise you in the name of Father Laide and Kevin Warren," while flinging the water west, south and east in tatters of brightness.

"Amen," I answered and I hope the Lord has forgiven me. No blasphemy was intended.

"Now we'll have the grub," I announced, thinking sadly of my lone orange in the rucksack.

"Never eat before swimming," he countered, wagging a dripping finger at me.

"Who said anything about swimming?"

"You did. You said I could go for a swim on the way down." Another debate had started and I already knew how it would finish. "I'm still hot but I'm not lighting so there's no danger I'll get a chill".

"But you have no togs, Kevin," I put in, using what I thought would be the strongest possible argument, the one based on convention.

"That's alright. It isn't Sandy Cove so who is going to see me?"

"I will, for one," I said.

"No, you won't. You won't look, sure you won't?"

"No. I won't". Without realising it, my flank had been turned again. "But I can't go away, either: I don't want you to drown, you know, however obstinate you are."

He would make the world's best player of snap: no matter how quick I was, he was always quicker. "I have a better idea," he said. "The two of us will go swimming, so you'll be near but you won't be looking!"

While this debate was ebbing and flowing I was gazing at the tarn: there was nothing to rival it for looks. It was as clear as glass, except for a slight glassmaker's fault down the middle of the pane where the current showed. And truly as I gazed, I forgot about Schubert and mosaics and Genesis and even Mary's eye itself, and all that I could see was what Kevin had seen an hour before: a means of cooling off. Any way, how could I ever have thought I could win an argument against a boy who had virtually pulled off "Lú na Lon" the notice that said "Skipper only."

"Alright so," I agreed, worsted in the battle of words. "That's what we'll do."

"Whoopee," he chortled in triumph.

"When you say swim, Kevin, you really mean swim, do you?"

"O, yes, I learnt in the pool in Bedford."

"Well, you have the advantage over me so," I confessed. "I can only do a few strokes. I'm a wader, more than a swimmer. You'll be a submarine. I'll be more like an oilrig, showing above and submerged below."

"You're gas, Father Brendan." He called me gas before but this was the first time he called me Brendan. "Where do you get the ideas from? Don't worry, my sub will not attack your rig."

"And to make doubly sure, let you go down to the far end, and I'll stay here. And there's a towel for you when you come out," I said as I pulled the towel out of the rucksack and draped it around his neck.

"Did you know all the time we were going to go swimming?" he asked in flattering amazement.

"Ah, not at all, Kevin, for goodness sake. I'm not that clever. When I put it in the rucksack I had no notion of meeting up with you. I had it in case I'd bathe my sore feet on the way down."

"But you need it for yourself".

"No, you have it. I'll use my vest. It won't be the first time."

"See you so," he said. "No, I mean I won't see you so. I mean I'll see you later."

That brain of his was really active, and his limbs too. By the time I had the double knots untied on my shoes — my policy of taking no chances with knots must have had something to do with the dread of seeing the jib halyard racing to the masthead minus the jib — and my socks pulled off and my shirt lifted over my head, the tarn at the other end was sounding with arms and legs. So I shed the rest of my gear in a two-handed hurry and slipped into the modesty of four feet of water. I did my pathetic dog paddle with my head higher and my legs lower than any dog had ever carried them in water, followed by a poor imitation on my back of a sandboat loaded to the gunwale and labouring in the current, and I wondered what in God's name I was doing trying to swim when I couldn't. So I took to walking instead and I sauntered from one bank to the other, looking down through the clear water at the shiny pebbles that quickly became the tesserae of the baths of Caracalla on a day in Rome when everyone except one man and one boy were at the naval fight in the flooded Colosseum.

Only once did I break my word to Kevin, and I would need to have been an Irish monk in the twelfth and final stage of mortification not to have done so. He came with an eager overarm stroke, considerably more than halfway up the tarn. 'The submarine is going to attack the oilrig,' I thought. But he must suddenly have realised that he had strayed into alien waters because he did a dolphin roll and kick that made for compulsive viewing. If it was really pulling up he was, it was the only braking manoeuvre I have ever witnessed that looked beautiful, but I rather think he was showing off.

I waited in the water with my back to the bank until I saw him reaching for the towel and scrambling out at the other end, and I lifted myself out by the palms of my hands at the very same time. Then he faced west and I faced east, but he had the advantage over me of pistoning hands and an absorbent towel, so I had to say "No, I'm not" when he called "Are you ready, Father?" Three minutes later, with all my gear minus the sopping vest on me again I hailed him and he came running up the bank with the look of someone who has seen a vision — and it definitely wasn't me!

"You swim really well, Kevin." I was going to add, "You are quite a performer" but I checked myself and instead I asked "What did you think of it?" I shouldn't have, because in reply I got a whole list of what lexicographers call informal words: "Fantastic," he said. "Fab. Smashing. Unreal."

"But what do you think Our Lady thought of it?" I asked, pulling his leg.

"How do you mean?"

"I mean 'tis her eye, isn't it?"

"Yes."

"I wasn't much trouble to her, I stayed here in the corner of her eye, just a tiny speck of dust, but you were moving all over her iris like some sort of white insect."

"Insect! What a way to insult your second-in-command," and then he came up with the perfect parry as usual. "She didn't blink at all anyhow," he said.

"That's true, so are you ready for the picnic now?"

"I sure am," he said.

He dredged up his Coke from under the little waterfall — not so little either, because when a dragonfly hovered over it, it became Niagara with a helicopter — and he sat on the bank opposite me with the rucksack in between us. My warm orange couldn't compare with his cooled Coke, but I didn't do too badly. I declined a share of the crisps — "they affect my innards almost as badly as Sergeant Miller," I told him — but I blunted my mountain hunger with a good many of his biscuits.

While we were eating I studied his face for the very first time, I think, since I met him. Aboard the boat we were always side by side sitting high, our backs braced against the wind, our feet in the well, and our eyes either on the set of the sails or on the next gust purpling the water, neither the time nor the place for the study of faces.

But now I began to look at him like a portrait artist before he settles to work. I didn't like his fringe: it was cut too high. His cheek bones were too prominent: they gave him a somewhat oriental look. I approved of his ears: they were small and shaped like a seashell I had seen in some book. But the finest features he had were his eyes: like the cascade jumping down from Súil Mhuire every smile that doused his face had its source in his eyes. They were expressive, they were luminous, there was awareness in the front of them and intelligence at the back of them. They had what St. John in a different context altogether called the light of life. In between biscuits he sensed my gaze. "What are you looking at, Father?" he asked shyly. And the only answer I could think of was the famous phrase from the most famous film of them all. "Well, in 'Casablanca'" I said, "Humphrey Bogart had a saying that went "here's looking at you, kid." So with me it was a case of "There's looking at you, kid". I'm not sure that he got the gist of my convoluted think-ing. In any case it was time to stop looking at everything except the watch, and we stirred ourselves to go home.

Two snatches of conversation brought the day to an end.

The first was when we got down from the mountain and back into the car. I attempted what tour operators call an evaluation and I regard it as an important item in my defence. Turning to Kevin I said to him, "Consider these five experiences we had to-day: the climb up the mountain, the lake, the view from the top, the swim and the descent, and give each of them a mark from one point to five, but without giving the same mark to any two of them. To which of the five would you give one point?"

"Coming down," he answered.

"To which would you give two points?"

"Going up," he said, and then he asked "What are the three left?"

"The swim,, the view and the lake."

"O, yes."

"To which would you give three points?"

"The view from the top."

"To which would you give four points?"

"Mary's Eye lake."

It wasn't necessary to ask the final question but I asked it, because I felt that he wanted to be asked: "And to which would you give the five points?"

"The swim" he answered, and he added, "Super."

The second bit of conversation that I remember took place just as we were arriving back in Kilbroney village.

"How long more have you left, Kevin?"

"I am going back next Thursday. Worse luck."

"Ah, well, there are a few days left. I am going to be busy all day tomorrow and all day on Sunday, so no sailing either day. But if the weather wakes up from its slumbers we'll go sailing on Monday. Would you like that?"

"O yes, Captain, I sure would." When the subject shifted from mountain to sea, he gave me back my brass and braid.

I brought the car to a stop outside "Chicago".

"See you on Monday, then."

"Monday it will be, Captain. Over and out."

Chapter 9

THE TOWEL

Monday came. When I pulled back the curtains, the first things I saw were the puffy white clouds. Good. The weather had woken up and it was throwing the pillows at the sun. The breeze was from the west, perfect for a reach to Carraig Aonair and for what I used to call the man on stilts, two long legs and two short legs coming home.

I wasted no time on lunch because I figured that Kevin wouldn't. A bowl of tomato soup and a tub of yogurt throttled my appetite and I drove to the pier. But there was no Kevin. I sat on the steps and read my breviary, the psalmist doing his regular job of filling in the time for me, but at the end of it there was still no Kevin. I went aboard and made all preparations in the firm belief that he would arrive in time for the command "Let go, for'ard," but he didn't come running down the pier road wheeling his sweater in greeting. "I expect that witch Catherine has marched him off to meet her hobgoblins of cousins now that the time is running short," I said to myself, and I sailed around the lone rock all alone.

Tuesday came. The pillows had become bolsters, there was a fresher breeze and an even more insistent reason for winking back at the light on Carraig Aonair but no Kevin came to make it two winks to the light house's one. "Gosh, I hope he hasn't got a chill from that swim in Súil Mhuire," I worried and I got tired of the sail to Carraig Aonair long before its exclamation mark became a mighty tower.

Wednesday came. The sky was advertising old fashioned featherbed mattresses rather than pillows and bolsters, the westerly was coming from further out in the Atlantic and the day was made for a litany of "O, wows." I went to the pier expecting for sure that the inflatable would already be giddy on the water waiting to ferry the skipper out to the barque that the little coastal cruiser had now become. But it wasn't, so I sat down as before on the steps with the breviary in my hands and a great lack of piety in my mind.

I kept lifting my head to look at the pier road instead of keeping it down to follow the route to heaven and I wondered at the end of each psalm whether I should read through another one before abandoning my wait for Kevin. Then psalm 102, the next one along, became real on the page, not just a reading: — "Hear my prayer, O Lord, and let my cry come to you. Do not hide your face from me at this anxious time but bend your ear to me and give me a speedy answer. The day is drifting away like smoke and my heart is wilting like grass under a blazing sun. My spirit is restless and I am like a lonely bird on the housetop."

That final sentence settled the issue: the lonely bird flew down from the housetop and shut the book with a flick of its beak. I got into the car and drove to Catherine Burke's bungalow. I rang the doorbell hoping that the God of psalm 102 would answer it.

Catherine opened the door. She was like a garden from the neck down and a gorgon from the neck up.

"Yes?" she said. No "hello." No "welcome." No "Father." Just "yes?" It was a bad beginning.

"Is Kevin sick, Mrs Burke?" I asked.

"I know who is sick," was her answer. I took that to be an oblique reference to the opening of the coffin, and as it was the first time we were exchanging words since she heard from Gobnait about the affair, I wasn't too surprised that her first words were sarcastic.

I tried again. "Has Kevin a chill, Mrs Burke?"

She gave no answer except a look that defined the word "chill," a look that was shaped by a March wind off Lake Michigan rather than an August breeze in Kilbroney.

I made a third try. "Will Kevin be coming sailing, Mrs Burke?"

"No, he won't," she answered, very bluntly. I felt a clip on the side of my head and then I walked into a big punch.

"Why is that?"

"Because he has gone back to England."

"Oh!" was all I could say until my senses cleared. "I thought Thursday was the day".

"The thought made a fool of you," she hissed, using a demeaning expression used by millions of children in billions of rows.

"He never said goodbye." My words came almost with a sob.

"He should never have said hello."

I was floundering utterly. "Never have said hello?" I repeated mechanically.

"No," she said firmly.

"Why?" I asked.

"You are not a fit companion for him, that's why."

"In what way?"

"You haven't heard?"

"Heard what? I've heard nothing".

"You will, Father, you will." This time she used the 'Father' mode of address but she used it in the disparaging sense in which gangsters say 'brother' when they are issuing a death threat — "you will, brother, you will."

And she shut the door on my face, bang, just like that. It was only the second time that happened to me in my fifteen years as a priest, and the first time in Kilbroney.

The lake Michigan wind which she stirred up blew all afternoon and I didn't go out in my boat. A man might read the breviary with distractions and hope that God wouldn't punish him, but there was no chance that he could sail a boat with distractions and hope to come home with all his gear intact.

What was I to make of the conversation? I sat in the garden thinking about it for a long time. Her key charge was that I wasn't a fit companion for Kevin. In what way? She had allowed him to go sailing with me eight or nine times so the unfitness couldn't have had anything to do with the white cloud flying and the flung spray and the blown spume and the sea gulls crying. Therefore the reason had to lie somewhere between the parked car and the top of the mountain.

The first thing I thought of was the popular belief that mountain lakes were bottomless, that they went down as far into the bowels of the earth as the mountain itself rose above sea level. Could my unfitness, then, be linked to a criminal negligence in permitting the boy to swim in those perilous waters?

The second possible reason for her attack on me was my attack on Miller. Stephen her husband had been a friend of Miller's. The sergeant used to visit them in Kilbroney twice or three times during their summer vacations, and Stephen used to exchange the hat as big as an umbrella for a deerhunter's cap to go tracking foxes and digging out badgers with the fur-and-feather man from Hilltown. Therefore — so my puzzled mind argued — my berating of Miller to Kevin on the mountain could be construed as a denunciation of her dead husband also. In that theory, pulverising a dead man's reputation was even worse than seeing a dead man's plasticated ashes.

The third arguable reason for my unsuitability as a companion for young Kevin — and it genuinely figured only third in my calculations — was that we had gone swimming in the nude. This was the most likely reason from the point of view of prudery but the least likely reason from the point of view of the facts, and surely Kevin had told her the facts as they occurred. Súil Mhuire could hardly be called a public swimming pool, and anyhow bathing costumes had only come into vogue with crowded beaches and full pockets.

Then again, I said to myself, maybe her open hostility and closed door had nothing at all to do with the climb up Slieve Mhuire; maybe it related to something totally unconnected with either sea or mountain. Had Gobnait in her mining operations come across some chancy uranium in my private life? But what? I trawled through my conscience and I netted a number of small fish but definitely no maneating shark.

"You haven't heard?" she had said to me." You will, Father, you will."

The question was: what would I hear and from whom?

* * *

That was on Wednesday, the 28th of August. On the following Friday week, the 6th of September, the postman opened the mouth of my letter box and the bishop stuck his coated tongue through it. The mere sight of the disciplined handwriting on the envelope set my heart scrambling out of control.

The letter read: —

Dear Father Laide,

A matter of very grave import has been brought to my notice about you. I wish to talk to you about it. Consequently, I am directing you to attend here at 11 a.m next Monday, 9th of September.

In Christo.

Yours truly,

+ Andrew Irwin,

Bishop of Demly.

On Saturday I went through the sad routine, now sadder than ever, of taking "Lú na Lon" off her moorings at the pier and steering her between the guide posts of my boat trailer at the slip, prior to getting Florrie Keane, who owned a tractor, to pull her out of the water from there on to the pier road and up to my house.

"This is the earliest you ever took her out," he said to me.

"Yes, and it was the latest I ever put her in, Florrie, but it has been that sort of summer for me. How would you say? Erratic? Topsy turvy? Sarah committed. Fr. Mac's death. The new man arriving. The revolution in the hall. All the old threads pulling loose, you know. Something tells me that there will be no more sailing weather for me this year."

On Monday, for the second time in seven weeks I drove to the bishop's house. I followed the usual protocol. I parked my car on the avenue — the steamed gravel forecourt was for rubber soles, not rubber tyres — and I sat in it until two minutes to eleven so that I would be putting thumb to bell at exactly eleven o'clock: Bishop Irwin had a mind like a sea captain's chronometer. In externals there was no change from my first visit; what was different was the dread which had been spawned by the uncertainty. On the earlier occasion I knew I would be hit by the boomerang of the money bag, but on this occasion I didn't know what weapon was waiting for me inside the intimidating door.

Once again the bishop opened the door himself and once again he seated me at the massive mahogany table where I felt suitably dwarfed and pauperised. He wasted no time on pleasantries for which I was thankful. If one is going to have one's head chopped off there is little point in telling that head about the admirable sunrise.

"Fr Laide," he began, "I have a number of items here which are central to the present issue," and he took some enclosures out of an oblong envelope and looked at them briefly, one by one, before putting them, one, two, three in line across the table in front of him, next to a page of notepaper which was covered with his own unmistakable handwriting.

"The first of these items is a letter from your parish priest, Fr O Donnell. I could describe it best by saying it is a covering letter, because it covers the circumstances in which he was given the other two items to send to me.

"The second item is also a letter. It comes from Mrs Catherine Burke. The burden of this letter" — he was scanning it as he spoke — "is that in spite of the deep seated reservations which she had about you since the incident of her husband's coffin she nonetheless entrusted her grandnephew Kevin . . . Kevin. . . ." He hesitated, searching for the name.

"Kevin Warren, my Lord," I put in, and it was ironic that the first words I spoke at the interview were Kevin's Christian name and surname.

"Yes, she entrusted her grandnephew Kevin Warren to your care. This was against her better judgement and only because the boy pleaded with her. Unfortunately the end result of it was that you betrayed her trust and took the boy with you to a lake where you and he were observed bathing in puris naturalibus. She concludes by insisting that I take disciplinary action against the miscreant. That is an exact quotation not a paraphrase: 'disciplinary action against the miscreant.' "

"She wrote that?"

"It is here in the letter."

"It may be in the letter, my Lord, but she didn't write it," and I emphasized the word 'she'. "She isn't capable of composing a sentence like that. She doesn't know the meaning of the word 'miscreant'. She couldn't even spell it. It was dictated to her."

"By whom?"

"Her companion-in-arms, of course, Gobnait O'Brien. It's a conspiracy."

"Co-operation, quite possibly, Father, but scarcely conspiracy on the evidence of one sentence in a letter."

"When you put two women together, two women who have grudges against a third party, what you have is a conspiracy." If a straw floats past a drowning man he clutches at it, and I clutched at that straw. "Catherine Burke has a grudge against me since the affair of the coffin and Gobnait O'Brien has a grudge against me...."

"Since the affair of the sprained ankle, you are going to tell me."

"No, I'm not, my Lord. The sprained ankle has nothing to do with it."

"No?"

"No." I had a strong feeling that he was playing a cat-and-mouse game with me and that he would haul me back and put his paw on top of me whenever he wished, but still my instinct was to make a run for it whenever I got the chance. I explained, "I thwarted her when she attempted to coerce a young man, who was mentally ill, into marrying her. He had no lack of acres but a complete lack of brains. It was unscrupulous greed on her part and I put a stop to it. That's why she hates me."

"And what about the man?"

"When I interviewed him he told me that he wasn't sure whether he would join Melleray or marry Gobnait."

"So you told him to join Melleray".

"No, I told him to do neither but to go home and have a bit of sense."

"The very thing I told you, Father, seven weeks ago but you didn't take my advice, as is quite clear from the third document here." Expert gardener though he was, my attempt to lead him up the garden path had failed.

He was back in the nettle patch and so was I.

"This is a statement signed by the boy concerned. It is written on official Garda Síochána paper and it was taken down from the boy by a Sergeant Miller of Hilltown Garda Station." The name hit me like an eighteen wheeler: I had made my assertion of conspiracy too soon.

The bishop continued "I do not gather from the statement that the boy is at all hostile towards you, but that is beside the point. The facts are what we must establish and the boy tells the simple facts: that the two of you swam in Suíl Mhuire lake, that ye were naked, and that you gave him a towel with which to dry himself."

I was about to object that while what Kevin had said was true it was nowhere near the whole truth, but the bishop forestalled me. "Say nothing now," he said. "I shall give you ample time to defend yourself, if indeed one can ever defend the indefensible. For the moment I want to thread those three items together in a coherent sequence.

"As I understand it from the evidence in front of me, this is what happened: — You, Father Laide, and this young boy, Kevin Warren, went on an outing to Slieve Mhuire. You were observed as you climbed to the summit where you spent some time and again as you descended. The man who observed you was Sergeant Miller who happened to be on the mountain the same day, shooting. He had no difficulty identifying both you and the boy whom he had met in Mrs Burke's house, through his telescopic lens. On your way down you made a long halt at the mountain lake. Both of you stripped naked and went swimming for some considerable time. You gave the boy a towel, and after you were both decent again you had a picnic and then you went back to your car which the sergeant also identified as yours.

"The sergeant is an old friend of Mrs Burke's and as a friend he went to Kilbroney that evening to tell her of the indecent exposure which had taken place. But he didn't let matters rest there. As a professional, well accustomed to investigating incidents and taking statements from the public, he questioned the boy and took a brief statement from him, which the boy duly signed. Whereupon Mrs Burke visited Fr O'Donnell and showed him the statement. He then, very correctly, in my view, advised the good lady to set out all she had gathered from Sergeant Miller about the incident in a letter addressed to myself, and he undertook to forward both the boy's statement and her own letter to me, which he did."

Although he was getting old, Bishop Irwin hadn't lost his professional knack of putting material in order. He was aiming at what he called a coherent sequence, and he achieved that, but in the long run — and it had run on for a long time — it was no more than a chronology of events, a very naked chronology of events at that, a sort of indecent exposure of them in fact, without taking into account the circumstances that had clothed them and had given them an entirely different appearance.

I felt cooler and more composed in myself than at any time since the bishop had opened the door to me, and I felt confident that with my complete knowledge of what had happened and what had not happened I could present that August day to him in such a way that he too would see it in an entirely different aspect.

"That, I believe," he said, after a satisfied pause, "is an impartial summary of the material in front of me here, but I intend to be completely fair to you, so I offer you the opportunity of examining the three documents for yourself. Do you wish to peruse the parish priest's letter, to begin with?"

"No. I don't, my Lord," I replied. "What I wish to do is to stay cool and if I were to read anything that he has written it would raise my temperature to a level where I couldn't think clearly. Ever since he arrived in the parish, his main aim, it seems to me, has been to diminish me in the eyes of the people."

"I disagree with you, of course, but if you want to use extra rope to hang yourself, that is your concern, not mine, Father. Right. What about Mrs Burke's letter? And may I remind you that it contains all the evidence presented to her by Sergeant Miller."

"No, I have no wish to read that, either. I accept unreservedly that you have given me an accurate summary of the letter, but I do not accept that either of those two people is interested in establishing the truth. They are patently hostile and prejudiced witnesses, working hand in glove, his hand in her glove, against me."

"I have to say, Father, that I find Mrs Burke's prejudice, as you call it, entirely understandable in the circumstances. I know nothing of Sergeant Miller's relationship with you."

"It could be described as a vendetta, my Lord,"

"That is a strong word."

"Yes, there are strong feelings on both sides."

"What about?"

'Killing birds and animals. I'm sure you noted that he was on the mountain for the purpose of killing."

"A person can kill something more precious than birds and animals, Father."

Once again I led with my chin. "What?" I asked.

"Innocence," he answered.

It took me a while to get up off the floor, but when I did, the words I spoke were the most earnest of the entire session, "I liked that boy." I said, "He was really mastering the art of sailing. I wouldn't have designed any evil against him. I didn't in fact commit any evil against him. His innocence is intact."

And after a pause I asked, "May I see his statement?"

"Yes, of course, but I think you may be disappointed."

I was. It was as though he could only come up with the bare facts because Miller had forced him to focus on bare bodies. It said: — "Fr. Laide and I climbed to the top of Slieve Mhuire on Friday 23rd of August, which was a very hot day. When we came down we swam in the lake called Súil Mhuire. We hadn't any togs with us so we went in naked. Fr. Laide had one towel with him in his rucksack and he gave that to me. (Signed) Kevin Warren."

"'Tis brief, my Lord".

"Yes, it is", the bishop answered. He was sharper on sociology than on Shakespeare. He didn't realise I was quoting, so I got back immediately on his literal level and I began my defence on precisely that point.

"It is so brief, my Lord, that it gives a very unfair slant to the whole incident. It is like telling the story of Adam and Eve in four short sentences and omitting the serpent."

"Adam and Eve, indeed. Are you admitting to a sin, then?"

"I am doing no such thing. I am invoking the principle in moral theology that circumstances alter cases, and in Kevin's statement no mention is made of the circumstances. The result is that his simple account, instead of establishing the truth, actually falsifies what took place.

"First of all, I had no intention at all of taking him with me to the mountain. He wasn't part of my plan for that day which was purely and simply to continue the old tradition of climbing Mary's mountain during the month of the Assumption."

"If you didn't intend it, why then did you do it?"

"Because I figured he might be expecting me to go sailing and I didn't want him to be wasting the whole sunny evening, so I went down to the pier to tell him the sailing was off."

"And?"

"He persuaded me to take him to the mountain instead."

"Persuaded you?"

"Yes, you have no idea how persuasive that child could be. When we reached the lake on our way up, he wanted to go for a swim straight away. He did. I didn't. I said no. When we had finished looking at all the sights from the top, I wanted to go back down a different way which would have taken us away from the lake altogether, but he said no, he wanted to see the lake again. See the lake. But when we got to the lake it was swimming was in his head, not viewing. He pleaded with me, and I just wasn't able to say no. It was his idea entirely, not mine."

"That may account for his being in the lake naked, but it doesn't account for your being in the lake with him."

"That is where a further circumstance came into play, my Lord. I just couldn't walk away from the lake and let him get on with his swimming on his own, because lake waters are very dangerous and that would have been to abdicate my responsibility for his safety. On the other hand, if I stayed on the bank as I was while he undressed and went swimming that in my view would have been voyeurism. Very much the lesser of two evils was for me to have a bathe as well. In fact, the only voyeurism indulged in on that day was the voyeurism indulged in by Sergeant Miller."

"You are impugning the man's honour."

"Saving your presence, my Lord, I am not. Either he wanted to see the little boy in the nude or he wanted to see me in hell. There is nothing honourable about either."

"You are back where you were before, back questioning people's motives."

"I know him better than you do, my Lord. In fact I know him inside out and he is rotten inside and out."

It is a wonder that at that stage the bishop didn't turn me inside out, didn't turn me out into my car from the inside of his house, but he showed extraordinary restraint and said, "You may go on with your defence, Father, but I shall not tolerate any further reference to Sergeant Miller. That is an order. Go back to where you were before you dragged Sergeant Miller into the picture again, and that was in the water."

"Very well, my Lord, but I must point out to you that before either of us got into the water I sent Kevin to the other end of the lake, so in so far as segregation was practicable I observed it. The main point I wish to make is that there was no compulsion on my part, no persuasion, or even the slightest suggestion. It was entirely the boy's own idea. He found it a wonderful experience and kept saying so afterwards. If I had caused him feelings of shame or embarrassment he wouldn't have voted it, as he did, the event of the day."

My defence rested. I thought myself that it was plausible and that there was no achilles heel protruding from the body of it. But the bishop found one.

"You have greatly eased my fears," he said "and you have answered the charges against you very effectively in many respects and I might believe you entirely if it were not for one factor."

"Which is, my Lord?"

"The towel."

"The towel?"

"Yes, the towel. Would you explain to me why you had it with you?"

"Well, as I explained earlier my original intention was to climb Slieve Mhuire on my own and I put into the rucksack only what I thought I might need for myself: my binoculars, my sunglasses, an orange and the towel."

"Yes, but why the towel?"

"Well, I thought I might bathe my sore feet on the way down."

"Or even have a swim?"

"I suppose the possibility was there but at the very back of my mind."

"If the possibility was there, why didn't you pack a swimming togs?"

'O, well, at two thousand feet above sea level and beyond the prying of human eyes" — I had to watch myself not to name that name again — "a swimming togs is hardly the most necessary item in a rucksack."

"You knew the lake was there then?"

"O yes, I had been up the mountain before."

"And it was a very hot day?"

"Yes, astonishingly hot for the end of August, twenty four, twenty five celsius."

"Why then, knowing that you were going to pass the lake on this extremely hot day, didn't you tell the boy to bring his togs and a towel with him?"

"Because when I told him I was going to the mountain I was thinking only of the mountain and not at all of the lake. As a matter of fact, it was only when Kevin, climbing faster than I could, 'discovered' the lake, as it were, that it came back to my mind."

"And with it the towel in the rucksack."

"I think that is a very unfair suggestion, my Lord. I used the towel in an honourable fashion. I could have kept it for myself, but in that case he would have had to stand in the sun to get dry and I would have had the chance to look at him for a pro-tracted period. That I did not do. On the contrary I gave him the towel and sent him to the far end of the tarn."

It was twenty five celsius inside my collar when I finished saying that, more especially because I felt the suffocating heat of that towel around my head like a hood before hanging.

"Is there anything else you wish to say?"

"No, my Lord".

"Are you sure?"

"Yes, I'm sure, my Lord".

"Very well, then." He scanned the notes he had at the start and some additional notes he had made during the interview and he said," I have been balancing all the various factors in my mind, what I knew before you came and what you have told me by way of explanation, and what I have to say is this:

"One. You did swim in the lake at the same time as the boy and you were both naked. That is an undisputed fact.

"Two. Even if there were no sexual overtones, which is something that cannot be either proved or disproved, and even though I accept without question that there was no close contact between you and the boy in the lake or on the bank, I have to say that you were indulging in activity totally at variance with the chastity expected of a priest.

"Three. The child's guardian perceives it as a very grave offence and I cannot ignore that. Perception does not, of course, overrule facts, but it is a key factor.

"Four," he counted. I never liked sums in school and as the numbers mounted my sense of despair mounted with them.

"Four. In the view of Sergeant Miller it was a case of indecent exposure in a public place. That is what he told Mrs Burke, but you declined to read her letter. I have the impression that he is taking no direct action, pending my decision on the matter. I therefore have to consider the scandal that would arise if the case came to court.

"Five. In spite of your submissions to the contrary, I am not satisfied in the matter of the towel. I see it as evidence of intent, to some degree.

"Six. I did warn you only a few short weeks ago that I would discipline you if there were another complaint of any kind against you. This is not a complaint of any old kind. This is a complaint of a very serious kind. I am committed to my word, you understand. Therefore. . . ."

"You are going to take disciplinary action against the miscreant," I put in, impudently and bitterly.

"Not miscreant, Father, so much as misfit. There is clearly no future for you as a priest in Kilbroney. You have too many enemies and too little sense". The man had a knack of summing you up and putting you down in one sentence. Of such are seminary professors made.

"You are giving me trouble, Father. You don't seem to realise that. Once upon a time I found trouble energising. Not any longer. Now I find trouble troublesome.

"I am sending you to a place where there won't be a great potential for trouble. I have looked up the most recent returns from Fr. Cleary and I find there are now 130 people on Inishnagaunogue."

Inishnagaunogue! So that is where I was headed for: an Island I had sailed to once on a summer's day but had never wintered on in a hundred nightmares.

He wasn't finished yet. "You priests have a phrase nowadays which wasn't current before I became bishop. Straight switch, I believe you call it. That is what I propose to do with you and Fr. Cleary. You will take up his position on Inishnagaunogue and he will take up yours in Kilbroney."

If, in the event, he sent notification of the changes to the "Western Orb," to wit,

Rev. Brendan Laide C.C. Kilbroney
to be Adm. Inishnagaunogue.
Rev. Brian Cleary Adm. Inishnagaunogue
to be C.C. Kilbroney.

he wouldn't have to add 'demoted' in brackets after my name because everyone in the west would know that the grandiose title Adm. meant only that the place was too insignificant to constitute a parish and support a parish priest, as they would also know that when a priest with fifteen years' service replaces a priest with two it spells demotion with a capital D.

Only a few details remained to be settled. My appointment at Kilbroney would be terminated at 12 midnight on Friday night; I was to be on the island for the week-end Masses; if Fr. Cleary and I couldn't shift our furniture on or before Saturday — and he granted that the passage to and from the island could create problems for both of us — we could postpone that chore until the following week; but, one way or the other, there were to be no organised goodbyes, sevenday presentation clocks or wallets of notes. The only smile I had all morning was when I thought — even as the bishop was speaking — of the words of appreciation the parish priest might have said about me at my now aborted farewell function!

The bishop gathered up his papers and said "I hope you will be happy in Inishnagaunogue".

Not being given to wearing a white feather as well as a white collar, I answered "I'll be happy anywhere, my Lord, where I can see the sea."

He led me to the door where he said "Goodbye, Fr. Laide" and held out his hand at a height suitable for the kissing of the ring, but I wasn't that much of a hypocrite and I merely said "Good bye, Bishop Irwin."

As I returned to the car I was hopping mad, as I used to say when I was young, but my anger wasn't directed so much at the bishop, who had given me a fair hearing, as at the four people who had taken the red skull cap off his head and put a judge's black cap there instead. On my way back to Kilbroney I dispatched hurricanes of curses in the direction of Miller, O'Donnell, Gobnait O'Brien and Catherine Burke, but, very strangely, in between the hurricanes there were periods of complete calm when I felt not so much the trickle of blood from my split skull into my eyes as a sense of relief that the sword of Damocles had finally fallen.

Chapter 10

EPILOGUE

The thing to have done, of course, would have been to sail to Inish — as everybody calls it for short. If I had known on the Saturday that the bishop had a St. Helena in mind for me, I would never have pulled "Lú na Lon" out of the water. I would have loaded it with my clothes, my radio, a few books, Sarah's cat The King of Siam and my own cat Fan-An, and I would have set a course for Carraig Aonair where I would have exchanged the customary winks with the lighthouse, and from there I would have sailed down the seaslope to Ardatroha Point on Inish. A pity. I would have made history – and history is more palatable in the islands than a feed of brill — because although every priest who had served on Inish for hundreds of years had arrived in a boat I would have been the first priest to bisect the headlands on the way into Inver in his own sailboat.

What is more, I think I would have guaranteed myself a memorable send off from the pier, because, in spite of what the bishop had said about organised goodbyes, the locals would never have allowed so rare an event as a curate literally cutting the cables to take place without being present in some numbers to mark it with appletarts and a few tenners at least. On the other hand, if my old charges' sense of humour got the better of their sense of occasion, my new charges in Inish might not have been very impressed at all with their new administrator's tastes, because only the year before, when Lorcan Tuohy and Siobhán, his bride of four hours, were setting sail for a cruise of the south on their honeymoon, they found their pookaun "dressed over-all" when they arrived at the pier: there were streamers of toilet paper of every colour ever devised for lavatory dilettantes, there was a pollack, higher than any pollack had ever been in the history of fishing, suspended from the masthead, and there were about two dozen beercans hanging like young monkeys from the stays. All of that was only a might-have-been in my case because having taken the boat out of the water it would have been altogether too much hassle to put it back in again.

But, in a sense, "Lú na Lon" made an even more impressive entry into the maritime life of Inish than she would have made beating diminutively up along the craggy shoreline from Ardatroha to Inver. She arrived at Inish mounted on her skyblue trailer as deck cargo on the mailboat. The passengers who were making the trip on the "Ringrone" that day cared not at all for the boat they were travelling on; they had eyes only for the boat they were travelling with. They were trying to estimate how many tons of pigiron there were in her fin keel; they were rubbing their hands along her smooth flanks as if she was some captive animal; and they were admiring her cutwater, shaped like the snout of a shark. But it was the people who were waiting on the pier at Inver who had the better view as the "Ringrone" came up the harbour. My boat was riding piggyback on the mailboat, they said. It was an image they will never forget.

* * *

That was in September. Now it is April. I spent the winter writing this account of my removal from Kilbroney and the events that led up to it. I started it in late October when the weather put an end to my walks along the cliffs and to my getting-to-know-you calls to the forty-eight houses. I had no experience of writing before I set down the opening sentence of this memoir, which was "The first nail in my own coffin was driven into it at the funeral of Stephen Burke", apart from writing my sailing log every summer, but I did find that particular discipline a help because in writing up my log I always aimed for accuracy.

As week followed week and chapter followed chapter and A4 pad followed A4 pad, the feature that was most surprising to myself was the total recall I had of the conversations that had taken place. It must be that when a person is fighting for what he believes in or when he is fighting for his life, there is an extra surge of blood to the brain and the words are written on the memory in that blood.

There is never a book without a title. I thought it would be clever to have something from Shakespeare and the first title I thought of was "Once upon the Hip" from "The Merchant of Venice".

"If I can catch him once upon the hip I will feed fat the ancient grudge I bear him", Shylock said, speaking of Antonio. I have no way of knowing how the Jew was familiar with the move in wrestling that would give him a winning advantage over an opponent, but it would have been apt to describe how Miller sought such an advantage, how he found it on Slieve Mhuire and how he then fed fat the ancient grudge he bore me. But on the other hand that would have limited the vengefulness to Miller alone, whereas there were several others in the ring against me at the same time.

That is why I opted for the title from "King Henry VIII." — Heat Not a Furnace.

"Be advised:
Heat not a furnace for your foes so hot
That it do singe yourself," Norfolk said to Buckingham. It threw the blame for creating the vengeful situation back on myself: I had heated a furnace for Catherine Burke, for Gobnait O'Brien, for Fr. Michael O'Donnell and for Sergeant Tom Miller and it got so hot that it did singe myself.

* * *

Much has happened since September. Bishop Irwin died in the middle of October shortly before I began this account of the wrestling match, the singeing, the nails in my coffin, the stones in the shepherd's pouch, the sword of Damocles or whatever. If he were still alive, I very much doubt if I would have put on record, word-for-word, the conversations we had on the two occasions when he summoned me to his house. Had I done so, he would surely have withdrawn me, boat and baggage, from Inish and packed me off to a silent monastery.

I had qualms about whether I had significantly added to the stress which brought about the massive stroke from which he died. I was, and am, very conscious of what were almost the last words he said to me: "You are giving me trouble, Father. You don't seem to realise that." I am very sorry now, that, when out of habit he presented his ring to me at the door, I did not, out of courtesy, kiss it.

* * *

Sarah has gone back to England to friends of hers in Hove and Fuchsia Cottage is up for sale. I visited her several times in St. Clare's and on the final two occasions it was she who was commiserating with me on my eviction from Kilbroney more than I was with her on hers. To be honest about it, in spite of my assertion to Dr. Morgan that she would be reduced to a chemical zombie there, she wasn't, and this was due mainly to the fact that she questioned every thrust of their needles and every proffer of their pills. She was as self-willed as her Siamese cat and there was nothing they could do to make a mouse of her. Two good things came of it, however: first of all, she ceased to look like a famine victim in Biafra, and, secondly, the medical people got in touch with the friends of her academic years in Hove and between them they persuaded her — how, I shall never understand, unless the Holy Spirit became directly involved in the discussions — not to the return to the squalor and the liquour of Kilbroney.

We write to each other frequently and in one of my letters to her I told her that I have hung her original painting "Grey Rock" in my study where the southern sun has been showing all the winter low that there is more to the grey rock than greyness. She gave it to me in Kilbroney as a reward for my acting as one of her donkey spotters, but I didn't hang it then with my other pictures because it clashed with them in theme and treatment. They were impressionistic and light; Sarah's was geometrical, and, as the name suggested, grey. But I have hung it with them now, precisely because it clashes with them: Sarah is a clasher and so, I have come to realise, am I.

It is in fact a better likeness than any photograph of herself that she could send me. It is oil on canvas, thirty inches by eighteen, and it is a study of the placement of nine rocks, irregularly shaped, one upon another. They are massive rocks, cyclopean rocks, the sort of rocks that went into the construction of the Lion Gate in Mycenae, and to me they are a symbol of Sarah herself: irregular, uncrushable, honest, unyielding and eccentric. But the canvas is not without colour anymore than Sarah is without colour. Although the huge slabs are edged with black, they are overlaid here and there with yellow lichen and green moss, the brightness of her conversation and the freshness of her views on life. We didn't beat the bastards in the sense that I meant on the day she left Kilbroney, but neither did the bitches and the bastards tame us, and her painting "Grey Rock" on my wall in Inish is a proof of that.

In another letter I told her about the King of Siam. The fact is that he has made a much bigger impact on the life of the island than I have done myself. Since the Roman traders brought Christianity to these parts, the priests who have lived on the island have been much of a muchness; maybe their hairstyles and their hobbies were different but fundamentally they were all the same. The King, however, was a totally new experience for the islanders: never before had they encountered a cat with blue eyes, cream fur and a husky voice.

Not a cat for sitting all day on a southfacing window, from the very start he leapt into a familiarisation programme of his own devising and there wasn't a yard that he didn't prospect or a field that he didn't cross from cliffend to cliffend of the island. His exploration brought him into very close contact with every dog at every house, but he was man enough for them all: their noses had a lot more blood on them than his had. There is only one way they will ever get the better of him, and that is if they organise themselves into a local defence force, but they won't do that: island dogs are like their masters: they keep their own counsel.

I would see the Irish Wildbird Conservancy people as a bigger threat to his future on the island than the dogs. I am a member myself and I have no wish for my incumbency to be noted as the period when the bird population fell dramatically but I fear the worst, judging by the number of trophies he has brought to my doorstep before tasting of the fruits of the hunt: unlike the boss he is interested in consuming, not conserving.

My hope is this: the Conservancy counters and taggers come here only in the summer, and now that spring is here the King's preferred diet has changed from feather to fish. The seagulls' wheeling and squawking have diverted him from the pastures to the pier, and he is establishing himself as a member of the welcoming committee for the fishing boats in the evening, so much so that when the fishermen, who are sorting their catch, see him leaping down the rocks towards them, they say "Here comes the priest's cat to collect the priest's dues!"

He is agile and virile and when I add vagrancy to agility and virility I think the chances are that in years to come there will be some very odd looking varieties of felis catus on this island to remind people of the time when Fr. Laide who was sacked from Kilbroney ministered on Inishnagaunogue.

In the meantime, the King of Siam has celebrity status here. He is a huge favourite with the schoolchildren especially, and in spite of Miss Brennan's obscurantist efforts to discourage his interest in education he sits on the window sills of the school for a while every fine day looking in to see how the lessons in geography, catechism and especially art are going. A month or so ago they submitted eight paintings for the Texaco National Child Art Exhibition: one depicted the mailboat, another the chapel, but six of the eight artists chose the King for their subject and one of the six, Mairéad Corcoran, entitled her painting "The King of Inish". I told Sarah in my letter about his new sobriquet and she replied "I am so happy to hear that His Royal

Highness's sovereignty is now acknowledged not only in the Far East but also in the Far West!"

* * *

But the best letter that came my way since I arrived in Inish came from Kevin in the middle of November. It eased a great ache. It said:

Tanner Close,
Brickhill,
Bedford.

Dear Father Laide,
I hope you are well. I am sorry to be so late thanking you for the great time you gave me in the summer. I read about you going to Inishnagaunogue in the Kilbroney Clippings. My Auntie Catherine sent us the paper. It didn't say why you left Kilbroney, but after reading it my Mum and Dad were using sort of secret language the way they always do when they don't want me to understand what they are saying and I knew by the looks they were giving me that it had to do with me. You will have to tell me what Inishnagaunogue means. 'Tis as long as a train. I know only three words in Irish so far, Slieve, a mountain, Súil, an eye and of course Lú na Lon, the fleetness of the hounds.

I am really sorry that I made trouble for you. It isn't fair. I didn't mean to. I couldn't make out what all the fuss was about. I mean, a few of my school chums and myself went on our bikes to St. Neot's in July and just before we got there we were so hot that we went for a swim in the river Ouse in our pelt and there was nothing about it. I couldn't twig why the sergeant was asking me so many questions about the same thing at Súil Mhuire. I told him over and over that it was all my idea and that you didn't want to let me when we were going up or when we were coming down, until I bulldozed you into it. He seemed to be set on getting me to say that it was your idea, but I didn't. Then when he wrote out the statement he would only put in the date and that we had nothing on and that you gave me your own towel. He said 'twas no big deal.

He must have tracked us from the time when we heard the shots, but 'twas only much later that I knew he was a spook. You warned me about him on the mountain but because he used to visit Auntie Catherine I thought he was O.K. The first that I really knew you were in trouble was when Auntie Catherine wouldn't let me go up to say goodbye to you. It just wasn't fair because you were the only friend I made for the whole month.

Anyhow, whatever they think, it was super on the mountain that day and it was the best swim I ever had in the sea or the river or the pool or anywhere. And the times we went sailing, I can remember every single day, they were all fab but the best day of the lot was the day that I beat the "Topaz" to the line between Seal Island and the Emperor rock by one minute and fifty three seconds. You didn't think I could beat that big a yaht. The spelling doesn't look right, should it be yath? Especially when she was carrying all that much sail. You said she had a belly on her like a sumo wrestler. But I beat her anyway, belly and all.

I hope I can see you next summer but I'm not sure if they will let me. It just isn't fair. Have you any photo of "Lú na Lon" that you could send me?

With love,

Your fond friend,

Kevin, also known to you as the Emperor Kevin the First.

* * *

I had made up my mind never again to get entangled with Miller but by the time I had read Kevin's letter straight through three times I had changed my mind. The sergeant had suppressed the boy's most vital evidence, and then on the basis of selective evidence he had manipulated him "to get" me, the phrase he had used on the day of the whale. I was so hot with rage that I decided to go back to the furnace and heat it again. Not very Christian of me, I admit, but there are some people so obtuse that there is no point in trying to converse with them in the lingua franca; one has to descend the linguistic ladder until one reaches their own crude patois. So, to be crude about it, how could I "get" him?

I had heard more than once that the answer to every question lies either in the Bible or in Shakespeare. I read the psalms every day and I knew I would come up with something apt there, and I did. Psalm 141 indicated that the sweetest redress is when your enemy falls into his own net. The idea appealed to me but what I didn't like about it was the accidental nature of the requital. "Falls into", the psalm says: that was too casual for my liking. I needed something more deliberate, something more dramatic than that. So I turned to the Sage of Stratford and there I found what I was looking for.

Rosencrantz and Guildenstern were commissioned to convey Hamlet to a pre-arranged death in England but he guessed their game and he put their names on the executioner's list instead of his own. "For tis the sport", he said, "to have the enginer hoist with his own petar". That was exactly the dramatic retribution I had in mind for Miller: to see the sapper blown at the moon with his own mine. The petar, the mine, the means of his own destruction were his ogling of Kevin and myself. I had actually tumbled on the stratagem during my cross examination by the bishop when I said to him that the only voyeurism indulged in that day was the voyeurism indulged in by Miller, but I didn't pursue it. I was intent on pursuing it now.

I have a friend in Hilltown and when it comes to pursuit she has the best tracking skills of anybody in the district. She runs the post office and has a small general trade on the other side of the premises. Her name is Chrissie Beglin. She is noted for her exceptional abilities in two spheres: the smoking of cigarettes and the spreading of gossip.

Gobnait O'Brien in Kilbroney had a big reputation for her ability to spawn gossip as prolifically as a salmon lays eggs, but in the matter of spreading it as distinct from spawning it, it was a case of no contest when Chrissie entered the arena. A shopper could give Chrissie a story as small as the flower of a speedwell, but that is what happened it, if she did: it sped well and spread well till like creeping jenny it covered a whole forest floor.

Her other prodigious aptitude is in the sphere of smoking cigarettes. Sixty a day is average on a busy day; on a slack day the number soars with the smoke. People who take government warnings about the danger of nicotine seriously regard a visit to her post office as a health hazard, perhaps not if they are buying a quick stamp, but certainly if they are sending a packet by registered mail or despatching a goose for Christmas. It is said that when she postmarks a letter for San Francisco it impregnates another fifty letters with the stink of cigarettes before it goes through the Golden Gate.

Such is the woman whom I called upon as my aide-de-camp in my renewed campaign against Miller, and basically because of cigarettes. Having enjoyed the solace of them for many years she hadn't it in her heart to refuse such a comfort to the young, but according to the law of the land she was not allowed to offer cigarettes for sale to the underaged. And so Miller in his capacity as a defender of the vulnerable — foxes and choughs did not fall into that category —twice summoned her for a breach of the tobacco licensing laws. On the first occasion she got off lightly, but on her second appearance at Hilltown District Court she was given a hefty fine and a warning that if there were a third offence her licence to sell cigarettes would be withdrawn. Chrissie wasn't interested so much in selling them as in stocking them so that she could have unhindered access to them day and night, and Miller became the bugbear of her life. Anytime she saw him passing by, she felt like a starveling in a besieged city, and she prayed for the day when somehow or other he would be forced to raise the siege.

I gave her that somehow-or-other early in December. One night late, when she had to contend no longer with distractions such as registered letters and postal orders, I phoned her.

"Chrissie Beglin here".

"And Brendan Laide here".

"Wisha, Father Laide, how are you at all since you left Ireland?"

"Not so bad at all, Chrissie. There is no devil to pull by the tail out here but I am keeping myself busy all the same. How's yourself?"

"Pretty good, but I'm not looking forward to the next few weeks. Thumping all those cards and making sure the guts of the geese aren't coming out through the parcels — you know how it is in a post office at Christmas."

"But just now, how are things? Quiet?"

"Yes, thanks be to God. I have time for the odd fag."

"Miller isn't troubling you?"

"No, bad cess to him."

"And maybe he won't any more!"

"How do you mean, Father?"

"I mean he is in a spot of trouble himself."

"For God's sake! What kind of trouble?"

"Scandal trouble."

"For God's sake! What sort of scandal?"

"Well, to put it mildly, he is not called Tom for nothing."

"You are speaking in riddles, Father. Can't you talk plain English?"

"Well, did you ever hear of a peeping Tom?"

"I heard of one but I never met one."

"That's where you're wrong, Chrissie. You met one as well. In the shop and in the court. Sergeant Tom Miller is a Peeping Tom Miller."

"For God's sake! Tell me more."

"Seems in the summer he spends time looking at people swimming in the nude."

"For God's sake! Where?"

"For God's sake, Chrissie, will you stop saying for God's sake?"

"I can't for God's sake. Wait till I get another fag." I could hear the sustained drag and the pursing of the lips at the other end, as she lit one cigarette off the other.

"Is it to calm your nerves, Chrissie?"

"No, this is more like the one after a good dinner. Go on."

"There's not a lot more to say, really."

"Where, I asked you, where?"

"O, yes. Up Slieve Mhuire, of all places. There's a lake up there. That's where."

"And who would be swimming up there?"

"Some class of hippies, I suppose."

"Yes, that makes sense: they wouldn't be wasting any of the dole money on swimming togs. And does he crawl up near them?"

"No, no, he is too cagey for that. He does his viewing through a telescope."

"For God's sake! Like an astronomer, do you mean?"

"Something like that. The heavenly bodies, don't you know."

"The heavenly bodies! Father, you're a gas man. Peeping Tom Miller! Who'd believe it?"

"Well, do you believe it, Chrissie?"

"I sure do. I always knew there was something slinky about that fellow, but I never knew what it was until now. Well, 'twas great talking to you, Father. I hope you will have a nice quiet time of it out there for Christmas."

One sure thing, her phone didn't have a nice quiet time of it for the rest of the night!

"Mischief, thou art afoot. Take thou what course thou wilt", Mark Antony said after he put his cat among Brutus's pigeons. What course the Hilltown mischief took became clear to me when Fonsie Leary's fishing boat chugged into Inver a fortnight ago. Fonsie comes from Cé na Cille which is the "port" of Hilltown so to speak. I was on the pier to run the line around the bollard for him when he edged in.

"What's new in Hilltown, Fonsie?" I asked him when he came ashore.

"Nothing very new, Father. Old people dying, babies being born, pints being lowered. All the usual things."

"How's Father Lucey?"

"Busy with the new school."

"And my friend, Sergeant Miller?"

The sarcasm wasn't lost on him and he replied in kind. "He isn't looking so well, you'll be glad to hear."

"Oh! Did he get the spring flu?"

"Ah no, nothing like that. It's a different class of bug that has bitten him."

"And what class of a bug would that be?"

"Well ... it's not something a person would like to be talking about, but the word is out, far and near, that he spends a lot of his time in the summer up Slieve Mhuire watching the hippies swimming in the raw."

"For God's sake!" Chrissie's exclamation seemed the most appropriate one.

"Everybody has it."

"Just watching them? For sport, you mean?"

"Yes. He is supposed to have a big telescope up there in some nook".

I carefully said nothing about the heavenly bodies: that crack might be common currency by now! Instead, I soberly suggested that, from what I knew of him with his sheaf of summonses for every session of the District Court, he would be more likely to be summonsing the hippies than staring at them.

"Ah not at all, Father. Sure in that case wouldn't the sport be over? If you kill off the woodcock, there's nothing to shoot at the next day."

"True for you, Fonsie. But he's not looking so well, you tell me."

"No, he's not. He has a sort of hunted look about him, don't you see? Maybe he will finish up in Court himself!"

"Wouldn't that be the sport now?"

"It would surely."

"For 'tis the sport to have the enginer hoist with his own petar."

"What's that you said, Father?"

"Twasn't I that said it at all, Fonsie. 'Twas Shakespeare."

"No better man", said Fonsie, and I went off for my chuckle, and he went off for his pint.

Now that the shove was on, I thought to myself that maybe it wouldn't be such a bad idea to put some more avoirdupois in the back row. I wrote to the Minister for the Environment, giving myself my full title of Administrator in the hope that whatever civil servant read it might conclude that I was somebody important in what is actually ninety per cent an administrative Church. I made three complaints, the first about the shooting of choughs, the second about the inflicting of awful and demeaning suffering on the dying whale, and the third about the harrying of hawks on Slieve Mhuire. I told the Minister straight out who the culprit was, went on to state that my regard for our natural heritage counted for more with me than my expectation of reprisals from the sergeant, and I concluded by saying that if he didn't believe me he could ask anybody living within fifteen miles of Hilltown and they would tell him that the said sergeant had been responsible for the mass slaughter of birds and animals over many years.

I had an acknowledgement from the secretary of the Department thanking me for my letter and assuring me they would shortly be putting an investigation in train into the alleged incidents. That should help to shift him, and if in the meantime, because of the lessening of his concentration, he falls when crossing over a ditch and his gun goes off and kills him, I for one won't be sending any messages of sympathy.

Whether Gobnait or Catherine will hear of his dismissal or death in due course is for God or Government to decide, but one sure thing is that they have heard of the peeping Tom affair. My certitude is based on the fact that Jim Lacy, the bus driver, Gobnait's favourite lodger, brings every crumb of news that he can gather in Hilltown back with him at night to Kilbroney, and the telescopic tastiness of Miller and Slieve Mhuire was no crumb: it was a whole Christmas cake, marzipanned, fruited, brandied and iced. I anticipated the route that the lubricious story would take getting from Chrissie Beglin to Catherine Burke: it would go via Jim Lacy's bus to Gobnait O'Brien's sewer and from there the muck would be conveyed down the village to Chicago. The seeds of doubt about the August swim in Súil Mhuire will have been sown in Catherine's mind long before now, and they will not lack for further dollops of manure from the same source to make them grow and grow.

* * *

The contentious bone of the parish hall is in the same condition, more or less, as I left it, when I got into my famous huff. Fr. O'Donnell didn't want me to have the bone all to myself, which was why he devised a system whereby other terriers would gnaw at it with me. His idea was that he himself would be the master of the kennel but would not actually get involved in the chewing procedures. I frustrated his plans by abandoning the bone completely, with the result that he had to pick it up and munch it even more vigorously than the rest of them!

When I was dismissed from the parish his intention was to appoint my successor, Brian Cleary, to the new committee as manager which would mean that he himself wouldn't have to sit at the draughty door, book the bands, repel the drunks, suppress the riots and keep the accounts, but again I frustrated his designs, because in the week and a half when Brian and I were sometimes here in Inish, sometimes there in Kilbroney and sometimes so confused with boats and baggage that we were neither here nor there, we were in each other's company a great deal and I gave him a suitably jaundiced diagnosis of the health of the hall. I rehearsed him on his role of new curate to O'Donnell, a role that did not include being a manacled manager of O'Donnell's hall, and, being one of the new brood of independent, nonconformist young priests, he withstood the pressure that the parish priest put on him, he evaded all the O-by-the-ways that came in his direction and he left O'Donnell still sitting miserably in the airy door!

O'Donnell got his own back on me by allowing the local branch of the Hilltown Gun Club to hold their monthly meetings in the hall. In my time they would have had to shoot me as well as the fox cubs in order to gain access to the premises, but as the old adage goes, you win some, you lose some. To me the most significant feature of those meetings is that Sergeant Miller attended only the first; Radio Chrissie was on the air before the next meeting was called!

From the point of view of the building itself, the major change has been the installation of new, indeed I am informed, luxurious toilets. Mark Sheerin who is the apostle of the W.C. and who had already brought his gospel to the outside of St. Brona's Church and the parking lot at Sandy Cove regards the hall job as the high point of his apostolate. It is perhaps a little odd that the sanitation now outshines the rest of the building for splendour: it is as if the cow's tail is shampooed and the rest of the cow is filthy. "O brave new world that has such people in it."

* * *

In his letter, Kevin asked me for the meaning of Inishnagaunogue and he said that the word was as long as a train. In fact, when I heard that I was being sent there, I had to ask for the meaning of the name myself and I learnt that the creature which had christened the island, far from being as long as a train, is only twelve inches in length. It is the puffin and Inishnagaunogue means the Island of the Puffins. If I had no other reason at the time – and I hadn't – for relishing the change, at least I was pleased to think that I was going to a parish named not for a saint, a scholar, a hero or a happening but for a bird: it was as if the Lord was saying to me, "Birds have always been welcome to your territory; now you will be welcome to theirs."

When I arrived here in the middle of September only a few laggards were left on the grassy slopes above the cliffs at the western end of the island. All the thousands of energetic ones, all those who had been listening to the ticking of the season clock since August had taken off for the Arctic. But about ten days ago I saw what I took at first sight to be an oil slick between Ardatroha and Carraig Aonair; however, when I fetched my binoculars I saw what it really was: a huge raft of puffins making its bobbing way towards landfall on its own island. Since then they have come ashore; and since then they have replaced the parishioners on my visiting list, my writing rate has fallen and I have beaten a path of my own to the western cliffs.

I take every chance I get to look at them, whether they are standing, walking, tumbling or flying. The puffin is no ballerina, for sure, but it stands as delicately as a ballerina on its tiptoes. In fact, it has a figure more like that of a well-beered sailor, and when it walks, the sailor quickly takes over from the ballerina, with a roll that you would think it had acquired, like the sailor, from much balancing on heaving decks. When it is frightened, it starts to tumble down the cliff slope as though it has no more choice in the matter than a stone, but at the last sensational moment, when you think it is going to finish up as mush on the rocks below, it checks its fall, spreads wings for thrust and legs for stabilisers, and takes off low across the water like an aircraft evading radar.

And then there is the face: what face can compare with the face of a puffin? Unless it is the face of a child streaked with facepaint in white, red, yellow and blue. And right in the middle of the face, like a bullseye in the centre of an archery target, is the fixed eye that fixes the watcher. "He holds you with his glittering eye" can be said as truly of the puffin as it was said of the ancient mariner. Add the orange legs, add the sergeant major chest, add the bill moustachioed with eels and you have a bird worthy of giving its name to a whole island not just a cliff, not just a cove, not just a rock.

I do not know all the terms that ornithologists use when they are describing puffins, but I know that no ornithologist who comes to visit Inishnagaunogue to count their numbers or map their tunnels will enjoy himself half as much as I will between now and August simply looking at these quaint and beautiful birds. There is a lot to be said, whatever my snickering fellow priests may think, for being the priest-in-charge on the Island of the Puffins.

* * *

And now it is time to wind in the line, as Conchúr Ó Síocháin said in the final chapter of his island book.

The appointment to Inish put me in touch with the puffins and it kept me in touch with sailing. If Bishop Irwin had been really vindictive, he could have sent me forty miles inland to where people think the sea is no more than a treat you give children on their confirmation day, or see it as the start of the trouble that ended with forty slates off the roof. To me the sea is the eighth sacrament, and sailing is the grace of the sacrament so my prayer for the bishop is that the Lord has brought him to the haven where he longed to be, the haven he had been reading about in the psalms for fifty years.

Whatever plans the next bishop may devise for me, my only plans just now are plans for sailing. As soon as a good set of weather hatches out of the Atlantic at the end of this month or the beginning of May, I intend to go down to the pier at Inver where "Lú na Lon" has herself been hatching out over the winter like a mute swan high on its nest.

I shall take her out of her winter mackintosh, polish her fibreglass, varnish her wood, oil her rigging, and slap her keel with the foulest of antifouling on the fairest of days, repeating to myself and to anyone else who comes along to watch the priest doing some real work for a change the words of Macbeth, "So foul and fair a day I have not seen". When all of that is done, I shall put her into the strange waters, which surround me here, for the first time.

Those strange waters are very open waters for the most part so I shall certainly be getting much more of a buffetting than I did out of Kilbroney. However, in spite of the vagaries of the

Irish summer there is bound to be one period of favourable weather at least and when it comes I am determined to make passage to Kilbroney early one day and return late on the next. My plans for that trip are all settled in my mind.

The first thing I shall do is to ring up my old telephone number in Kilbroney and ask Fr. Cleary for a bed for the night. I know he has a second bed, because as a result of those days in September when we were involved in a combined operation to get his stuff from here to there and mine from there to here, I know everything that he has and he knows everything that I have! I shall pack a few hardboiled eggs, a packet of digestive biscuits, and a bar of Nestlé chocolate to munch on the trip to Kilbroney and a small tin of indelible paint for use when I get there.

My mooring buoy won't be in the middle of the creek any more, so I shall tie up at the pier astern of Pad Murray. We shall have a natter about how the crabs are behaving themselves, and, if they are being cooperative, I shall ask him once again to tell his famous story of the fright he got on the Falls o'Garry reef when Sarah suddenly appeared in the mouth of the cubby like the Virgin in a grotto. "Only that I couldn't swim I would have given the order to abandon ship", is how he always sums up the intensity of the fright. Pad hadn't been in such close proximity to a woman since his mother was dressing him as a child, and he was convinced that the crabs were equally disturbed by her presence. And I know how he will end his tale. "The sliced banana she gave me was something grand but although I couldn't see any banana skins in her basket I knew I was walking on a very slippery deck and I decided to make for solid land".

After that I shall walk up the hill to greet Fr. Cleary and toss in my overnight bag, removing from it one vital item, the small tin of indelible red paint which I shall take with me to my next halting place. That will be Gobnait O'Brien's newspaper shop. No, I shall not be going inside to enquire about the suppleness or otherwise of the ankle that was damaged on the Day of the Arab, but the unregenerate imp in me will take up a position in the street at precisely the point where she and her tin of paint hit the ground together.

I shall winkle a paintbrush out of the pocket of my sailing jacket and get to work painting a red cross on Gobnait's landing site. I shall have to work briskly because this wonder product, which I got from America to paint LÚ NA LON on the transom of my boat some years ago, is not only indelible but it is quickfixing: "nondrip, quick as a wink" the tin informed me. If Gobnait comes to the door and asks sharply "What are you doing there?" the stressed adverb implying trespass, I shall answer "I am on County Council property; you have no right to ask me that question." If she merely asks "What are you painting?" I shall answer "X marks the spot". She is very very unlikely to ask the further question "What spot?". Even if the American paint does not live up to its claims entirely, and the red loses some of its ruddy boldness with all the traffic that will be passing over it, it can always be renewed on a yearly basis like insurance against falling off ladders!

It will only be a short walk from Gobnait's to my next stop, the most frequented premises in the village, Florrie Keane's. The first thing I shall do is to go around to the western gable, where traditional hitching rings are fastened to the wall, to see if Jack o'Lantern is tethered there. If he is, my stay at Florrie's will be a long one; if not, I shall make my excuses over a Seven Up and explain that I have a long walk before me to Dunsheen because whether he is seated high on a stool at Florrie's or seated low on the car seat which is his fireside chair at Dunsheen, I am determined to meet Connie Con O'Leary on the day. He and Jack o'Lantern were the co-stars of the best bit of drama I was ever involved in while in Kilbroney and I couldn't imagine myself going back there without having a reprise of Connie Con's evidence to the court.

I can foresee exactly how I am going to stage it. I shall say to him, "Connie Con, I'll do Judge Crowley and you'll do yourself." I remember exactly the questions that the judge asked him, and Connie will remember all his answers, if only because they have been repeated over and over for him in Florrie's and further apub. I can hear the dialogue now, every line of it, and that is what I want to hear when he places me in the car seat in Dunsheen:—

"A very self respecting donkey, you say. What do you mean by that, Connie?"

"Well, he's very particular about what he will carry on his back. He will carry wrack after a storm. He will carry furze for the open fire. He will carry baróid from the bog. He will even carry a new mattress for the stations. But there is one thing that he won't carry."

"And what is that?"

"Stones".

"Stones?"

"Stones!"

And so on and so forth and so extravagant all the way to my final triumphant line "Case dismissed!"

After my stroll back to the village, my next scheduled stop will be for what I might call, for want of a better word, a performance in the hall. Because Fr. Cleary is only an ordinary member of the committee he won't have the keys hanging on the hook in the kitchen where I used to keep them, so I shall have to get a loan of them from Bernard Lowry. Canadian maple floor and many memories notwithstanding, I shall make a beeline — should that be a peeline? — to the new toilets and there I shall have a derisive piddle in Mark Sheerin's pissoir.

After the relief of that, I shall wander around a bit seeing some of my friends. They haven't featured much in this memoir because friends make for affection, loyalty, support and ease rather than for drama, and one of them that I shall spend a lot of time with will be May Connell the chapelwoman. I shall arrange with her to have the church opened up the next morning half an hour earlier than usual so that I can get my Mass finished before O'Donnell arrives to pace up and down the aisle in the rosary patrol. For certain I know that she will ask me, "Will I tell Fr. O'Donnell that you are here?" "Of course,

May," I shall answer, "it will make his day!" I shall then call into the Emporium and invite Bill too to come to my Mass so that the three of us can have the church to ourselves without either Gobnait or an empty coffin next morning.

Mass over, I shall go to May's for breakfast but not immediately, because she will have to stay on to lead the responses at the parish priest's Mass and tidy up afterwards. That will give me the chance to take a walk along the road that I almost haunted when I was curate in Kilbroney, the road following the bends of the coastline from the village to Croghan. I shall pass Fuchsia Cottage and by midsummer the "For Sale" sign will surely be gone and somebody else will be trimming the hedge, and, no doubt, trying to solve the mystery of the hecatomb in the garden. I hope the new owner will be another English eccentric — every parish should have one! — and that she will swim in all her clothes in the cove beneath the cottage.

I won't have my breviary with me at that hour of the morning but I know I shall finish up at that stretch of road under the granite cliffs where I used to walk up and down reading the divine office on days when the wind would be around to the north. I shall have two ends in view: first of all to see Croghan harbour which the whales mistook for a strait on the day when they made the dormant waters erupt like geysers, and, secondly, to open up the harbour mouth and to draw an imaginary line across it between Seal Island and the Emperor rock, that gorgeous line which Kevin and I crossed one minute and fifty three seconds ahead of the "Topaz". All of that will give me a big appetite for May's breakfast. I am already looking forward to it because no one in Ireland makes scrambled egg like May: not only does it taste better than anybody else's but it looks different as well: she has some knack of whipping it up into the most amazing conical shapes and when it is presented on the huge plate it looks like the mountains of Montserrat on a saffron evening.

There will be one other item of great piquancy in addition to scrambled egg during the breakfast, and that is the response that Fr. O'Donnell will have made to May when she tells him that I have said Mass. My guess is that his only immediate re-mark will be a neutral "Is that so?" but in the days to follow I am certain that he will call her aside in the sacristy and with eyes resting on the picture of the Sacred Heart, rather than on her, he will say, "O, by the way, any other time a priest comes along to say Mass tell him he cannot do so without consulting the parish priest first!"

When the mountains and hills of the scrambled egg have been laid low, I won't be hungry but I shall go into the Emporium nevertheless to buy some pocketable snack for the long haul back to Inish. I could have the wind on the nose all the way — at this long distance in time even Pad Murray wouldn't be able to say! — so I might need a lot of time and a good supply of chunky bars to get me home.

The final item on the programme is this:— when I head out of the creek into the bay I shall cut in as close to Cláirseach as I can manage, and as I am sailing past the cliff-face shaped like a harp I shall recite a stanza from John Masefield's "Sea Fever". It won't be the first stanza because that will be forever Kevin's. It will be the third.

I must go down to the seas again, to the vagrant gipsy life
To the gull's way and the whale's way where the wind's like a whetted knife;
And all I ask is a merry yarn from a laughing fellow-rover
And quiet sleep and a sweet dream when the long trick's over.

Unfortunately I shall not have a laughing fellow-rover with me, but I hope for a quiet sleep and a sweet dream when the long trick is over.

ISBN 141201720-3